Two
Times
as Hot

Two Times as Hot

An Oklahoma Nights Romance

CAT JOHNSON

BRAVA

KENSINGTON PUBLISHING CORP.

www.kensingtonbooks.com

BRAVA BOOKS are published by

Kensington Publishing Corp.
119 West 40th Street
New York, NY 10018

All Kensington titles, imprints, and distributed lines are available at special quantity discounts for bulk purchases for sales promotions, premiums, fund-raising, educational, or institutional use.

Special book excerpts or customized printings can also be created to fit specific needs. For details, write or phone the office of the Kensington special sales manager: Kensington Publishing Corp., 119 West 40th Street, New York, NY 10018, attn: Special Sales Department; phone: 1-800-221-2647.

BRAVA and the B logo are Reg. U.S. Pat. & TM Off.

ISBN-13: 978-0-7582-8540-9
ISBN-10: 0-7582-8540-X

First Kensington Trade Paperback Printing: October 2013

10 9 8 7 6 5 4 3 2 1

Printed in the United States of America

First Electronic Edition: October 2013

ISBN-13: 978-0-7582-8541-6
ISBN-10: 0-7582-8541-8

*For all the romantics who share my belief
that dreams can come true, at any age.
May every one of you find your own happy ever after.*

*And for all those who helped make my dreams come true—
my military consultants, my wonderful readers, and
all the folks at Joseph's Fine Foods in Drumright, Oklahoma.*

Prologue

Ten months ago

It had turned out to be an extremely promising evening. Heck, the whole trip to Oklahoma was going even better than she'd planned. Emma decided she deserved an award for this one. She envisioned the inscription on the plaque. *Emma Hart—Sister of the Year.* That was her. What in the world would her sister Becca do without Emma to straighten out her life?

As Emma walked to the rental car in the parking lot of the rodeo arena, she glanced back to see Becca holding hands with the bull rider they'd met that night. What a nice, tall drink of water that Tucker Jenkins was. Emma's main purpose during this spur of the moment trip to Oklahoma was to get her little sister a new life far away from all the disappointments Becca had suffered in New York.

It looked as if Emma's plan was working perfectly.

Step one—get Becca a man. *Check.*

That part had been easy enough. It seemed the tickets Emma had purchased for tonight's rodeo were as good as buying an all-access pass to the hottest men in the state of Oklahoma, all corralled under one roof. In fact, the ten-dollar tickets had gotten them a two-for-one deal on hot men, because Becca's rodeo cowboy came with an equally sexy sidekick. Being a good sister and wingman—or rather wing-woman—Emma was more than happy to keep bull rider Jace Mills occupied so Tucker and Becca could get to know each other better tonight.

Tomorrow would bring the second half of Emma's plan to right the wrongs in Becca's world.

Step two—make sure Becca nailed her interview for the associate professor position in the English department at Oklahoma State University.

That shouldn't be a problem. Becca had a doctorate degree. She was qualified for the job and had the résumé and recommendations to prove it. Equally important as Becca's credentials was the crucial choice of the perfect interview outfit, which Emma had supervised. Her sister was going to shine at this interview and get the job. Emma felt it down to her bones, and her intuition about things such as this rarely proved wrong.

"So I'll follow you to the bar. You said it's next to your hotel?" Jace paused next to a truck bigger than two of Emma's rental cars put together. Then again, more than half of the vehicles in the arena lot were humungous pickup trucks.

Didn't these people know or care about their carbon footprint? People said things were big in Texas, but Emma had found that so far, Oklahomans were no slouches in the size department.

Naughty, sex-deprived girl that she was, Emma wondered what else might be oversized on Jace. Her gaze traveled from the black cowboy hat pulled low over his sandy-colored hair, all the way to his boots. She suspected there was a pretty nice body hidden beneath the denim. Hopefully she'd get to find out for sure firsthand tonight.

"The bar is inside the hotel where we're staying, but it's

got an entrance from the parking lot. So, yeah, you can follow me, and Tucker and Becca will follow you in his truck."

Jace glanced past her and grinned. "Yup. If Tuck ever gets his hands off her long enough to be able to drive."

She followed his stare to where Tucker was boosting Becca into the passenger seat of a truck that was possibly larger than Jace's. Emma noticed definite hand-to-booty contact. Perfect. Her plan was progressing just as she'd hoped.

"Ah, sorry about that comment." Jace cringed. "I shouldn't have said that with her being your sister and all."

"No apology necessary. I want nothing more than for Tucker to take complete advantage of Becca tonight. Even if it takes all night long." She caught his expression of surprise. "Believe me, Jace. Becca needs to let loose a little. I think a night of good old-fashioned sex with a man like Tucker is perfect."

His eyes opened wider. "Um, okay."

Judging by the shock evident on Jace's face, Emma figured she had better explain. "Don't tell Becca I told you this, but she got dumped by both her job and her live-in boyfriend on the same day."

"That sucks."

"Yeah, it does." Emma agreed with Jace and continued. "But even before that happened, Becca was living her life like she was some boring old shut-in. I swear my grandmother in the rest home has more fun and a better social life than Becca does. Becca needs someone to turn her world upside down and, you know, maybe clear out the cobwebs down there."

She made a sweeping gesture in the general region of her own pelvis.

A laugh burst out of Jace as he watched her hand motion and shook his head. "Damn, woman. I think I could love you."

Emma smiled. She'd been hoping for some loving for herself tonight, too, and Jace seemed like just the man to give it to her.

All right, maybe the beer she'd drunk at the arena had ramped up her sexual neediness a little, and erased her inhibitions. But why should Becca get to have all the fun?

Beer or no beer, Jace would have caught Emma's eye on any night. A real cowboy, and a hard-bodied, good-looking one at that, was hard to resist for a native New Yorker who spent her days surrounded by pale, soft-bodied men.

The men at work at the graphic design firm back in Poughkeepsie didn't move anything heavier than a computer mouse. They sure as hell didn't have the golden skin or big calloused hands that Jace did. Emma suspected Jace's healthy glow came from being outdoors working the ranch or whatever he did when he wasn't riding bulls in the rodeo.

There was no way Jace's deep tan was of the spray-on variety. Everything on this man was God-given, natural, and sexy.

Nope, she'd had enough of metrosexuals and geeks and their smooth hands that had never seen a day of hard labor. Emma wanted a real man's hands on her body. Big and rough hands belonging to a strong, tough man who would grab her and throw her onto a bed where he'd spread her thighs wide, yank her head back by the hair, and kiss her breathless while loving her until she was senseless.

Phew. That image had Emma's insides turning molten hot. She glanced at Jace's hands. Emma treated him to her sexiest smile. "Come on, let's go. The hotel waits. The bar, too."

With a well-practiced flip of her shoulder-length blond hair, she headed toward her car. Knowing for sure he would watch her walk away, she put a little extra sway into her hips. She smiled when, behind her, Jace muttered a soft curse.

The drive from the arena to the hotel was a quick ten minutes. During that time, she let her mind wander, fantasizing about a romp with the cowboy following her.

The glow of the hotel sign caught her attention just as she'd almost driven past the exit. More than ready for some sex, Emma needed to forcibly wrestle her attention back to driving where it belonged or she'd end up in an accident. She flipped on the turn signal seconds before taking a fast, sharp turn into the parking lot.

Seeing a couple of open spots next to each other, Emma maneuvered the rental car into one and parked, not quite straight but at least within the painted lines.

Jace pulled the truck into the space next to hers. Before she even had time to check her reflection in the rearview mirror and grab her purse off the passenger seat, he was there to open the door for her.

A gentleman. Emma liked that trait in a man, as long as he wasn't too much of a gentleman in the bedroom. In the boudoir, she liked a bit of a caveman. A man who took what he wanted and gave back as good as he got.

"Thank you." She smiled at him and stepped out of the car.

"My pleasure." Jace hooked a thumb in the direction of the road. "Tuck got caught at the red light back there."

It took Jace pointing it out to her for Emma to notice her sister and Tucker hadn't pulled into the lot after them. She hid the cringe at that realization and felt a little guilty. Apparently, all the blood had left her brain in the presence of a hot cowboy. She'd forgotten about her younger sister.

Emma glanced from the lot's entrance to Jace. "I guess we can go on in and get a table. They'll find us inside."

"Sounds good." Jace proved himself a gentleman once again by jogging ahead to pull the entrance door open for her.

She could get accustomed to this kind of treatment. If Becca got the job at Oklahoma State and moved to Stillwater, Emma would have to get used to it. She'd be able to visit Becca and get a cowboy fix whenever she felt the urge. That seemed like an excellent plan. Emma was feeling some urges right now as she led the way inside.

The hotel bar was buzzing with quite a few patrons gathered on barstools watching some game on a big screen television, but the place was by no means fully packed. They had no trouble finding a table with seating for four and a waitress standing by ready to take their order.

Jace turned to Emma. "What would you like, darlin'? Another beer?"

"I think I'll switch and have a glass of white wine." Beer was appropriate for drinking out of big plastic cups while watching a rodeo, but Emma was a wine drinker at heart.

"White wine for the lady and one of whatever beer you've got in a bottle for me."

The waitress named a few brands and Jace chose one, but Emma was more interested in wondering what his stubble would feel like when she kissed him than listening to the selection.

After the waitress left to get their order, Jace turned in his chair to face Emma. He caught her watching him and smiled until his hazel eyes crinkled beneath the brim of his cowboy hat. "So, you told me that Becca no longer has a boyfriend, but what about you?"

"No boyfriend for me either." *Totally single. Free as a bird and completely available. Hint, hint.* "And you? Girlfriend?"

"Nope. Well, not anymore." He lifted a shoulder in a half shrug. "I had one for quite a long while, actually."

That was an interesting piece of trivia. It made Emma curious. "How long is long?"

"We would have been going on seven years if we hadn't broken up." The waitress arrived, and Jace took the longneck and raised it to his mouth. It gave Emma a moment to digest that information and think of about a dozen new questions she wanted to ask.

Seven years would be a considerable portion of his adult life. To invest that much time in a relationship and have it end was a pretty big deal. She tried to judge Jace's age. He was probably about thirty, or maybe at the tail end of his twenties. Being in the sun all the time might have aged him.

"That is a long time. When did you break up?"

He planted the bottle on the table but left his hand wrapped around it. "A few months ago."

Okay. That was probably long enough ago for him to be back in the game. Men were different from women. They bounced back pretty fast from a breakup. At least she hoped so.

"I'm sorry to hear that." Not really. Emma was happy he was single.

"Eh, it's fine." He took another swig of beer and glanced around the bar, as if he was avoiding eye contact with her.

Hmm, maybe a few months weren't long enough, after all.

Jace brought his attention back to her and donned a smile. "So, do you have any other plans for while you're here besides turning your sister's world upside down with my best friend?"

A blatant change of subject. Good. Emma was more than

glad they'd moved on from the depressing ex-girlfriend talk. "Nope. Although, maybe I wouldn't mind shaking things up in my own life a bit."

"Is that so?" He lifted one sandy brow. "Hmm. Lucky for you, I might know just the guy to help you do that."

His gaze captured and held hers. Emma's chest tightened. She took a gulp of the cold wine to cool her overheated insides and glanced at the entrance. "Where the hell is Becca?"

Jace laughed. "Knowing Tuck, they're—uh, never mind."

"They're doing what?" Emma frowned.

He looked around, toward the bar, at his beer, pretty much at anything except Emma before his gaze settled on her. "Nothing. I'm sorry. I shouldn't have said anything. I don't know what they're doing."

Emma's eyes opened wide when realization struck, and she figured out what Jace had assumed was happening between Becca and Tucker. "You think they're *doing it*? In the *truck*?"

"Don't know. Don't care. None of my business." Jace shook his head, leaving no doubt in Emma's mind this was a subject he didn't want to discuss further. That was too bad for him, because she had no intention of letting the topic go.

"Well, I do care. I'm texting her." Emma dug through her purse and found her cell phone. She punched in the message and hit send.

Jace cringed. "What did you say in the text?"

"I just asked if she's okay and where she is." Emma hadn't outright asked if her sister was having sex with a cowboy in the parking lot, which showed a lot of restraint on her part.

"Okay. I guess we'll see what she says, won't we?" He took another sip of beer as the bottle hid his smile.

The expression on Jace's face told her that he already

knew the answer. Emma could believe Jace knew Tucker well enough to guess what they were doing, but Jace didn't know Becca. She would no more have sex in a truck in a hotel parking lot than book a seat on the next space shuttle.

The phone buzzed and Emma looked down at the incoming text from Becca.

I'm fine. Don't wait up.

A winking smiley face followed Becca's response. Maybe Emma didn't know her sister that well after all. Or perhaps it was just the lure of these cowboys making both city girls want to do all sorts of things they wouldn't normally do.

Emma turned the phone toward Jace. She watched him scan over the words as a grin spread across his face.

He let out a short laugh. "No surprise there. Darlin', I hate to tell you this, but you won't be seeing your sister until tomorrow morning."

"You know Tucker well, huh?" Well enough to know his skills with women had the power to loosen up even the most tightly wound female Emma knew—Becca.

"Oh, yeah. Aside from his friend Logan—he's a guy who grew up next door to Tuck and his family—I probably know him better than anyone else in this world. Tuck and I used to rodeo together right outta high school. We were traveling buddies."

Emma pursed her lips and considered that. "So you're saying, based on your long-standing knowledge of your friend, that I have a hotel room upstairs all to myself for the entire night?"

Jace's brows rose high beneath the brim of his hat, before he recovered enough to say, "Seems like it. What ya gonna do about that?"

His eyes narrowed, and he sent her a smoldering look filled with desire. She may have been wrong about her sister, but Emma knew one thing, and that was when a man was interested in her. Brokenhearted from his recent breakup with his girlfriend or not, Jace was interested.

"I have an idea or two. How long before you finish that beer?" She glanced at the level of the white wine filling her own glass and then eyed the longneck on the table in front of him.

Jace knocked the bottle back, swallowed a few times, and then slammed it, empty, on the table with a clunk. "Done."

Two swallows and she was done herself. Good thing the bar served their wine in tiny glasses. Usually that would piss Emma off. Not tonight. "Good. Let's go."

He wrestled his wallet out of his jeans pocket and threw down a twenty. The waitress had seen them stand and rushed over.

"That cover it?" he asked.

"Yeah. Let me get your change—"

"Keep it." Jace waved her off and reached for Emma's hand. "Shall we?"

Emma smiled at his enthusiasm. "Oh, yeah."

They left the well-tipped waitress standing by their table and headed out the back exit, which led into the lobby and the elevator.

The ride upstairs was silent, but not without some flirtation and a hell of a lot of sexual tension between them. Emma peeked at Jace standing beside her. He caught her looking at him and grinned at her. He ran a hand down her back, letting it rest at the base of her spine. Her stomach fluttered in response to his touch.

The doors swooshed open on her floor, and they stepped out. A short walk down the hall, and the locked door of her room stood in front of them.

Emma's common sense returned, and she realized she needed to find her keycard or they weren't getting inside.

A bit of rifling and she was able to excavate it from amid the clutter collected at the bottom of her purse. She managed to get the card into the slot facing the correct direction on the second try. The automatic locks slid open as the light turned green. Green for go.

Emma pushed open the door and a moment later, she and Jace were standing inside the room. She should have thought to straighten up after she and Becca had gotten dressed for the rodeo. The room was a shambles, but Jace didn't seem to notice the two suitcases open on the floor, or the clothes strewn on the chair, or much of anything else.

He stepped closer, his eyes focused on Emma. Just a few inches taller than she was in her boots, he had to only dip his head to brush his lips across hers.

Their first kiss was soft and slow, but all consuming. It had her dragging in a breath. What would it be like to make love with a man who could kiss so thoroughly? It had been a long time since she'd been kissed like that. Slow and deep.

Hell, it had been a long time since Emma had been kissed by anyone in any way at all. She wanted to savor every taste, every touch. This was a memory that would last forever—

The obnoxious sound of Jace's phone chiming in his pocket interrupted her enjoyment of his talented mouth. Emma pulled back from the kiss, just far enough to say, "That's your phone."

"I heard it. It's just a text. I'm ignoring it." He pressed closer and wrapped his hands around her waist.

Two sides warred with each other within Emma. She wanted nothing more than to go back to kissing Jace. But the other half was dying to know if it was a text from his friend Tucker. It could be something to do with her sister.

Maybe it said something about her level of nosiness, or she could pretend it was concern for Becca, but either way Emma let curiosity get the better of her. "Maybe you should check. It could be Tucker looking for us."

Jace let out an exaggerated sigh that lost all authenticity when he rolled his eyes and smiled. "All right. If you want me to."

He read the text and his grin disappeared. His drastic change of expression had Emma immediately worried. "What's wrong? Is it Tucker? Is Becca all right?"

"It's not Tuck. It's my ex. She has a flat tire and needs me to come and put the spare on for her." He punched in a reply and then glanced at Emma. "I'm sorry. She's stuck on the side of the highway. It's dangerous sitting there in the dark. People drive like lunatics on that road. I have to go help."

"Um, yeah. Sure. Go. You should definitely help her." A call to the auto club would have been a better idea. Or to a local towing company, if his ex didn't belong to AAA. Or to one of her friends or family. Any number of alternatives came to mind. Yet this girl had instead texted Jace, her ex-boyfriend. And at her summons, he was going to come running.

"I really am sorry." With literally one foot out the open door, Jace paused. "Do you think I could have your number?"

"You want my number?" Emma's eyebrows shot up. "You know I'm leaving tomorrow."

"I know, but you'll be back." There was that smolder, lighting his eyes and making him irresistible again.

Dammit. She should be mad at him, not admiring how sexy he was. "Why are you so sure I'll be back?"

"Because after one night with Tuck, your sister will want to come back for more. I'm thinking there's a good chance you'll be with her."

That was a very definite possibility. Emma hadn't told Jace about Becca's interview at Oklahoma State tomorrow. It was not a secret; it just hadn't come up. But if Becca got the job—which Emma had every confidence she would—she would be back.

Maybe this was a one-time thing with the ex-girlfriend. Jace could be just a good guy who felt obligated to help because of their long history together. She probably shouldn't fault him for being nice and helping out a friend. Even if that friend was an ex-girlfriend with the worst timing on earth.

"All right." She scribbled her cell number on the top page of the notepad next to the bed. He took a step forward and grabbed the paper she held out to him.

"Thanks." He shoved it into his pocket and opened the door again, cocking his head toward the hallway. "I'd better go, but I'll call you. I promise."

He sounded sincere enough, but she'd believe that when she saw it. "Okay."

Hand still braced on the door, he glanced back at her one more time. "Bye."

"Bye." It was a hell of an effort to sound upbeat as she said good night to the man she thought she'd be waking up next to in the morning. She wasn't sure if she managed it or not.

Just when Emma thought he was about to take his final leave, Jace stepped back inside the room. He strode to where she stood by the bed. He grabbed the back of her head with one big hand, and covered her mouth with his.

It ended too quick, barely after a few seconds. He pulled away, and with a small smile, left. The click of the door latching behind him gave the act a definite sense of finality.

He'd kissed her breathless and then had gone to ride to the rescue of another woman. Emma had the worst luck with men. She flopped back onto the mattress and blew out a big breath. Apparently chivalry had its downside when the sexy knight rode off to save another damsel and left his ladylove primed, ready, and sexually frustrated.

Meanwhile Becca, Miss Prim and Proper, was off somewhere getting lucky. The English professor who didn't even like to get her hands dirty pumping gas for her own fuel-efficient car was most likely getting laid in the front seat of Tucker's huge bad boy pickup truck. There was irony if ever Emma saw it.

After the events of tonight, she sure could use another drink, but there was no way in hell she was going back down to that bar alone after the promising public exit she and Jace had made together.

She glanced at the phone on the desk in the room. Maybe the bar delivered.

Chapter
One

"To Tuck and Becca." Logan Hunt held the stem of the fluted glass between his thumb and forefinger and raised it in a toast.

The glass contained champagne when he'd much rather be drinking beer, but what could he do? It was a celebration, and celebrations traditionally called for bubbly. Tuck's mom had poured a glass for them all before she'd run off to the kitchen to check on something in the oven for tonight's party. Maybe Logan could refill his glass with beer. Who would notice? The two drinks basically looked the same. At least to him, they did.

The bride and groom raised their glasses to take a sip, but Logan wasn't quite done with his toast. "May your marriage be long and happy and far less tumultuous than the past . . ." He frowned and glanced at the happy couple. "How long has it been since you two first met?"

"Ten months." Becca screwed up her face. "And it hasn't been *tumultuous*."

It seemed like far longer ago that Tuck had sprung the news on Logan that the new English professor at OSU had been his rodeo one-night stand.

"Maybe not for you, but for me it sure as hell has. Ten months? Really? That's all? Jeez." Logan laughed. As head of OSU's Military Sciences department, Logan could only turn a blind eye to Tuck and Becca flaunting the university's non-fraternization policy for so long, hence his stress. But that wouldn't be a concern any longer, once Tuck and Becca were married. "Anyway, I'll be more than happy when you officially tie the knot."

"So will I," Tuck agreed. Becca opened her mouth to say more, but Tuck silenced her with a kiss before he pulled back and tipped his glass toward Logan in salute. "And thank you, Logan."

A chime sounded and Becca glanced at the cell phone she held in one hand.

"That must be Emma getting back to me." She glanced down to check the text. "It is. She's still at the hotel and needs directions to the house. Of course she does. I knew she'd forget to print out the ones I e-mailed to her last week."

"Go on. Call your sister." Tuck gave Becca a pat on the bottom that would have earned any other man who tried that a black eye. "Logan and I have a lot to discuss anyway. You know, all the bachelor party plans for tonight after this family party is over."

"Bachelor party . . ." She let out a humph.

Tuck grinned. "Yes, ma'am. Bachelor party."

"I'm still not sure I approve of that." Becca's blond brows furrowed.

"Too late to object now. It's already planned." Tuck hooked an arm around her neck, planted another hard kiss on her mouth, and then gave her a little push toward the door. "Go call. Emma's waiting. You know she gets pissy when you don't get right back to her."

Becca narrowed her eyes. "We're talking about this bachelor party thing more later."

As she left the room, Tuck shook his head and glanced at Logan. "I'm sure we will talk more about it later."

"No doubt." Logan commiserated with his friend.

How many times had he and Tuck stood together in this house in the past? It would be impossible to count the number. Logan had taught both Tuck and his own younger brother, Layne, how to pitch a fastball in the backyard here. All while he'd tried to occupy Tuck's little brother Tyler, who insisted on being in the middle, trying to keep up with the bigger boys. Being ten years older than Tuck and Layne, Logan had been the referee for many a scuffle between the boys.

Come to think of it, it wasn't just the boys he had to referee. Tuck's little sister Tara was always right in the mix, too. It didn't matter if they were digging worms to go fishing or playing war, Tara wanted to be with them.

It felt good to be back in his old hometown and here in the Jenkins' house for the happy occasion. Having grown up next door and being the oldest of the neighborhood kids, he had served as a built-in babysitter at times. But with the three Jenkins kids, he was more like an older brother.

A wave of nostalgia hit Logan hard, along with something else. Loneliness, maybe?

After their marriage, Tuck and Becca would be building a family. They'd have kids of their own, and it would be Tuck teaching them to throw a ball or bait a hook. For the first time, Logan felt his single, childless status. It left him feeling a little empty.

It was crazy for Logan to feel lonely, because he was almost always surrounded by people. He had his fellow faculty and cadets, and his family was just a couple of hours away. He could visit home anytime he wanted. Still, Logan hoped he'd be involved in some way with Tuck and Becca's kids, whenever the time came. Maybe he could be an honorary uncle. He'd fill whatever role they gave him.

Logan found himself a little choked up as he said, "I'm happy for you, Tuck."

"Thanks, man." Tuck put his champagne glass down on the table. "You ready to trade in these sissy bubbles for something with hops and barley in it?"

"Oh, yeah." Logan pushed his champagne flute toward Tuck's before he ended up tipping over the too tall, stemmed glass and breaking it. Give him a nice solid long-neck bottle any day. Something he could wrap his fist around and not worry it would snap or get crushed. "So what's the plan for tonight?"

Besides Tuck's eventual, inevitable negotiations over the bachelor party with Becca.

"Well, most of the guests we invited to the wedding are local, but the ones coming from any distance have arrived in town already and checked into the hotel. They should all be here within the next hour for this . . . whatever this party is called." Tuck shook his head, looking as baffled as Logan as to why there was a smaller party tonight before tomorrow's big party—the wedding reception. "I guess we're supposed to spend a few hours eating and drinking here to welcome the out-of-towners, before we head out for the bachelor party. Then tomorrow—"

"Tomorrow your days as a free man are over." Logan finished Tuck's sentence. "You ready for that?"

It had hardly been two years since Tuck's divorce from his first wife.

"Yeah, I'm more than ready. If Becca didn't want the white dress, church wedding, and big reception, I would've dragged her off to Vegas and had Elvis marry us on Valentine's Day when I proposed to her."

"But then you couldn't have had the bachelor party." Logan laughed at Tuck's expression of dread at the reminder.

"I have a feeling that is going to come back to bite me in the ass. Becca doesn't look all that happy about the whole idea. I don't know if it's worth the hell I may have to go through. What in the devil did y'all plan anyway?"

"Me? Nothing. Jace and your brother did all the planning."

"Jace and Tyler together? Crap." Tuck cringed and took a swig out of his bottle.

"Aw, come on. What are you so worried about?" Logan grinned and took a sip of his own cold brew. It hadn't been a serious question. Logan knew very well Jace being involved was something to worry about in itself.

Tuck released a burst of air. "Jace . . . Well, he's just Jace. Him alone planning this thing would be bad enough, but my brother's no better. Tyler's what, twenty-four now? And he's never had a girlfriend for longer than two weeks. He can't appreciate what Becca could put me through if she's unhappy about this party."

Logan laughed and enjoyed Tuck's torture. "Where are the two party planners, anyway?"

"Tyler drove to pick up my sister at college. Don't know where Jace is. He should be here soon, I guess." Tuck glanced at the old grandfather clock that had stood in the corner of the Jenkins living room forever. Or at least for as long as Logan could remember.

"Maybe he's busy finalizing plans. You know, for the nekkid dancing girls and all." Logan couldn't resist a little more teasing.

"Oh, God, I hope not." Tuck hissed in a breath and glanced in the direction Becca had disappeared. "And don't even joke about that where she might hear you."

Seeing Tuck as a taken man again sure was making for some good entertainment for Logan in his own unencumbered state. It made a man happy to be free. He'd be even more grateful of that fact at the wedding when all of the available female guests were feeling romantic after the nuptials. Maybe some would be looking for someone to slow dance with or kiss. Logan could definitely oblige.

Becca, the woman responsible for Tuck being off the market again, came back into the room. Luckily she arrived well after the discussion about dancing girls was over. "Emma's on her way. She figured out her outfit so she's happy."

"Thank God for that. Nobody wants Emma unhappy about her outfit." Tuck rolled his eyes before glancing at Logan. "This'll be your first time meeting Bec's sister, won't it?"

Logan dipped his head in response to Tuck's question. "Yes, sir. It sure will be."

"I'm not worried about Emma fitting in. Everyone loves her. It's the rest of the relatives I'm concerned about." Becca screwed up her face into a scowl. "My father, Mr. Punctuality, is beside himself they're not here an hour early, and it sounded like my mother was already well into her sherry. She bought a bottle at the duty-free shop at the airport."

"A bottle? Sounds like a hell of a good start to a party," Jace said as he walked through the door.

Speak of the devil.

"Hey there, darlin'." Jace scooped Becca into a hug that lifted her feet right off the ground. He gave her a kiss on the cheek and set her back down. "You look great, as usual."

Becca laughed. "Thanks, Jace. But you'd better save a few compliments for later when my family is here and I'm tearing my hair out. I may need to hear them then."

"You got it. And just send me the signal and I'll sneak you some booze, too, if you want it." Jace winked at her and slid a flask partway out of his pocket.

"I'll keep that in mind. A visit with my parents might

require some alcohol." Becca glanced at Tuck. "I'm going to go see if your mom needs any help in the kitchen."

"Sounds good, baby." Tuck nodded.

Jace watched Becca leave as he walked over to Tuck. He stuck out one arm to shake the groom's hand. "Hey, man. How you holding up? You ready to bolt yet? I got the truck filled up with diesel and coolers full of ice-cold beer. It's parked right outside, just in case."

Logan shook his head. Typical Jace, as changeable as the wind. He was sucking up to the bride with one breath and offering to help the groom escape with the next.

Tuck's gaze cut to the doorway Becca had gone through before he answered, "Not at all. I love every minute of this. Nothing more fun than planning a big ol' wedding. You want a beer? I'm getting myself another one."

Logan glanced at his bottle. He wasn't even halfway done with his own beer yet but Tuck's was empty. Tuck might pretend he was calm, cool, and collected about the wedding and all it entailed, but the empty bottle told another story.

Out-of-town relatives. Nervous brides. Crazy groomsmen. Saying *I do* for the rest of your life . . . Yeah, Logan sure was happy he'd be on the ushers' side of the altar rather than directly in the line of fire like the groom.

"Definite yes on the beer." After he answered Tuck, Jace turned to extend a hand toward Logan. "Lieutenant Colonel Hunt, sir. What's the status of the Oklahoma State ROTC program?"

Logan laughed at how Jace lowered his tone of voice and spoke more like a battalion commander than a bull rider. "A little slow right now since we're on break between semesters, but thanks for asking. How you been, Jace?"

"Good. Rodeoing quite a bit now that it's summer.

Dragging Tuck with me when I can get him away from Becca and convince him to ride."

"Just don't break him, please. Tuck may be a bull rider part of the time, but he's one of my soldiers full time, and one of my department's best military science instructors. I need him with two functioning legs when we go back to PT with the cadets. Got it?"

"Sure thing. Let's just hope Becca doesn't break anything on him during the honeymoon." Jace waggled his eyebrows. "As for rodeo, he usually ends up breaking his ribs when he wrecks, not his legs, so we're good. Broken ribs hurt like a son of a bitch, but he can still run with 'em."

"Thanks for the vote of confidence, Jace. And I only broke my ribs once or twice, thank you very much." Tuck scowled.

Jace grinned and accepted the bottle Tuck handed him. "Once or twice, my sweet ass. You can't seem to keep yourself out from under hoof. You're too tall for a bull rider, if you ask me. You need to be small and quick like me. You should have stuck with team roping."

Watching the two men bicker, Logan sipped his beer and stayed out of the fray. He wasn't about to enter that debate. Bull riders were insane.

Sure, Logan had joined the army knowing there'd be times during his career he was going to be up against an enemy who wanted him dead, but to get on the back of a bucking bull knowing you were going to be thrown in the dirt every damn time? Even when you won? Nope. Not for him.

While Jace and Tuck continued to banter—something about which bull Jace drew last time he rode—motion out in the driveway caught Logan's eye. He turned to watch through the window. A hot-as-hell woman in a short, black dress reached one long leg out of the car and stepped from behind the open passenger door. Even doing nothing but standing in the driveway, she was sexy enough to make a man take notice. Her blond hair and the family resemblance told him this must be Becca's sister, Emma.

Logan glanced at Tuck and wondered how bad a friend he was that Tuck's soon-to-be sister-in-law was giving him a hard-on. Just from his thinking about how the curves that dress accentuated so nicely would feel beneath his touch.

Imagine if he ever got his hands on her . . .

An older woman and man exited the front doors of the sedan and joined the blonde. They had to be Tuck's new in-laws. Their presence should have diminished Logan's amorous fantasies about Emma. It didn't.

It seemed Emma had captured his attention and she wasn't letting go. He managed to block her parents right out as he wondered what her hair would feel like against his cheek while he ran his tongue down her throat.

"Hey, Tuck. It looks like Emma's here." Jace came to stand next to Logan at the window. He blew a slow whistle. "Boy oh boy, is she looking good."

The tone of Jace's voice made Logan turn to get a good look at him. The man had a knowing expression on his face that didn't sit well with him at all. "You know her?"

"Oh, yeah." Jace dragged the two short words out to be suggestively long.

What the hell was that about? Logan's brows rose. He turned to glance at Tuck.

"Emma was here with Becca the first time she came to Oklahoma for the job interview at OSU. You know, the night Becca and I met at the rodeo."

Tuck had answered without Logan's having to ask, but that sure as hell didn't explain the rest. Such as why Jace was acting as if he and Emma had done more than just meet that night.

Those were details Logan was more than interested in having.

"Yeah, I remember you telling me about the rodeo." But not that Jace and Becca's hot sister from New York had had a little one-night rodeo of their own.

Of course, Jace liked to exaggerate. It didn't matter if it was about conquering a bull or a woman. Logan had known the man for years through Tuck. Ever since the two had ridden on the rodeo circuit together before Tuck had enlisted in the army. If nothing else, he knew Jace could throw the shit with the best of them. It was very possible nothing at all had happened between Jace and Emma, except in Jace's own overactive imagination.

Logan decided to run with that theory and see how things progressed. It was far better than the alternative—assuming Jace had a prior claim on this woman and having to back off. A lot could happen over a short period of time. Look at how one night between Tuck and Becca had changed both of their lives. Logan had an entire weekend and a wedding reception to work with. There'd be sentimental speeches and tears, music, and a fully stocked bar. Everything to put the partygoers—and Emma—in the mood for romance.

Not to mention Logan had Tuck on his side, pulling for him, putting in a good word. At least Tuck had better be on his side. Jace was Tuck's friend, yes, but Logan was like a brother. Not to mention his boss and commanding officer. If it came right down to it, Logan would pull rank. Hell, he could order Tuck to put in a good word for him with Emma or else.

When leggy blondes with curves like Emma's were involved, a man had to bend the rules.

How the hell long was it going to take Becca's family to get inside so he could meet Emma officially? Logan glanced out the window again and noticed Tyler's truck was now parked in the drive, as well. If people continued to arrive at this rate, it was about to get very crowded in the Jenkins' house, but there was only one guest Logan was interested in now.

"We're here. Now this party can get started." A familiar voice brought Logan around as Tuck's younger brother came through the door. "Sorry I'm late, bro. *Somebody* wasn't ready when I got there."

Tyler's sister, Tara, followed him in. She delivered a backhanded smack to Tyler's gut after shooting him a look over his comment. "Hey. I had to pack a lot of stuff for this weekend."

"You sure as hell did. My truck was riding kind of low. Of course, that could be from you putting on some weight last semester." Tyler grinned.

"I did not." A punch this time rather than a slap had Tyler frowning and rubbing his shoulder where she'd hit him.

"It's good to see you. Both of you. I'm glad you're here." Tuck stepped up to hug Tara. "Now quit the arguing. Becca's parents and sister just got here. Don't show them what heathens we are before the wedding. Okay?"

"Afraid she'll want to call it off? Don't worry, Tuck. I'll be sweet as pie. I promise." Tara's attempt to appear sweet made her look more devil than angel.

She ignored Tuck's burst of laughter at her declaration as she glanced at the others in the room. When her eyes reached Jace, standing and drinking his beer while wearing his usual amused grin, she scowled.

"Jace."

"Tara." Jace's tone was as low and flat as hers had been.

Those two were like oil and water, and always had been. Most likely, they always would be. The only thing they had in common was their love of Tuck, and their inexplicable dislike of each other. Logan figured they were all lucky they'd left their greeting at a single word and that it hadn't been accompanied by the usual string of insults.

Logan smiled. Some things never changed. Jace and Tara still fought like cats and dogs. The two younger Jenkins siblings still bickered, even at the age of—how old were they? Tuck had already said Tyler was twenty-four. Tara was two grades behind Tyler in school so she should be about twenty-one, or maybe twenty-two by now.

God, that made Logan feel old. He'd changed Tara's diaper once or twice when she was a baby. He'd been seventeen years old and babysitting on a Saturday night instead of being out with his friends—at that time, changing a diaper full of baby shit was the dead last thing he wanted to do.

"Logan." Tara moved across the room. She wrapped her arms around him and aimed a kiss at Logan's mouth. He turned his head a fraction of an inch at the last minute. If he hadn't, it would have been a full-on lip-lock.

What the hell was that? Her greeting to him was a far cry from the pouting, juvenile one she'd given Jace.

Logan still thought of Tara as a child, but pressed up against him as she was, from tits to thighs, it was obvious she was all grown up now, and she wanted him to know it. He cringed at his own thoughts—he didn't even want to think of the word *tits* in relation to the girl he'd spent most of his life thinking of as a sister.

"Hi, Tara." He pulled back, though her arms stayed around his neck.

"I've missed you. It's so good to see you again." Her face remained a little too close for his liking.

"Good to see you, too." He took a step back until she was forced to drop her hold. "How have you been? How's school going?"

"Great, but I can't wait to graduate. You know, get on with my life. Get a job and my own place. I'm thinking about moving to Stillwater once I've gotten my degree. You like living there, right?"

"Sure. It's a nice enough place." He shrugged. Far better than a few places he'd endured while deployed, so he certainly couldn't complain.

A wide smile bowed her lips. "Maybe I could come visit and you could show me around. You know, so I could get a feel for what it would be like to live there."

As a single man going on forty years old, Logan knew damn well when a woman was flirting. The problem was this was not just any woman. This was Tara, the closest thing to a little sister he'd ever have. Not only was he almost old enough to be her father, but when he looked at her he still saw the sweet little toddler who used to hold his hand while they walked. She used to run to him crying when Tuck or Tyler or even Layne had been mean to her, or she'd fallen and scraped her knee.

He needed to nip this little crush in the bud and right quick. "I'm sure if you came to Stillwater, Becca would love to show her new sister-in-law around. She knows where all the good places are. I pretty much only go to the shooting range and the fast food joints right off campus."

"I like to shoot. You taught me." She kept her gaze leveled on his. "Remember how we'd line up empty pop cans on the fence as targets and see how many we could each knock off with the BB gun? I always beat Tyler."

He'd obviously done too good a job as surrogate big brother. He'd created a tomboy with the determination of a pit bull. Though Tara sure didn't dress like a tomboy any more. Gone was the old holey denim. In its place were fancy jeans with rhinestones on the back pockets.

Come to think of it, it wasn't only Tara's attire that had altered. She'd also been showing him a lot more attention the past few times they'd seen each other. In his blissful bubble of denial, he hadn't noticed how much it had changed from sister-like devotion to that of a female on the prowl. He sure as hell noticed now. She was obviously fueled by a good dose of adult female hormones.

Logan glanced around for help and found it in the group walking through the door. "Oh, look. Becca's family is here. I haven't met them yet. As one of the groomsmen, I guess I should ask Tuck to introduce me. Don't want to be rude."

He didn't wait for a response from Tara to make his escape. He downed the last slug of lukewarm beer en route to Tuck and hoped the introductions would keep him busy until Tara had moved on to something or someone else.

While he'd been fending off Tara, Logan had fallen behind in his number one pursuit of the evening—Emma. Just moments after she'd walked through the living room doorway, Jace had already zeroed in on her.

One thing was for sure—at least it wouldn't be a boring evening. Not with the unwanted attention from a girl he thought of as a sister, and another man after the woman Logan had his eye on—who could have ever imagined this weekend would turn out to be so damn complicated?

Chapter
Two

Becca squeezed Emma's hand as they followed their parents through the doorway of the Jenkins living room. "I'm so happy you're here."

"Finally." Emma sighed. "The one dress I'd put on didn't look right, so I tried a few others I'd packed. I thought Dad's head was going to pop off when I wasn't ready the moment he wanted to leave."

Her father knocking on the hotel room door every five minutes, tapping his foot and complaining they were going to be late, hadn't made getting ready any easier or faster for Emma. Being a man, he couldn't understand that, but Becca would, which was why Emma looked to her sister for commiseration over the trying ordeal.

"It doesn't matter, because you're here now and you look great." Becca smiled.

"Thank you." At least one member of their family appreciated all the effort Emma had put into getting ready for tonight's party. She reached out and fixed a twisted strap on Becca's dress, and then glanced at the people already gathered in the living room. "Small group. Are more coming?"

"Oh, yeah. Like two dozen more. Everyone's not due for another hour or so."

"Another hour?" Eyes open wide, Emma turned to stare at Becca. "Dad said—"

"I know." Becca shook her head. "Believe me. I told Dad what time Tucker's parents expected them, but you know Dad. If he's not at least fifteen minutes early, he considers himself late. It doesn't matter. Tuck's friends are here early, too. It's no big deal."

It was a big deal because their father had stressed Emma to the point she was ready to rip her hair out. She should be used to him and his idiosyncrasies after thirty-plus years, but Emma still couldn't help the sigh that came escaped her. "Is there wine?"

"Yes." Becca laughed. "Did you have any doubt of that?"

"Uh, yeah. I did." Emma wouldn't say it and insult their hosts, but how could she know if Tucker's parents were teetotalers or not? This was Oklahoma. What did a New Yorker know about Midwest traditions? Life in the heartland could be very different from the coasts.

"Relax, there's plenty. I went to the liquor store myself. We set up a bar in the corner of the room. There's champagne, white wine, and soda chilling in a cooler under the table. The red wine is out and open. Oh, and there's Tucker's favorite beer for him and the guys."

The mention of alcohol and men brought a smile to Emma's lips. "Then lead the way to the bar." And to the cowboys.

"Gladly. As soon as we can slip past Mom and Dad." Becca tilted a head toward the two sets of parents in front of them, blocking their path to the wine.

It seemed they were all stalled in the doorway as Tucker's mother and father were in a deep discussion with the bride's parents.

"How old did you say the building was?" Emma's father asked Mr. Jenkins.

"Parts are from the 1800s. You can still see the original beams." Tuck's father gestured toward the ceiling and every member of the group glanced upward in unison.

Emma looked up as well, but she would have been much more appreciative of the structure if she had a glass of wine in her hand. She peered around the group of ceiling-gazers, who were apparently fascinated with the history of the architectural details. Over by the bar, she spied something far more interesting than two-hundred-year-old beams. "Becs, who's that guy talking to Tucker?"

Her sister bobbed a bit to get a look. "That's Logan, Tuck's boss. Or commander or whatever." Becca waved one hand in the air. "I still don't have all that army lingo straight yet. I doubt I ever will."

"*That's* Logan?" Emma strained to get a better view of him past her father's broad back.

"Yes. I told you about him. He grew up next door. Logan's younger brother and Tucker were in the same class in school. Logan's parents still live there. They should be here any minute, but his brother couldn't make it."

"Yeah, you told me about Logan, but you didn't tell me he was so cute." Emma had envisioned some stodgy old military man as Tucker's commanding officer, like a kind of General Patton-type of character. Not this tall, dark, and handsome hottie.

"Sorry. I didn't realize any time I mentioned a male to you I had to include a cuteness rating."

Emma didn't bother to look at her sister. She didn't need to. The tone of that comment told her Becca was being a smart ass. Instead, Emma kept her eyes on the newest object of her interest. "Well, now you know."

"What should we go by, do you think? A scale of one to ten perhaps?" Becca asked.

"Is he single?" Ignoring the sarcasm in Becca's voice, Emma shifted a bit farther to better peer around her dad, but not so far that Logan, or anyone else, would notice her staring.

"Yes, he's single."

"Never been married?" Emma took note that Logan had maybe an inch or two on Tucker, who was no slouch himself in the height department. That probably put Logan at just over six foot. Nice. Emma liked a man tall enough she didn't have to be afraid to wear heels. A man big and strong so a woman could feel safe and really held while in his arms.

"Not that I know of."

"Hmm. At his age, that could mean he has commitment issues." Or that he was gay, but Emma didn't get that vibe from him. Maybe he was just a player, sailing around the world with the military. A different woman in every port. Though he was in the army, not the navy.

"Jeez, Emma. Do you have to judge every man you meet on his marriage potential?"

Emma drew back at that insulting statement from her sister. "Forgive me, Miss About-to-Get-Married. I'm sorry it bothers you that I want a social life of my own."

"Forgive *you*? Are you serious? Ha! I could say the same thing." Becca's bitching interrupted Emma's fantasies about Logan.

Emma frowned. Since she hadn't been paying all that much attention to her sister while she'd been drooling over the hot military man in the room and wondering what was wrong with him that he was still available, Emma was confused. "What are you talking about? You could say the same thing about what?"

"I could say forgive *me* for assuming that if you were going to be interested in any man here this weekend, it would be Jace." Becca threw out the name of the one man Emma had refused to discuss since that fateful night at the rodeo last July.

At least Becca had kept her voice down to a low whisper so the whole room wouldn't hear. Particularly the man in question, whom Emma could see was already there. The parent blockage worked both ways, and Jace hadn't been able to get to her from his position across the room. That didn't stop him from continuing to glance and smile in her direction as she ignored him and pretended she didn't notice.

"Humph. We'll have to see about Jace." Emma wouldn't admit it to Becca, but she couldn't deny it to herself—one big reason she'd taken so much time getting ready today was because she knew she'd be seeing Jace again. Not that she was still interested in him. Her concern over her appearance was strictly to let him know what he'd missed out on last year.

"Emma, what happened between you and Jace?" Becca obviously wasn't letting this topic drop.

She decided to play it off light. "Wouldn't you like to know?"

"Yes, actually. I would." Becca nodded, eyes wide.

"Then you'd better wish for something else when blowing out the candles on your next birthday cake, because you're not going to find out." There was no way in hell Emma was going to tell her sister that literally on the way to her bed, the man had up and left. To go change his exgirlfriend's flat tire, no less. And that on top of that, he'd asked for her number, promised to call, and never did. All while Becca and Tucker were off having a wild night of passion and falling in love.

It was humiliating. She couldn't be happier that Becca had found the love of her life, but still, as the older sister, it would have been nice if she'd gotten to her happy ending first. Or at least at the same time.

But it was almost a full year later. Things might have changed. Perhaps Jace was finally untethered from his ex and ready for a relationship. It didn't matter at this point.

For this weekend, Emma didn't need or want Prince Charming, a perfect man she'd hope would drop down on one knee while holding an engagement ring.

Looking for happily ever after was exhausting. She'd be happy with some good, old-fashioned, sweaty sex. If she went into a fling with no expectations other than a good time, afterward she could fly back to New York happy and satisfied. And most importantly, unencumbered by worries about some guy who would never call even after he asked for her number and promised he would.

No more dreams of white dresses. No more hoping for promises of tomorrow. Well, perhaps a man for just one tomorrow—she was here for the entire weekend—but definitely not past then.

Logan was a possibility for that man. It would be nice to get to know him better. A whole lot better. If only she could get over to him to say hello, or at least get a closer look.

There was a jostling of positions within the wall of bodies in front of them. Emma found herself free of the blockage obstructing her view of the hot military guy still speaking with Tucker.

Shame Logan was in normal clothes—khaki pants and a blue button down shirt. Emma would have loved to see him in his uniform.

What was even more of a shame was that there was now some cute young thing hanging on him. Literally. She was holding onto his arm with a two-handed death-grip as if her life depended on it.

What the hell? Emma scowled at the sudden change of events. "Becca, who's that girl next to Logan?"

Becca followed her gaze. "Oh, I'll have to introduce you two. That's Tucker's sister, Tara."

"Ah. Of course." That figured. It seemed there was always a girl from the past getting in Emma's way. First, Jace's ex-girlfriend. Now, Logan's girl-next-door.

Becca turned to frown at her. "What's that supposed to mean?"

"Look at her, Becs. She's all over him. It's the classic little sister with a crush on big brother's friend scenario."

"No. I don't think so." Becca shook her head. "I've never gotten that impression from Logan. Besides, she hasn't even been around him. He lives in Stillwater now, and she's been away at college for the past three years. Tyler just drove her home from school today."

College. God, that made Emma feel old. It was hard not to feel old next to a perky, fresh-faced coed.

"Yup." Emma nodded. "That sounds about right."

Classic romance trope. Emma had probably read the story in some form or another a hundred times in paperback novels. There was an older neighbor boy, and his best friend's younger sister who had an unrequited crush on him since puberty. He falls for her after she returns home from college, a woman now instead of the girl he remembers. With her pigtails, braces, and knobby knees gone, they fall madly in love and live happily every after.

Emma watched as Tara took every opportunity to touch Logan. The girl made skin-on-skin contact each chance she got. Even after he moved away to get another beer, she followed and put a hand on his arm while she spoke to him.

"Hey there, darlin'."

The voice from the past interrupted Emma's observations of Tara's obvious pursuit of Logan. Emma might not have heard the voice for nearly a year, but she would know that *darlin'* anywhere.

"Jace. Nice to see you again." The words were pleasant

enough, but her tone didn't exactly say she welcomed him with open arms.

Next to her, Becca watched the situation unfold, her eyes shifting from Jace to Emma. "Um, I'm going to go get us some wine."

"That's an excellent idea." With Becca off getting them drinks, Emma didn't have to pull any punches should she decide to put Jace in his place.

Apparently unperturbed by her tone, he grinned as he took her in from head to toe with one thorough perusal. "You look real nice."

"Thank you." She didn't mind an honest compliment, even if she was still pissed over that night.

He dragged his focus back up to her eyes. "I'm glad you could make it in from New York."

"Of course I could make it. My only sister's getting married."

He nodded and took a swig out of his beer bottle. The wrap dress had definitely been the right choice. Emma took great satisfaction in how his gaze kept settling on her cleavage.

She decided to throw him a bone and make some small talk . . . and remind him about that night. Let him stew over what could have been his. "It's funny, isn't it? Almost a year ago, when we all met, did you ever imagine we'd be here now for Tucker and Becca's wedding?"

"Oh, hell no." Jace laughed. "No offense to Becca, but I never thought Tuck was getting married again. I figured he'd be single 'til the day he died."

"I guess love changes a man." Emma hoped that little tidbit sank in to Jace's cowboy brain.

He snorted out a laugh. "If you say so."

Same old cocky cowboy. Some things never changed. She wondered if the situation with his ex-girlfriend had. Emma glanced around the party. Aside from Tuck's sister, who was still staring at Logan like a puppy looking for attention, there were no other extraneous females. She had thought that maybe by now Jace's ex-girlfriend might no longer be an ex, but she wasn't here yet, if she were coming at all.

"So, you here alone?" Emma asked.

"Yup. All alone. Totally solo. For the wedding, too. What about you?"

Interesting how he'd stressed his single status so obviously. "I've promised a dance at the wedding to that very handsome gentleman shaking hands with Tucker, but otherwise, I'm solo, too."

Jace followed her gaze and grinned. "Your pa?"

"Yes. Of course, I'll have to share him with my mother. And I suppose Becca, too. As the bride, she'll have the father-daughter dance with him during the reception."

With Logan all tied up with Tara at the moment, Emma hoped Tucker had lots of good-looking, single male friends and relatives. Jace didn't deserve to think he had no competition for Emma's attention.

"You know, we should go to the reception together, you and I." Jace's invitation surprised her, though it probably shouldn't. She knew from what little time she'd spent with him that he wasn't shy.

She shrugged. "I figured I'd just catch a ride with my parents in the rental car from the church to the reception, but thanks."

Emma knew that wasn't what Jace meant but she wasn't about to make this easier on him. There'd been no apology of any sort on his part. No sorry I didn't call. Sorry I left you needy and wanting alone in a hotel room. Just an invite which amounted to not much more than saying they should probably just go to the wedding together since they'd already both be there. He was going to have to step it up a bit to win her over again.

"I wasn't talking about driving there. I meant we should *be there* together at the reception."

"Oh." Emma played it as if she'd misunderstood again. "No worries about that. We will. I laid out the seating chart on the computer for Becca. We're both sitting at the same table with the wedding party so we'll be together at the reception."

"I mean like a date."

"*Like* a date?" She cocked a brow. "But not a date?"

He grinned and shook his head. "No, I meant an actual date. Will you be my date to the wedding?"

Emma leveled her gaze on Jace. "Are you planning on staying for the whole reception or will you be leaving early for some reason?"

"Yes, I'm staying. And I apologize for last time. I won't run out on you again."

That's what she'd been waiting for. That, and a reason why he hadn't bothered to call, but one out of two wasn't bad. "All right. Since I have to be there anyway, I guess I can be your date."

He grinned. "Good. I look forward to a dance, when you're done with your pa, that is."

"What kind of dance will we be doing? Western line dancing? The Texas Two-Step?" Yeah, she was giving him a good dose of New York attitude, but he deserved it. She couldn't have him getting too confident. He wasn't out of the woods yet. Not by a long way.

"First of all, we're in Oklahoma, not Texas. And second, real cowboys don't line dance. We like to dance nice and close. Close enough to polish our belt buckles." He winked at her. "Here's your sister with your drink. Excuse me while I go grab myself another beer."

Cowboy to the bone, Jace tipped his hat and spun on one boot heel to make his way toward the bar. Emma blew out a breath. So much for keeping her resolve to not give in to this particular cowboy's charms.

"So? Tell me everything." Becca thrust one wine glass toward Emma and kept the other for herself. "Why did Jace look so happy?"

"He asked me to be his date to the wedding."

"And?"

"I said yes." Emma sighed and wondered if she'd made the right choice. She hadn't exactly taught him a lesson. When it came to men and playing this whole dating game, she stunk.

"Good." Becca broke into a wide grin, her voice high the way it used to be when she was little and excited. "Oh my God. Imagine if you and Jace hit it off! You could move here. You two could get married. We could buy houses next door to each other and have our kids at the same time."

"Whoa. Wait a minute. Don't put the cart before the horse. First of all, I'm not looking for anything serious this weekend. Second, I still have many, many doubts about the relationship potential of that one." Grave doubts after last year's encounter.

If Jace could keep his butt, and his other parts, in the same room as Emma without running off, which had yet to be proven, then maybe they could have one hot night together. But a long-term relationship? Probably not. It would depend on whether he was ready for commitment again after his last relationship, and she seriously had concerns about that.

"All right." Becca sighed. "I won't start looking at apartments for you quite yet."

"Yeah. Good idea." Emma laughed. She turned and noticed Tucker was on his way over with Logan.

Damn, Logan was handsome. Tara's schoolgirl crush on

the man might make him ineligible for Emma's amorous pursuits for the weekend, but she could still appreciate him as a fine male specimen. Not just his rugged good looks, but his entire demeanor. He oozed testosterone.

Logan. Jace. Tucker. Oklahoma was full of gorgeous men, but they weren't model perfect. They were manly men, all tanned and toned. Their bodies were firm, not flabby, and from honest hard work, not the gym.

With a flutter low in her belly as Tucker and Logan got closer, Emma once again had to appreciate the differences between the men she was used to in New York and the ones here. Maybe she should take a quick look at the *Help Wanted* and the *Apartments for Rent* listings in the local paper. Just to see.

"Hey, baby." Tucker reeled Becca in with one arm around her shoulders and brushed his lips across her forehead. "I wanted to introduce Emma to Logan."

Logan didn't wait for the introduction. Emma found herself captured in his intense brown gaze even before Tucker made it official. He didn't break eye contact. Not when he extended his hand to shake hers. Not as his deep, warm voice washed over her as he said, "Very nice to meet you, Emma."

The sound of her name on his lips sent a thrill through her. "Pleasure's all mine. I've heard a lot about you."

One dark brow rose. "I'm not sure if that's good or bad. Perhaps we need to discuss it, in case I need to redeem myself."

Oh, she could definitely discuss it and more. She'd do anything to keep Logan talking to her. Looking at her. Touching her would be nice, too. Emma swallowed past the tightness in her throat and hoped her voice wouldn't come out sounding like a frog. "Anytime you want. I'm available."

"No time like the present, I always say." He smiled and drew her attention to his lips. Good strong lips made for kissing. "Have you seen Mrs. Jenkins' rose garden yet? It's the pride of the county. She was telling us how it's just come into bloom."

"I haven't seen it, but I'd love to. It sounds beautiful." Emma yanked her gaze away from the temptation that was Logan and found both Becca and Tucker staring, watching as if she and Logan were on stage and this conversation was the show.

"Good." He touched her arm and she couldn't have cared less anymore about Becca and Tucker or the twin expressions of shock they wore, until Logan frowned and dug into the pocket of his khaki pants. He pulled out a ringing cell phone. Emma flashed back to Jace and the incident with his ex. She got a feeling of dread as Logan glanced at the name on his phone.

He looked up at Tucker. "It's Layne."

Emma's brain spun, wondering if this Layne was a male or a female. And more important, a friend or a girlfriend.

"Layne's calling from Okinawa?" Tucker asked, surprise evident in his voice.

"Yeah. He wants to congratulate you since he can't be here." Logan turned to Emma. "Excuse me a moment? I have to take this."

He? Phew.

"Of course." Emma couldn't stop her sigh of relief. Whoever this Layne was, he wasn't a *she,* or Logan's girlfriend, and that was very good news.

Logan stepped through the doorway as he flipped open the phone. Tucker followed him out into the hall and Emma could breathe freely again.

She turned to Becca, not concerned, but still curious. "So who is Layne and why is he calling from Japan?"

"Logan's little brother. He's in the marines and stationed over there, and don't change the subject." Becca glared at Emma.

"I didn't realize I was."

Becca very pointedly glanced at Logan and then back to Emma. "What's going on?"

"What do you mean?"

Her sister checked the hallway, then leaned in. "The chemistry was so thick between you two, I could cut it with a knife."

It had been, hadn't it? Emma smiled. She was glad it hadn't been her imagination. Even if all evidence indicated Logan wasn't the marrying kind, she sensed he was definitely interested in a little extracurricular activity. She could handle a bit of that.

Emma shrugged. "I don't know what's going on. We're just talking."

"Maybe you'd better figure it out." Becca shook her head. "You just made a date with Jace to the wedding. And now you're making a date to see the rose garden with Logan. It's getting a bit hard to keep up with you and the social life you claim not to have."

Crap. Jace. Logan's presence had so consumed Emma, she'd forgotten the date she'd agreed to with Jace. The irony wasn't lost on her. She'd gone months upon months without a date at home. But on her first day here, she'd found two men she was interested in, and they both appeared to be interested in her. Now what?

A female laugh from the corner of the room caught her ear and Emma turned. She saw Tara talking with Tyler and their parents. That was a vivid reminder that as strong as the chemistry had seemed between her and Logan, Emma was still late to the party.

Tara had grown up with Logan. They had history together and Tara had an obvious crush on Logan. Even if it was yet to be determined whether the feeling was reciprocal, Emma wasn't about to put all of her eggs in one basket. She knew darn well from past experience that things that seemed like a done deal could change in an instant. All it took was one little text message.

Emma turned back to Becca. "Eh, you know. A girl's got to keep her options open. Might as well play the field. Besides, how in the world could I choose between a soldier and a cowboy, anyway?"

Becca gazed at her fiancé in the hallway. "Luckily, I didn't have to choose. I've got the best of both worlds with Tucker."

"Yes, you do." Emma glanced again at the conversation happening among the Jenkins family in the corner. Tara's light and cheery laugh filled the room one more time as she flipped a silky fall of long dark hair over one shoulder. "We'd better go and mingle with your new in-laws so we don't look like rude New Yorkers."

Time to size up the competition a little closer.

Chapter
Three

As the party began to wind down, Emma put the empty glasses she'd collected from around the house into the sink and then turned to frown at her sister. "I can't believe you don't know any fun places to go around here."

The boys were all going out, and Emma would be damned if the girls sat home and did nothing. Though, the more she thought about it, the more she realized Becca never went out. Not when she was a teenager. Not as an adult. It was Emma who snuck out the window of their shared bedroom so her parents wouldn't know she was meeting her friends. Becca was always the one who stayed home, studying or reading.

It would have been easy for Becca to go out, too. They looked so much alike, once Emma turned twenty-one she could have said she'd lost her driver's license, gotten a duplicate to replace it, and given the old one to Becca to use to get into bars until she reached legal drinking age. But, no. Emma had suggested that once and Becca had lectured her about it being illegal and rattled off all the possible consequences.

Becca probably should have been born the older sibling. Some strange twist of fate or nature had put Emma in the wrong position in the Hart sibling lineup.

"Emma, why would I know the bars around here? I live in Stillwater."

"So?" Emma asked.

"So, Miss New York is the Center of the Universe, we're a couple of hours away from Stillwater here. I've only come to visit Tucker's parents a few times, and we don't take them out barhopping while we're here."

"Maybe you should." Emma scowled as she got another look at Tara pawing Logan. "When are the guys leaving for the bachelor party?"

"I don't know. Soon, I guess." Becca glanced at the cow-shaped wall clock hanging above the kitchen cabinets. "At least, I hope it's soon. I don't want Tucker out all night. He'll have dark circles under his eyes for the pictures tomorrow."

Emma sent her sister a glance. That's what Becca was most worried about? That Tuck would look tired in the wedding photos? She should be more worried about what kind of adult entertainment his twenty-something, single brother, Tyler, who was also the best man, had come up with.

Best to keep that reality check to herself. Emma knew Becca too well to bring up that. Her sister could worry herself into a hysterical tizzy in no time, and Emma knew who would have to play babysitter to the nervous bride all night.

Nope. Best to go out and get them both drunk enough to forget about what might or might not be going on at that stag party. And while she was at it, Emma wouldn't mind feeling out Tara to see what was going on between her and Logan.

In vino veritas. In wine was truth. Emma noted Tara was drinking beer, not wine. She didn't know the Latin for beer, but she figured enough of any alcohol would work just as well as a truth serum.

"I think we should ask your new sister-in-law where there's a fun bar. She's the right age to be going out partying. She must know a good place." Emma put into action her plan to get Tara drunk to draw some information out of her.

"Why are you so eager to go out?" Becca frowned.

"Because my only sister is getting married tomorrow and I'm her maid of honor. It's my job to make sure you have one last girls' night out. The boys get to have a bachelor party, so you need a bachelorette party. Tit for tat." When Becca didn't look convinced, Emma added, "Besides, it's pretty selfish of you to deny me the opportunity to go out and see some hot Oklahoma cowboy scenery while I'm here, just because you've already found your perfect man. You owe me for that, you know. Need I remind you who's responsible for your meeting Tucker?"

"I know. You are." Becca rolled her eyes. "You're going to remind me of that until the day we die, aren't you?"

"Maybe. Or maybe if you'll just agree to let me take you out on the town tonight, I could be convinced to never mention it again." Emma dangled that hint of a promise like a carrot.

"Fine, go and talk to Tara about a bar. Though I don't know why you're looking for a cowboy or any other man. You agreed to go to the reception as Jace's date. A fact you seem to keep forgetting."

Emma dismissed Becca's criticism with a wave of one hand. "I only agreed to that so I could show him what he can't have."

"I'll never understand you." Becca shook her head.

"As it should be. My brilliance shall remain a mystery. So we're going out then?" Emma asked just to confirm she'd won this battle.

"Yes. But we're not staying out too late. I don't want to have bags under my eyes for the pictures, either."

"That, dear sister, is what makeup is for." Emma grinned and saw through the kitchen doorway that the men had begun to gather in the front foyer. "Looks like the herd is forming for the stag party exodus. You go kiss your man good-bye and then grab your bar purse."

"I didn't pack a special purse for barhopping. I'll have to use my regular one."

That figured. Becca never thought ahead about fashion necessities the way Emma did. She, of course, had packed not one but two small purses for going out. They were just big enough for her ID, lipstick, some cash, and a cell phone.

"I'll loan you one of mine. Now, go. Say good-bye to Tucker. I'm going to talk to Tara about the local hotspots." Emma headed toward Tara. The girl had finally released her hold on Logan so he could join the rest of the guys.

Emma donned what she hoped was a smile that appeared sincere and prepared to make nice, satisfied this evening was going to go her way.

An hour later, it was obvious the night was not going at all as Emma had planned.

"Logan looked great tonight, didn't he?"

Emma couldn't stifle her sigh at Tara's dreamy-eyed question. "I don't know. Did he?"

"He totally did. I was away at school all year. I haven't seen him in what feels like forever." Across the tiny cocktail table in the dark corner of the bar, Tara sighed. "He looks so good out of uniform. I wish he'd just retire. Then he could move back home again and work at his pa's shop." Tara looked to Emma for a comment.

Emma had to scramble to come up with something to

say. "Sorry. I only met him tonight so I don't have a basis of comparison on how good he looks, in or out of uniform." Though she wouldn't mind seeing him out of his uniform, and she didn't mean in his civilian clothes either.

Tara nodded. "Jeans look so much better on him. Even the khaki dress pants he had on tonight are an improvement over those camouflage pants he and Tuck wear."

"Well, that's the uniform. It's my understanding they have to wear it. It's, you know, kind of the rules." Emma had tried to temper her answer, but it still came out sounding snarky. Luckily, Tara didn't seem to notice.

Damn, had Emma ever been this young and naïve? Maybe a million years ago. She willed Becca to hurry back from the ladies room before she lost patience with the college coed with the stars—or rather Logan—in her eyes.

"I know it's their uniform, but I'm used to Logan from before he joined the military." Tara's voice took on a faraway quality. "When we were younger, Logan was always in jeans and a cowboy hat. He had this old pair of boots that he loved. He said he'd never find a pair like them again so he wore them until the sole flapped when he walked. Even then he didn't want to part with them. He nailed the sole back on and wore them until his mother made him stop."

Instead of the country song blaring out of the jukebox, Emma wouldn't have been surprised to hear a sappy soundtrack to accompany Tara's memories. Violins or maybe a harp, like the background music from a television show dream sequence.

It was obvious the girl was lost in the distant past. Her crush on Logan had apparently been the result of a surge of prepubescent hormones. Tara wanted the Logan of her youth back. The young cowboy version, not the mature adult soldier he was now.

In Emma's opinion, Tara was barking up the wrong

tree. Logan had to be in his mid to late thirties, so he was obviously a career military man. From what Becca had told her, he was an officer. He wasn't going to up and retire to hang around in holey boots with Tara.

Or maybe he would. Considering Emma's bad track record with men, she might not know as much as she thought she did. After all, she never would have guessed Jace, or any living breathing man, would have given up a night of sex to change a flat tire.

That depressing thought left Emma torn between calling it a night and ordering more drinks so she could get drunk enough to forget about this day. All of it. Every bad decision she'd made. Accepting Jace's invite when her gut told her it was a bad idea. Noticing Logan when Tara was obviously already in love with him. And now, going out, just the three of them.

"Hey. What did I miss?" Becca finally returned from the bathroom.

About damn time. Becca had taken long enough that Emma regretted not going with her, but even as much as Emma had hated their conversation, it would have been rude to leave Tara sitting alone at the table.

Emma let out a sigh. "Nothing. Just talking about boots."

Becca sat. "You must be in heaven. You love boots."

"Not this kind." The flat tone of Emma's reply had Becca glancing at her.

"Oh. Um, so, any interesting scenery show up while I was gone?" Changing the subject. Smart girl. Her sister knew Emma well enough to know when something was up.

"What kind of scenery are you looking for?" Tara asked Becca.

"Not for me, it's for Em—" The kick in the shin under the table shut Becca up.

Becca glared at Emma, who opened her eyes wide and mouthed, "Shut up."

Becca frowned and continued, "Um, you know. Just some authentic western scenery. Like farmers or . . . stuff. I want Emma to get the full Oklahoma experience while she's here."

"Then you should take her to a rodeo. Logan used to take Tuck and Layne to rodeos all the time, back when Tyler and I were so little we had to fight to go along and not to be left home with Ma."

If this girl said the name *Logan* one more time . . .

Emma gritted her teeth. "That sounds fun."

Becca shot Emma a glance and then turned to Tara. "Ah, we've actually both been to a rodeo. It's where I met Tucker last year."

"Oh, that's right. I heard that story. I'd forgotten because I assumed when I heard where he met you that you were a buckle bunny. Then when it turned out you weren't . . ." Tara shrugged and let the sentence trail off.

After that strange comment, Emma wasn't sure whether to feel insulted on Becca's behalf of not.

Tara wrinkled her nose as she glanced at the collection of men gathered there. "You'll find more guys at the bar on the other side of town. The one with the pool table. There are a few cowboys in here tonight. No one as cute as Logan, but at least there's some authentic western scenery for you. That way when you're back in New York you can say you saw some."

"Yup." Oh, yeah. That would make a hell of a story for Emma to tell around the water cooler at work. How she went out and saw a guy in a cowboy hat sitting at a bar. Simply riveting.

Emma drew in a deep breath. She was being ridiculous and acting like a child. She knew that. Honestly, Tara was being perfectly nice and polite. Tara didn't know Emma was interested in getting to know Logan better. Why should she? Emma had only met him a few hours ago, had only spoken a handful of sentences to him. And, as Becca kept reminding her, Emma had a date with Jace. Aside from his unbelievably huge *faux pas* with her last year, Jace seemed to be a decent guy.

So why wasn't Emma happy to be going to the wedding with Jace?

Because talking to Logan, even for that short time, had made her heart beat faster than it had in years, that's why. What did that mean? Love at first sight? Or just lust because, like it or not, Tara was right—Logan had looked good in those khakis and the cotton button-down shirt that complemented his rugged suntanned complexion so perfectly.

It must be Emma's inner competitive spirit set off by the challenge Tara presented that had her blood pressure rising every time the girl mentioned Logan's name. Certainly not what Emma feared—that after meeting Logan once, she'd developed a schoolgirl crush on him to rival even Tara's.

What if Emma had said no to Jace's invitation? Or if the cell phone hadn't rung with that call from Japan and she had gone outside for a walk in the rose garden with Logan? What if Emma didn't give a flying fig that Tara had an insane crush on Logan—probably the biggest crush that Emma had ever witnessed firsthand—and went for it with him anyway?

What if Emma was doomed to wonder for the rest of her life, *what if?* That would stink. There was nothing worse than living with regret.

Maybe all this introspection was alcohol induced and by tomorrow, Emma would forget all about Logan. That would be good. She didn't believe in love at first sight anyway. Lust maybe, but not love.

Still, Emma decided to investigate that concept further. "Becs?"

"Yes?" Becca looked a bit wary when she turned to Emma. She knew to tread lightly when Emma was cranky. Most likely Emma's bad behavior tonight had given her sister that impression.

"When you first met Tucker last year at the rodeo, did you know then, that night, that he was—you know—the one?"

That brought Tara's attention whipping back to the conversation at their table, just when she'd been busy looking around the bar, probably for someone better to hang out with.

Okay, that was mean. Emma mentally took the nasty comment back and waited for Becca's answer.

"Looking back, I think I did feel it then, but I didn't realize it. At least, I didn't admit it to myself. I sure tried to keep it casual. Just a one-night"—Becca's gaze moved to Tara as she cut herself off—"um, just a casual meeting."

Emma smiled at how Becca scurried to not tell Tucker's little sister how she'd planned on one night of hot sex and nothing more.

Tara leaned forward in her chair. "So then how did you and Tuck end up together?"

"Once we saw each other again and I discovered we both worked at OSU—"

"You couldn't keep it casual anymore," Tara finished.

"No, we couldn't. I guess it was inevitable we'd end up with each other. I just was too . . ." Becca searched for the word.

"Stubborn?" Emma had no problem supplying it.

"Yes, thank you." The look Becca sent her was not at all grateful. "Too stubborn to realize it."

"That's how I think it is with me and Logan. I can tell he's trying to keep it casual, probably out of respect for my

parents or something, but it's inevitable we'll end up together. I know we will. Hopefully by the end of tomorrow night." Tara looked confident in her prediction.

Unable to take any more of Tara's youthful exuberance
when it came to the topic of Logan, Emma stood. "I'm
going to get us another round. We all ready? Maybe some
shots, too. What kind do we want?"

The room tilted slightly to the right, which made Logan's decision for him. He'd considered standing up, but
on second thought it might be best to stay sitting right
there. Possibly all night.

"Dude, another Alabama Slammer?" Tyler stood before
him holding a glass shaker of something red in his hand.

"No. Thanks."

"You want a different kind?" Tyler asked. "I've got
Jaeger if you want."

"No. I'm good." The four shots Logan had been talked
into doing had been a bad idea to begin with.

Shots—and sweet, red-colored ones at that—were for
college kids and young guys like Tyler. Not for a man
about to turn forty. Logan could handle his liquor, just not
so much of it in so short a time and definitely not Alabama
Slammers. Give him some straight bourbon or whisky.
Or hell, even tequila. That Logan could metabolize. But
sticky, sweet crap? Not so much.

He probably should have eaten more at the party at the
Jenkinses', too. If he hadn't been so busy drooling over
Emma, and being pissed that Jace was doing the same, he
might have enjoyed the food and had more.

Not enough dinner, sugary sweet shots, and a belly full
of beer—the perfect storm for one hell of a hangover tomorrow. Crap. Logan groaned when his fuzzy brain remembered what tomorrow was—Tuck's wedding day.

Jace and Tyler had gone all out in their planning for this

shindig. A hotel room crowded with old friends, an exotic dancer—who had come and gone so fast that maybe they'd be able to get away with not telling the bride a stripper was ever there—beer and, of course, the infamous shots. But it was getting late.

Logan frowned at his watch and realized it was harder to read than it should be. Damn, he was drunk. This party needed to break up. Or at least Tuck needed to quit drinking. The groom couldn't crawl down the aisle reeking of booze and looking like death warmed over because he'd been out drunk all night. He scanned the crowd for Tuck and found him talking to Jace.

Drawing in a deep breath, Logan braced a hand on each arm of the chair and hoisted himself up. He stood for a second until he knew he could walk without stumbling, and then made his way over.

"Logan. You need a drink?" Jace glanced down at Logan's empty hands.

"No, thanks." Logan eyed the big red plastic cup in Tuck's hand. "What are you drinking?"

"Pop."

"Really?" He glanced into Tuck's cup and saw it did indeed look like cola. "With bourbon in it?"

Tuck laughed. "No. Just plain old soda pop. Becca would kill me if I was hung over tomorrow."

Well, crap. Logan had been trying to keep in the party spirit. As one of the groomsmen, it was his duty to participate in all the activities, but if the groom hadn't even been drinking, then why the hell had he?

Logan shook his head. "Then she's not going to be too happy with me." Good thing the wedding was later in the day or he'd be in big trouble.

"You'll be fine. She's so happy this day is here, she won't even notice that all the men are moving a little slow." Tuck grinned.

"And wearing sunglasses," Jace added. "Nothing worse than a sunny day after a long night."

True that. Logan cringed at the thought of the headache he'd suffer from in the morning and glanced at Jace's drink. "What're you drinking?"

"Unlike the groom here, my soda pop comes with bourbon." Jace grinned and raised his cup. "I couldn't handle any more of that red shit Tyler's pouring."

Jace had been smarter than Logan, and that knowledge didn't sit any better in his gut than those shots. At least Jace was drinking something alcoholic so Logan would have company in his hangover misery tomorrow. He should probably find some water and get home. Sooner rather than later.

He glanced at the desk. There must be a phonebook in here somewhere. Hotel rooms had two things, a bible and a phonebook. He'd get his dose of the first at the church tomorrow during the ceremony, but right now he had to find the second because he really needed to call a cab.

"So, Tuck. I asked Emma to be my date tomorrow and she said yes." Jace's declaration brought Logan's head around from his visual search for the phone directory.

Tuck glanced at Logan before saying to Jace, "Really? I didn't know you were planning that."

"I didn't know it myself, until I got a look at her in that dress."

Logan set his jaw, trying not to punch Jace in his grinning mouth for talking about Tuck's sister-in-law like some piece of ass he'd picked up at a bar.

"You do know my parents invited Jacqueline's whole family to the wedding, right?"

"Uh, what?" Jace looked ready to vomit up his bourbon at Tuck's news.

Logan sifted through his alcohol-soaked brain and retrieved a fuzzy memory. Jacqueline was the girl Jace had dated for years, until they broke up a year or so ago. Judging by how Jace had paled at the mention of her name, the breakup hadn't been all smooth sailing.

"They belong to our church, so my parents invited them."

"And are they coming?" Jace swallowed hard. "All of them?"

"Yup. You gonna be okay with her being there?" Tuck eyed Jace, probably afraid there could be trouble with the two ex-lovers in the same room.

"Sure. Why wouldn't I be? We're still friends. We talk. She's called me a few times when she needed help with something or another."

If that were all true, then why didn't Jace look happy? Could it be because his former girlfriend who still called him would be there while he was on a date with another woman? Logan got the distinct feeling Jace had hoped to have his pie and eat it, too. Have what fun he could with Emma while she was in town, all without Jacqueline ever knowing. That way after Emma left town, Jace could go back to whatever post-breakup dance he and his ex-girlfriend were doing together.

If that had been Jace's plan, Logan took great satisfaction that it had been ruined. Emma deserved better than that. She deserved a date to the wedding who would be focused solely on her. Logan could definitely have been that guy. The army was the only other commitment in Logan's life, and this weekend he was on official leave, so even Uncle Sam wouldn't demand his attention.

Still looking disturbed, Jace took another big swallow out of his cup and then glanced at the desk where the booze was spread out. "I need another drink."

Logan would bet he did. He couldn't help his smile as stone-faced Jace made a beeline for the bar. "Hmm. Interesting turn of events with Jace's girlfriend being there to-morrow."

"Isn't it?" Tuck laughed. "So . . . did I kick that door open wide enough for you?"

"What door would that be?"

"The one Emma's behind. Now that Jace will be worried about Jacqueline being there, you and she might get that walk through the rose garden after all. That is what you're hoping for, no?"

So much for his poker face. Logan laughed. "I can't fool you, can I?"

"No more than I could fool you."

Logan shook his head. "Guess not. But damn, open door or not, I'm going to be useless tomorrow if I don't get home, find some water and aspirin, and get some sleep."

"Come on, I'll drive you. I need to get out of here, too. Knowing Becca, she's waiting up for me."

Knowing Jace, and that he was partially in charge of this bachelor party, Logan didn't blame her. "Can you drive?"

"Yeah. I only had one beer here. I switched to this hours ago." Tuck raised his cup of pop.

"Okay. Then let's go." His own bed, or at least the bed in his old room at his parents' house, sounded very good to Logan about now.

"Just let me tell Jace and Tyler I'm leaving."

Logan leaned against the door as Tuck said his good-byes, amid plenty of protest from the guests that the groom shouldn't leave his own party.

Most of the guys were so drunk, Tuck was able to skirt the issue and get away. "All right. We can go."

"Good." Because the sleepy stage of being drunk was starting to creep up on Logan, and he could hardly keep his eyes open.

"It was good to see you loosen up tonight." Tuck grinned as Logan stumbled out the hotel door and toward the parked truck.

"Don't get too used to it." Good chance Logan wouldn't be drinking again for a long time. And once the semester began and they were surrounded by ROTC cadets, he'd have to act more like Tuck's superior officer than his friend.

"Believe me, I won't. But it was nice tonight." Still wearing a smile, Tuck clicked open the door locks.

The truck ride lulled Logan into a hypnotic state. Before he knew it, Tuck was jostling him.

"Wake up, Sleeping Beauty." Tuck's voice came from across the dark cab. "You want me to drive you right to your door?"

Logan dragged himself up from sleep and realized the truck was parked in the Jenkins drive. He straightened his spine, stretching sore muscles. It hadn't been a long drive from the hotel to the house, but it had obviously been long enough for him to fall asleep, or pass out, and for his back to get stiff. "Nah. Thanks. I can walk home."

"You sure? It's dark. Don't want you to trip and fall."

"Yes, smart ass. I'm sure. I'll be fine. It's almost the full moon." Logan glanced over and saw the swath of illumination from the floodlight outside his parents' house next door. "And Mom left the porch light on for me."

This felt like he was a kid again. Hanging out at the Jenkins house until after dark, and then walking home across their lawns by the glow of a single bulb.

"All right. Don't want you to break something before tomorrow." Even in the dimness of the truck, Logan could see Tuck's cocky grin.

"I won't." Logan reached for the handle and swung the

passenger door wide. Before he stepped down, he turned back to Tuck. "Have fun explaining the late hour and that stripper to your bride."

Tuck groaned. "Thanks."

With a smile of satisfaction, Logan got out, slammed the door shut, and aimed slightly wobbly legs for home. He did pretty well. The path he walked wasn't exactly straight, but he didn't trip and end up facedown in the grass so Logan was feeling real proud of himself as he neared the mecca that was his bed.

"Logan! Wait up." Tara's voice had him stopping in mid-step before he'd crossed the property line.

"Tara?" He turned and saw her jogging toward him. "What are doing creeping around in the middle of the night?"

She came to a stop in front of him and swayed a bit. When she reached out and regained her balance with a hand braced on his chest, Logan figured it out. Tara was drunker than he was. Or at least more unsteady. "I was sitting on the back porch and heard you and Tuck in the drive."

He grabbed her hands to stop her as she moved them down his sides. "You shouldn't be up. It's late and tomorrow is a big day."

"I know. My big bro is getting married." Tara was dressed in a shirt he'd never seen before, and it allowed him to see much more of her than he wanted to.

He yanked his eyes up and away from her cleavage. This girl was and always would be in the sister category in his mind. "What I meant, Tara, was that I think we both need to get to bed."

"My thoughts exactly." Wearing a sly smile, she took a step closer.

As she pressed against him, Logan stepped back. "Tara. You've had too much to drink."

"Don't sound so judgmental about it. Everyone else was drunk, too." She dropped her hands and folded her arms across her chest.

This was good. He could handle an angry Tara much better than an amorous one. Now that the immediate danger of her fondling him had passed, what she'd said struck him. "Everyone else is drunk, too? Like who?"

When he and the guys had left the party to go to the hotel for Tuck's bachelor party, there'd been friends and relatives milling around drinking coffee and eating cake. What could have possibly happened after that to get everyone drunk? Shots of after dinner cordials? Doubtful.

"We girls went out for drinks for Becca's bachelorette party. It was Emma's idea."

The mention of Emma got Logan's attention. He pictured how different things might have been if Emma had appeared out of the darkness and wrapped her arms around him instead of Tara. That thought had his body starting to wake up, just when he'd assumed it was as drunk as his brain and ready for sleep.

"Is Emma staying here with Becca tonight?" He glanced at the house, and pictured Emma inside.

"Nah, we had the cab drop her at the hotel then bring us home. Becca's in Tuck's room, and because she won't let him see her in the morning before the wedding, Tuck's on the sleeper sofa in the den. Full house over here, but your house isn't. And your room is all the way at the other end of the hall from your parents' room." Tara ran her hand up his chest.

"Tara, listen to me. You need to turn around, go inside, and head directly for bed. Your own bed. Tuck and your parents are counting on you to be in top shape for tomorrow."

"But I'm not tired." She pouted, which reminded

him of a time when she was five and he'd told her she couldn't play baseball with the big boys.

"Then just lie down and close your eyes." He'd used that line a few times during his babysitting days when Tara and Tyler had refused to go to sleep. Hopefully it worked as well with drunks as with children. With a hand on each shoulder he turned her to face her house.

She glanced back over her shoulder, her lids sagging heavily over her eyes. "Want to join me?"

Logan was truly in hell.

"No." He hadn't used the scary commander tone that he used with cadets, but it was stern enough to leave no doubt that what she'd suggested was not happening.

"Party pooper."

"Yeah, whatever."

She took a few steps and then called back. "See you tomorrow. Save me a dance at the wedding."

Logan had a bad feeling all of this—the drinking, the flirting—was going to be repeated tomorrow and there wasn't a damn thing he could do about it.

Feeling a lot more sober now, he watched until Tara disappeared around the corner of the house, and then he made his way to the safety of his own parents' home unmolested. The whole way there he envisioned Emma, back in her hotel room after the bachelorette party, all tipsy and tempting in a big king-sized bed all alone.

Good thing Emma wasn't spending the night with Becca, temptingly close next door. So close Logan might have been tempted to knock on her window. Maybe invite her on a moonlight stroll in the rose garden. Drunk as he was, he could have done it. Probably the only thing that would have stopped him was the fear of running into Tara again.

The encounter with Tara, and now all these thoughts of

Emma, had knocked the weariness right out of Logan. That figured. Chances were he wouldn't fall asleep anytime soon. He'd be tired and hung over tomorrow for the wedding.

Resigned to his fate, he headed for bed. Logan had faced worse in his career. He'd get through this.

Chapter
Four

"Ugh." Emma glared at her reflection in the hallway mirror. "Becca, next time you get married, can it be in a month when the relative humidity is less than eighty-percent? Would you please look at my hair?"

Halfway up the staircase in the Jenkins house, Becca paused and cocked a brow. "There isn't going to be a next time. I'm getting married once and only once. And your hair looks fine, just like it always does, so stop worrying. I have to touch up my nail polish. I somehow managed to chip a nail last night."

Probably when they all stumbled into the taxi to get home after the shots at the bar. Emma had woken up in her hotel room this morning feeling less than stellar. The cotton mouth, headache, and exhaustion she could handle, but not having a bad hair day. Today's wedding pictures would be around for decades and Emma was going to look good for them even if it killed her.

She glanced into the mirror again and sighed. She'd been planning to leave it down, but the weather had managed to make even her pin-straight hair do some puffy, frizzy kind of thing she was not happy with.

It was early in the day. They didn't need to get dressed and leave for the church for a little while yet. She could still make a change.

Emma called up the stairs after her sister, "Maybe I should run into town and see if someone at the salon can do a quick up-do."

"You look beautiful. I wouldn't change a thing." A very male voice behind Emma had her spinning around.

"Logan. Uh, hi." Emma swallowed hard. She'd been caught complaining and by Logan of all people. "Thank you. That's sweet of you to say."

She smoothed the skirt of the sundress she'd thrown on at the hotel to wear until it was time to put on the official maid of honor dress that was hanging upstairs next to Becca's wedding gown.

"You're very welcome and it's true." He held a big box in his hands, but Emma was more interested in noticing how his dark eyes had swept her from head to toe. "So I'm here on a very important errand on behalf of the groom, since he's not to come within twenty feet of this house."

Emma smiled. "That's right. Becca won't let Tuck see her until she walks down the aisle."

"Yes, I'm well aware of that. He woke me up at dawn knocking on my door after he was kicked out of here because he's not allowed to see Becca. So where would you like it?"

Emma would *like it* in the bedroom, and in the shower, and maybe in that hammock in the back yard—but Logan probably was talking about the box, not sex. "I don't know. What is it?"

"The flowers. I took out the boutonnières for the groomsmen, so all the rest are for you ladies here. Oh, and I also left in the corsages and boutonnières for the parents of the bride and the parents of the groom."

"Impressive organization. Thank you." Emma smiled. A man who was organized and hot was a rare find indeed.

"Eh, it's nothing. Seems like planning a wedding isn't all that much different from planning a mission, and that I've been well trained for." He shrugged, the brown cardboard box still in his hands.

She cringed and glanced around the foyer, at a loss. "Sorry. You need to put that somewhere. I guess the flowers should go in the fridge so they don't wilt, but it's pretty packed with last night's leftovers."

"Not a problem. I can solve that. Follow me." Logan tilted his head toward the back of the house. He led Emma to the door that opened into the garage. "Can you just grab the door?"

"Sure." She swung it wide enough for him to walk through with the oversized box.

He glanced over his shoulder as she followed. "There's an extra fridge out here and I'm betting it's turned on because of the party last night."

Emma hadn't noticed the big white fridge humming against the wall. She'd been too busy ogling Logan's butt. She hated to admit it, but Tara was right—Logan did look really good in jeans. The worn denim pulled just tight enough across his ass to make her mouth water. Then there was that kind of swagger that the cowboy boots put into his every step.

Emma wrestled her attention away from his assets and back to what should be her priority given her position as maid of honor—keeping Becca's bridal bouquet from dying before the ceremony. She skirted around him to pull open the refrigerator door and sure enough a cloud of cold air drifted out.

"Wow. I had no idea this was even out here. You're handy to have around." She shot him what she hoped was a casual and maybe a little bit sexy smile.

This flirting business required a light hand and a delicate balance. Juggling flirting and flowers—good thing she'd had coffee that morning so she was alert enough to handle it all.

"I try." He laughed and put the box down on a tool chest while Emma bent to move a few six-packs of soda and beer to the bottom shelf so the flowers would fit on the top one.

"Well, you do a very good job." She turned, prepared to do some more flirting while she had the chance, when she came face to face with the bouquet Logan held out.

She stopped and stared as her throat grew tight from the sight and smell of the floral arrangement. She and Becca had gone through dress fittings and a bridal shower in New York together, but it hadn't truly hit Emma until she saw those perfect white roses punctuated by the deep blue delphiniums and dark green ivy in Becca's bridal bouquet. That's when it felt real.

Her little sister was getting married today. Never again would they be the two single sisters, banded together against the world. No more girls' night out. Becca was Tucker's now.

"Emma?"

At the sound of Logan saying her name, Emma snapped back to reality. She reached out to take the flowers and realized her hand was shaking.

"Sorry. I'm just being a girlie girl. Getting choked up about Becca's flowers. Silly, huh?" She forced out a wobbly laugh.

She bent to put the bouquet in the fridge and while hidden by the door, swiped at the moisture in her eyes. There was no way she was going to cry in front of Logan. Especially not over a stupid bouquet.

"Not at all. You know, right before I left my house Tuck was putting on his tuxedo. Seeing him, standing there all decked out and looking like a groom, I got a little choked up myself. I've seen him in his dress uniform a dozen times, but the tuxedo and the boutonnière? It kinda got to me." Logan shrugged and looked absolutely adorable. "Guess I'm a girlie girl, too, huh?"

"No. Definitely not." That idea made Emma laugh. He was possibly the manliest man she'd ever met, even when holding a handful of flowers.

"All right. I'll take your word for it." His smile made her heart flutter.

She took the next bouquet he handed her and put it in the fridge, changing the subject until she could get her emotions under control. "Tucker's dressed in his tux already?"

Between worrying about her hair, and lusting after Logan, had it gotten later than she'd thought?

"He is. As soon as these are safely put away, I'm going to head home and get dressed myself. The photographer wants to take the pictures of the groomsmen early so she can come here and take some pictures of you girls while you're getting ready." He smiled. "See, told you. As many details as a military invasion."

"I guess so." The thought of what Logan would look like in his tuxedo was a very tempting image. Emma loved a uniform but she had to agree with Becca's thinking. Having Tucker and Logan in uniform and Tyler and Jace in tuxedos might have looked disjointed for the pictures. It seemed Becca's obsessive compulsive disorder extended to needing even the groomsmen to match. Uniforms or not, it would certainly be a good-looking group of men.

Emma took the clear plastic box holding two wrist corsages and two boutonnières and rested it on top of one of the six-packs. Beer and flowers. It made for an interesting arrangement.

"Thank you for bringing these over." She swung the door closed and turned to find Logan much closer than he had been before, his arm braced on the top of the fridge.

"My pleasure." He smiled, his lips temptingly close. "Can I just sneak past you and grab a pop?"

Emma's mouth grew dry. She licked her own lips and couldn't seem to keep from staring at his. "Um, a pop?"

His dimples grew deeper as he smiled. "That would be soda to you northeastern girls."

"Oh, sure. Of course. Sorry." She liked right where she was, under the arch of his arm, but she moved out of the way so he could get into the fridge.

He opened the door and grabbed a can, glancing at her over his shoulder as he did. "I already had a cup of coffee, but I could sure use the extra caffeine this morning."

She nodded. It seemed the closer Logan stood, the less she had to say, and Emma rarely found herself speechless.

"So, I guess I'll see you later?" His eyes focused on hers. "I look forward to it."

He didn't move. Emma didn't feel compelled to, either, unless it was to step into his arms and see if his kiss was as good as she imagined it to be.

His gaze moved away from her eyes as he reached out and brushed a piece of hair that had fallen over her cheek. He tucked it behind her ear. The move felt as intimate as a caress. "You'll look perfect however you decide to do your hair for the wedding, but I think it looks great just the way it is."

Emma imagined Logan pushing her up against the fridge and kissing her while he tangled his fingers in her hair. She swallowed hard. "Thanks. I'll keep that in mind."

The door from the house swung open and Tara stood in the opening. "Logan. What are you doing here?"

"He just dropped off our bouquets. They're beautiful. Want to see yours?" Emma answered Tara's questions for him, hoping her thoughts of a quickie in the garage with Logan weren't written all over her face.

"Sure." Though her focus never strayed from Logan, Tara moved into the garage. She reached out and looped an arm through his. "You're so sweet to bring them to us. Isn't he the best, Emma?"

"Yup, the best." Emma did her best to tear her gaze away from where Tara touched Logan.

Emma had to remember she had no claim on this man. Heck, she even had another date for the wedding, so who was she to complain if Tara touched him and acted like he was hers, the way she was doing right now as her hands remained clasped around his muscle. Tara and Logan had grown up together, after all. They were friends. They had a history.

None of Emma's lectures to herself worked. The green-eyed monster still took hold and squeezed.

Logan shook his head. "Not at all. Just doing a favor for Tuck. I, uh, gotta run now, though. I'll see you ladies later."

"Definitely." Tara shot him a wide smile even as he disengaged her hand from his arm. "Remember, Logan, you promised to save me a dance."

"We gotta get through the ceremony first. I better go. The photographer's waiting on us." Logan's gaze cut to Emma. "See you later, Emma."

At least Logan wasn't hanging on Tara the way Tara hung on him. That was something. Emma retracted her claws. "Bye. Thanks again."

With a nod, Logan departed and for better or worse, she was left alone with Tara. Emma yanked hard on the handle of the fridge. "So yours and mine are the two matching smaller ones. The big white bouquet is Becca's."

The door to the kitchen had slammed completely shut behind Logan before Tara would even look inside the fridge at what Emma was trying to show her.

"Oh, nice. Just wanted to get myself a pop. See ya."

Tara reached inside and grabbed a soda before she scampered off with her pop, probably in pursuit of Logan, if Emma had to venture a guess.

Emma was competitive in work. Even in play—don't get her started in a heated game of Scrabble or the tiles might start to fly—but her love life was a different situation. She was in no mood to compete with Tara for Logan's attention. Just as she had never wanted to compete with Jace's ex-girlfriend for his time.

When it came to Oklahoma men, it seemed Emma was routinely too late. There was always a woman from the past. A woman who drank *pop* not soda.

She would always be the interloper, and there wasn't anything she could do about it.

Logan strode across the lawn and into the house as fast as his legs could take him. He'd faced down the deadliest of enemies during his army career, and yet he was running away from a twenty-one-year-old girl.

A man had to do what a man had to do.

How else could he react besides run? He couldn't tell Tara he could no more kiss her than he could Tuck or Tyler. If it came to it, he'd sit Tara down and explain he felt nothing toward her except brotherly affection, but he'd rather not do it mere hours before the wedding. That's all he would need—a pissed off or worse, crying Tara ruining Tuck and Becca's day.

Meanwhile, to complicate things further, just a few moments alone with Emma had made him crave hours more. If Tara hadn't walked in and interrupted them, chances were good he'd still be there, imagining kissing Emma, and late for the pictures.

Logan cleared the property line between Tuck's and his own house without being waylaid by Tara again, thanks to his near sprint, but it was only to see Jace's pickup truck in the driveway. A two-ton reminder that Emma was going to the reception with Jace.

Hell of a fucked up weekend this was turning out to be, and the day had only just begun.

"Logan? Is that you?"

He heard his mother's voice from inside the kitchen even before he pushed through the screen door.

"Yes, ma'am."

She glanced at him from her position at the kitchen sink. "Your friend Jace is here."

Logan held back his opinion on that statement and hooked a thumb at the door leading to the hall and his room. "Okay, thanks. I gotta go get dressed."

"All right. Let me see all you boys once you're ready."

Had he been transported back to his senior prom? "Will do, Mom."

Logan turned the corner and headed into his bedroom and, like it or not, almost into Jace, who was blocking the doorway.

"Admit it, Tuck. You nervous?"

Logan walked into the room just in time to hear the question and see Tuck frown in reaction to it. "No. Not at all. Why should I be?"

"This isn't your first time." Jace cocked his head to one side and shrugged.

"No, it isn't. Which is why this time I'm sure." Tuck's tone left no doubt of his sincerity.

Had Jace been raised by wolves? He was seriously bringing up doubts about getting married on the man's wedding day? Couldn't he see Tuck didn't need any more stress right now?

Time for Logan to end this conversation. He wedged himself into the space between Tuck and Jace and reached for his tuxedo, which was hanging from the frame of the wall mirror. "Excuse me."

"Sure." Jace had to take a step back or be whacked in the face with the tux.

Logan glanced at Jace. "Aren't you going to get dressed?"

"Now?" Jace raised a brow and glanced at the digital clock on the dresser. "Do we have to? The wedding isn't for hours. I figured we could have a drink first."

A drink? Logan had woken up on the rough side this morning. Thank God he had had the presence of mind to take that ibuprofen and drink a bottle of water before passing out last night or things might have been worse. But there was no way in hell he was starting off his morning with a drink.

"The ceremony doesn't start for a while yet, but we have to get to the church an hour early to go over things with the preacher." Logan ignored the drink comment and reviewed the schedule. "And we have to meet the photographer before that to take some pictures of the groomsmen without the girls."

It never failed. It seemed he always ended up having to be the leader. Didn't matter if he was in charge of a unit in Afghanistan, or running a training for the ROTC cadets at OSU. Or here and now, herding the groomsmen to get them to the church on time.

"Fine. My tux is in the truck. I'll go get it." Jace left with a pout worthy of a child.

Petty as it might be, Logan enjoyed Jace's displeasure. He glanced at Tuck, too busy trying to put on his cufflinks to have paid much attention to the conversation. "Here, let me help you."

Logan felt every inch the surrogate older brother as he helped Tuck. Twenty years ago, when Tuck and Logan's little brother, Layne, had been inseparable and had both been Logan's shadows, they all might as well have been blood brothers. Back then Logan could never have imagined the grown man standing before him now dressed for his wedding and ready to start a new life and a family of his own with the woman he loved. As much as it made Logan feel old and sentimental, the thought made him smile.

Tuck glanced up and saw Logan's expression. "What?"

"I'm just thinking about the old days. Back when you and Layne were in little league together. Things have sure changed."

"Yeah, they have. Unlike in the past I now restrain myself from running down the road after the ice cream truck." Tuck grinned.

"Thank God for that. You skinned more knees than I could count running after that damn truck." Logan laughed at the memory. "And now here you are getting married."

Tuck shrugged. "I've been married before, as Jace keeps reminding me."

"That wedding was . . ." Logan searched to put a name to it.

"A mistake?" Tuck's brows rose.

"No. What I was going to say was . . ." Logan shook his head. "Okay, maybe it was a mistake. Either way, that time was nothing like this."

"Yeah, I know. This feels different." Tuck stood still as Logan continued to wrestle with the tiny cufflink. Was there no invention to make putting these things on easier?

"It is different, Tuck." Logan finished the job on one of Tuck's wrists and moved to the other. "And I'm not saying that because the first one was at the courthouse and this time will be in a church. It's not about where. It's about who."

"You're right. It's different because I'm marrying Becca."

"Exactly." Logan finished with the final cufflink and stepped back. "You two might have started out a little unconventionally, but you did good finding her."

Tuck adjusted his sleeve and then his gaze met Logan's. "I'm glad you like her."

"It would be hard not to. She's likable."

So was her sister. Damn, Jace—Logan hated that Jace had gotten to meet her first. Logan fought the scowl threatening to settle on his face.

"I know something you don't know. Something Emma said to Becca." Tuck waggled his eyebrows. "Wanna hear?"

Logan broke out into a laugh. "Are we both twelve-year-old girls now?" But dammit, he did want to know. "All right. Tell me."

"She called you a hottie."

One look at Tuck's grinning face told Logan his friend was enjoying this way too much. Meanwhile, he couldn't deny his heart sped at the revelation of what Emma had said to her sister about him. Logan opened his mouth to reply when the door swung wide.

"Who called you a hottie?" With his usual annoying timing, Jace was back.

"No one." Logan's answer came out as more of a warning for Tuck to keep his mouth shut.

Tuck's grin widened.

Jace frowned. "Come on. Who?"

"My Aunt Matilda," Tuck answered and shot a smirk in Logan's direction.

"Your grandmother's sister?" Jace slapped Logan on the back. "Wow. Good for you, big guy. I'll make sure to keep an eye on you, Aunt Matilda, and her walker on the dance floor. It might be hard though, while I'm grinding against Emma's hot little body."

Logan set his jaw and drew in a bracing breath through his nose.

"Hey, guys." Tyler came through the door, already dressed for the wedding. "The photographer just called the house and talked to Ma. She's meeting us at the church in fifteen. Better get a move on."

Lucky for Jace, though he'd never know it, that Tyler

had chosen that moment to come in. Otherwise, after that comment about Emma, there was a good chance Jace would have been sporting a black eye for the wedding pictures.

Chapter
Five

"I'm going to cry off all my makeup." Becca was a vision in white, even with her red eyes.

Emma wiped at her own cheek as a tear slipped down. Good thing no one could see them in the tiny room off the back of the church. It was the perfect place for brides to hide—and cry—until it was time to make their appearance.

"Becs, you have to stop. You're making me cry, too." Thank God for waterproof mascara or Emma would look like a raccoon.

"I know. I'm sorry, but I can't stop." Becca drew in a shaky breath. "I didn't even get down the aisle yet. What's going to happen when I'm standing next to Tucker and have to say my vows?"

"That man waiting for you at the altar doesn't care if you do sob your way through the ceremony, because he loves you." Emma's voice cracked as the sentiment brought a fresh wave of tears to her eyes. "Oh, no. Now I made myself cry."

Becca let out a laugh through her tears. She reached for the tissue box the church provided. Pulling two from inside, she handed one to Emma. "Quite a pair we make."

Emma took the tissue and nodded. "I know. We're pitiful. And we both had better stash a spare tissue in our cleavage for during the ceremony."

"Good idea." Becca pulled two more out of the box.

"This morning I was worried about my hair." Emma turned toward the mirror. She pointed at her reddened eyes and turned to Becca. "I should have been more concerned about looking like this."

The door to the room swung open as Tara returned from the bathroom. She stood in the doorway, looking from Becca to Emma. "What's wrong? What happened?"

"Nothing." Becca shook her head.

Emma drew in a long breath, determined to steady herself. "We're being silly and crying over nothing and we're going to stop. Right now. Right?"

"Right." Becca nodded. "I hope."

"Phew. Okay. I got scared for a second." Tara stepped inside and closed the door behind her.

Emma tried not to hate her as her perky little breasts stood up just fine on their own beneath the sky blue taffeta dress. The halter style Becca had chosen meant Emma had to wear a bra with convertible straps to contain her own C-cups. That strap, and the weight of the breasts it supported, cut into the back of her neck and made the dull headache she'd woken up with—probably from the shots at the bar last night—worse.

It was going to be a long night, but she'd get through it. She'd suffered for fashion before and she was sure she would do so again. Tara, on the other hand, was braless and no doubt far more comfortable. It must be nice to be twenty-something with the breasts to match.

"I peeked inside. It's really filling up in there." Tara glanced at her own reflection in the mirror.

"Good." Becca blew out a breath. "I'm ready to get this ceremony going."

Emma heard the tension in Becca's voice and glanced at her sister. "You okay?"

"Yes. Fine. It's just after all Tucker and I have been through this past year, I'm ready to be married to him." Becca dabbed the corner of her eye with a tissue. "Crap. We better stop talking about Tucker. It makes me cry more."

"Okay." Emma smiled and willed the fresh wave of moisture in her own eyes to go away. Becca's love for Tucker was heartwarming enough to make anyone cry—at least they were happy tears.

She glanced at Tara and saw her flick away a teardrop of her own. Maybe they weren't so different after all. Emma drew in a big, steadying breath, or at least as big as the tight dress allowed. "Should I go out and find someone to tell us how much longer before we start?"

"I guess—" A knock interrupted Becca. She eyed the door and then spun toward Emma. "Who could that be?"

"The preacher. Mom and Dad. Who knows? Answer it." It could be any of a number of people, but Emma could see Becca was too flustered right now to reason that out. Not that she could blame her sister. She was pretty flustered herself.

"You're right." Becca pressed her hand to her chest. "Come in."

Tyler's smiling face greeted them when the door opened. Dressed in his tux with a fresh haircut, he looked like a young clone of Tucker. "Ladies. You all look stunning . . . even you, Tara."

Tara scowled at her brother. "Thanks."

"So." He clapped his hands together. "We all ready? Everyone's here who's coming. It's showtime."

"Wait. I need my father. He's supposed to walk me down the aisle." Becca turned toward Emma. "He's not here. I knew we needed to have a rehearsal. But you didn't fly in until so late and Tara was still at school and I didn't want Tucker to see me this morning—"

"Becca. Stop. Calm down." Emma took Becca's hands in hers. "We went over everything. You even drew us a map of the church and put an X on it where each one of us is to stand. And the guys came early and went over their part with the preacher. Right, Tyler?"

He nodded. "We did. And I can go find your pa for you. No problem."

"Find him? Is he missing?" Becca's eyes opened wide.

This was a clear case of bridal nerves. They probably all should have had a drink on the way over. It would have calmed Becca down, or it could have had the opposite effect and they'd all be bawling their eyes out. Oh, well. Too late for that, anyway.

Motion in the doorway caught Emma's attention and she smiled. "Dad. Come on in."

Becca pivoted toward their father. "Dad."

"You all look perfect." His eyes looked a bit misty, too. "So are we set to go?"

It seemed weddings could choke up the best of them, even a tough old former New York City police sergeant. Emma smiled. "Yes, sir. We were just waiting for you."

"I'll run up and tell them you're ready to start." Tyler took off out the door.

That was it. The only thing left to do was wait for the organ music to play the first strains of Pachelbel's "Canon in D." And try not to cry. Emma shoved another tissue into the front of her dress, just in case.

Emma's hair brushed her shoulders, a cascade of golden silk that framed her face.

She'd left it down like he'd suggested instead of having it put up. It was a ridiculous thought, but that's what popped into Logan's head when Emma appeared around the corner and stopped in the doorway as the processional music began. One measured step at a time, she made her way up the aisle toward him.

Once he got past noticing her hair, he couldn't deny the rest of her looked pretty great, too. The dress did some amazing things to her already curvy figure, as if it had been made for her. He felt like a letch standing in church and imagining how those curves would feel beneath his hands.

Sinful or not, he couldn't seem to tear himself away from watching Emma until she turned and followed the path Tara had taken off to the opposite side of the altar.

"You doing okay, bro?" Tyler whispered to Tuck over the processional music.

"Never been better." Judging by the calm confidence in Tuck's voice, Logan believed he spoke the truth.

Once Emma was out of his field of vision, Logan wrestled his focus back to where it should be as a groomsman, on Tuck and anything he might need. He glanced sideways and saw Tuck's attention riveted to the aisle. One glance told Logan that Becca had come into view. The music changed to "The Bridal March" and Logan turned to see that the bride, on the arm of her father, had indeed made her appearance.

Logan spared a glance at Tuck and saw a smile bow his friend's lips, his attention glued to the aisle and Becca. That was the look of a man in love. No denying it. The military could be tough on a marriage. Logan had seen that time and time again with the soldiers he served with, but this marriage—this one might just have a chance. He felt like a cynical bastard even thinking that, or maybe he was just a realist. Either way, he'd do what he always did. Hope for the best and plan for the worst, and be there for Tuck no matter what happened.

"I've got a flask in my pocket if anybody needs it," Jace hissed next to him.

Logan resisted the urge to clock him one. "Jace, I swear to God, if you dare drink that here . . ." He kept his voice low but there was no mistaking he was serious.

"Fine. I'll save it for later." Jace rolled his eyes, until something in the direction of the pews caught his eye. He paled. "Crap. There's Jacqueline."

Jace's ex-girlfriend. Logan smiled. Good thing Jace had that flask. By the stricken look on his face, he was going to need a drink.

Tuck, good-natured as always, grinned wider at Jace's whispered comment, and then all of his attention was needed for far more important things. He stepped forward as Becca stopped at the end of the aisle in front of them. Her father kissed her on the cheek and then moved aside so Tuck could take her hand. She looked up at Tuck with love in her eyes so evident, Logan had to swallow a lump in his throat.

What Emma had said this morning in the garage was right. It was the littlest things that made it feel real. That could get a person all choked up. Even a man like Logan, who'd thought, until now, that he was perfectly content being single.

Logan cleared his throat and turned his attention to the preacher, happy to have something else to focus on.

Chapter
Six

Before leaving the bridal room, Emma had to worry about straightening Becca's train, keeping her own cleavage appropriate for church, and fixing their tear-stained makeup. But once she was assured Becca was all set behind her, Emma stepped out into the aisle behind Tara.

The start of the ceremony was a jumbled blur of music and motion during the processional. That was preferable, actually, to the long stretch following it, which consisted of nothing more than the steady drone of the preacher's voice and long moments of standing and inactivity. Emma tried to concentrate on the words spoken and not focus on how her feet hurt in the uncomfortable satin pumps she'd had dyed to match her dress.

Then the ceremony was over. One moment Emma was holding both her flowers and Becca's while biting the inside of her lip desperately trying to squelch her tears as Becca and Tuck recited the traditional vows and exchanged rings. The next thing she knew, the recessional music had begun and they were all on the move once again.

Emma had to pull herself together and scurry to help Becca. Things seemed to speed up in fast motion. She handed the bridal bouquet back, then juggled her own in one hand as she bent to sweep the train of her sister's gown out of the way. She had to scramble to straighten the folds in the tail of the gown so the bride and groom could turn and exit to begin their walk out of the church.

As maid of honor, Emma found herself walking down the aisle behind the bride and groom escorted by Tyler. Behind her, Jace, Logan, and Tara followed. Once outside the church, the bride and groom paused to greet all the exiting guests.

Emma's heels sank into the grass. Losing her balance, she slipped her hand onto Jace's tuxedoed arm and held onto it to steady herself. Make that Jace's incredibly *stiff* arm. Now that Emma had stopped crying long enough to pay attention to her date standing next to her, she realized his entire body seemed tense. She glanced sideways at him. His jaw was clenched tight and a small frown creased the forehead beneath the cowboy hat he wore. This was not the Jace she knew.

"You okay?"

Jace jumped at her question. He barely glanced her way when he said, "Yeah. Fine."

That wasn't very forthcoming or reassuring. He was definitely not fine, but there wasn't much Emma could do about it now anyway. Not with a church full of people filing out into the churchyard. Then there would be photos before they headed from the church to Tuck's parents' house for the reception that was being catered in the backyard under a tent.

The sound of a shutter brought Emma's attention to the photographer, snapping photos. Emma realized she had more important things to worry about than what was up with Jace. Such as her makeup. Her lipstick was probably in need of repair before they got to the formal posed shots that would immortalize this moment for Becca and Tuck—and haunt Emma if she didn't look good in them.

They were heading into a long night of speeches, dancing, and socializing with the hundred plus guests, most of whom she didn't know. Emma definitely did not have time to deal with Jace or his unexplained frowning now.

She slipped the lipstick she'd hidden in her bra out and swept on a quick application before stashing it back. "This part will be over soon. Just smile for the pictures."

"No worries." Jace's words didn't match the continued tension radiating off him.

Emma squeezed his arm and made sure to take her own advice and smile.

Jace remained just as strange during the photos as the photographer arranged the wedding party on the church steps. Meanwhile, Emma didn't miss how Tara was trying to get close to Logan; it was as if she were trying to get inside his tuxedo with him. In fact, Tara's hand was inside it at one point as she slipped her fingers beneath the lapels of the tux.

Emma tried to determine how Logan felt about that as she watched him—smiling for the camera the entire time—take Tara's hand off his chest and hold it in his. She sighed and glanced at her own tuxedo-clad date. He stood far enough away from her that the photographer had to ask him to move in closer a few times.

Were all weddings this complicated? With this being her first gig as part of a wedding party, Emma couldn't be sure. But if this were par for the course, she'd definitely consider eloping when her time came. Whenever that would be.

A tropical island would be nice. The ceremony on the beach. A simple white sundress and some flowers in her windswept hair. Becca and Tuck would fly down with them for the wedding, she was sure.

The only thing missing from her mental picture was the groom. She glanced sideways at Jace and saw his smile was as stiff and forced as his posture. A look toward Logan on the other side of the bride and groom told her Tara had now resorted to pressing up against him until the halter top of her dress began to gape. These photos were in real danger of showing exposed nipple if someone didn't adjust Tara's dress.

Emma tried to subtly get Tara's attention to warn her, but the girl had eyes only for Logan. After a moment, Emma gave up and glanced at the photographer, who wasn't any more responsive from behind the lens as she tried to coordinate the group.

A sigh of frustration escaped Emma. She felt like a failure in her maid of honor and sister of the bride duties, and the ache in her feet and lower back was beginning to be unbearable. Emma could appreciate the enticing view Tuck's groomsmen made, lined up in their matching black cowboy hats, boots and tuxedos, but all the standing around in heels and not moving was getting to her. The photographer needed to finish up already.

Emma leaned toward Jace. "Someone should supply us with some alcohol for this part."

One sandy-colored brow rose beneath the brim of his hat as he patted his pocket. "I've got a flask. Want some bourbon?"

She'd been thinking more of a glass of champagne, but she was in so much pain, Jace's offer was tempting. Emma dismissed the notion. There was no way she could take a swig out of a flask here and now. Not in front of her parents, Tucker's parents, Becca and the preacher. Besides, bourbon wasn't her drink of choice, but if this thing went much longer, it might become so.

Emma shook her head. "No, thanks. I'll wait."

Jace nodded just as the photographer put the camera down and said, "I think that's it for here."

Thank God. Emma released the frozen smile and realized how sore her jaw was. At least with the photo session done, the families and the wedding party were starting toward the vehicles. They'd make their way to the Jenkins house and Emma could sit down.

She turned to Jace. "Shall we go?"

"Uh, would you mind very much riding to the reception with your parents?" he asked.

She frowned. "Why?"

"Um, uh, I just realized the front seat of my truck is filthy. You'll ruin your dress. It's not a big deal, is it? I'll meet you there."

"All right. Sure." Hell of a date this was turning out to be. Sober, with a sore back, and now, hitching a ride with her parents like she was twelve and going to the middle school dance. Oh, well. She'd just have to drown her misery in wedding cake.

Emma wasn't sure how it had happened that she ended up in her parents' rental car for the trip, rather than in her date's truck, but that was fine with her. Jace was acting so strange as it was, he was starting to piss her off. There was enough pressure on her today. She didn't need to babysit him, too.

When they arrived, she slid out of the backseat and stepped into the driveway. She could see guests were already milling around on the lawn, enjoying cocktails and appetizers served up by the black and white clad caterers.

In a little while there'd be the official introduction of the new bride and groom, followed by the first dance and then dinner. Until then, Emma had a second to breathe and take in the transformation that had taken place, turning the Jenkinses' peaceful, private property into a reception venue bustling with over a hundred guests.

Emma swept her gaze toward the long buffet table. It was laden with chafing dishes filled with so much barbecue, it looked in danger of collapse. The smell of the smoked meats permeated the tent set up in the yard. She had to admit the aroma alone was making her mouth water. Of course, that could also be from the sight of all these cowboys in their tuxedos, even if her date was missing.

A waitress plodded past Emma carrying a bowl so heavy with coleslaw she nearly didn't make it all the way to the table. It was an interesting reception menu choice her sister had made.

Becca stepped up to her. "Phew. I'm glad the official part is done. Now we can have fun and *eat*. I'm starving."

Emma cocked a brow and glanced at Becca. "Yeah, about the food . . . I always thought you'd serve something like, I don't know, salmon in dill sauce with *haricot vert* at your wedding. Or maybe a nice surf and turf selection of lobster tail and filet mignon."

"You're right. That probably would have been the menu if I'd married Jerry." Becca glanced toward the buffet the waiters were still setting up.

"Jerry. Ugh. Thank God you didn't marry him." Emma screwed up her mouth in distaste at even the thought of Becca marrying that ball-less asshole of an ex-boyfriend of hers.

Becca let out a short laugh. "Amen to that, and good riddance. But anyway, the menu for today was kind of a sentimental decision."

"Oh, really? Sentimental barbecue? Interesting." Emma looked toward the buffet again, raising a brow as two waiters carried out what appeared to be an entire pig—feet, snout, tail and all.

"Mmm, hmm. And don't tell Tuck but I'm having them serve him a special surprise during dinner." Becca kept her voice low. "A fried bologna sandwich."

"Um, a what? Don't, like, kindergarten kids eat those after school?" And Emma's sometimes snooty, New York born and bred sister was serving it to her groom on their wedding day?

"Fried bologna is a Joseph's Fine Foods specialty. The restaurant and that sandwich are kind of special to Tucker and me, too." Becca's expression turned to the one she always wore when she was being naughty. Since Emma couldn't think of anything naughty about a fried bologna sandwich, she was confused.

She turned to her sister. "Oh, come on now, Becs. You have to explain that one to me."

"Let's just say that Tuck and I ate at Joseph's on what I guess you could call our first date. We'll leave it at that." Becca wore a secretive smile that made Emma even more suspicious. "But we were lucky they agreed to come all the way here to cater. Drumright is quite a distance."

"Where is my real sister and what have you done with her?" Emma shook her head. "Becca, even before you had a boyfriend, you used to size up the ballroom in the Plaza for your future wedding reception. Every time we went into Manhattan for dinner and a Broadway show I'd have to hear about it. Did they brainwash you somehow? What's growing out here in Oklahoma? Are you smoking peyote or something?"

"People change." Becca shrugged. "Besides, I think everything turned out absolutely beautiful."

"It does look beautiful. You did a great job, Becs." Bologna and all. Emma drew in a breath and let it out slowly. She'd get used to this new and strange Becca eventually. The one who chose a buffet barbecue in the backyard rather than French service at the Plaza.

She had to admit Becca had made the Jenkins backyard magical. The ceiling of the big white tent was strung with tiny white lights to create the perfect atmosphere. The rental tables and chairs, all uniformly clothed and covered, completed the sea of bridal white punctuated only by the centerpieces made from blue hydrangea tied with matching ribbon and set in clear mason jars filled with water and river rocks.

It made for a surprising setting—simple and elegant like Becca, with a touch of rustic cowboy, like Tucker. Speaking of Tucker . . . as he came across the dance floor toward them, Emma watched Becca's face light up just at the sight of him. True love if ever she saw it. Emma could only hope that lightning had a tendency to strike twice here in Oklahoma, and that she'd find her true love, too.

"Here's my wife." Tuck wrapped one arm around Becca and bent to plant a pretty heated kiss on her.

The word *wife* sounded strange used in reference to her little sister. It made Emma's heart flutter. She could only imagine what it did to Becca to have the man of her dreams, her new husband, say it to her.

All right, maybe love was worth it, even if it meant there was a vat of barbecue sauce on the buffet and fried bologna sandwiches were being served at the wedding reception.

"They're just about ready to officially introduce us," Tuck announced when he managed to disconnect from the lip-lock with Becca.

Emma resisted the urge to be snarky and tell them to get a room. Instead she asked, "Where's my date? They're going to want to introduce the wedding party, too."

Tucker glanced around the tent, specifically toward the bar set up in the far corner. "I don't see him with Tyler at the bar. I'm not sure where Jace is."

That figured. Jace seemed to be making a habit of skipping out on Emma. She screwed up her mouth. "I'll just walk in with Tyler. As maid of honor and best man, I guess we should have the first dance together anyway, after you two."

"That's fine, Em." Becca touched her arm. "I knew

there'd be some juggling for the first dance since Tuck has three attendants, and I only have two. It's not a problem."

Not a problem except that Jace had asked Emma to be his date and now had disappeared. It looked as if he'd stood her up both as her date and as a groomsman. Emma pasted on a neutral expression for Becca's sake.

"All right. As long as you're good with it." Emma, however, was not. "I thought Jace knew enough to be here for the beginning of the reception but I guess not. Where could he have gone?"

"Hmm." Tucker's gaze zeroed in on a group of people off to the side of the dance floor.

Becca narrowed her eyes at him. "Uh, oh. I recognize that *hmm*. What is it?"

"Uh, nothing." He shuffled a bit in his black cowboy boots.

His expression said it definitely wasn't *nothing*. Emma's brows shot up and she silently willed Becca to pursue this point with her evasive new husband.

Becca didn't disappoint Emma as she turned toward him and with one hand still holding her bouquet, planted the other on her hip. "Oh, no, you don't. Tucker Jenkins, we're married now. You have to tell me everything."

He laughed. "As if us not being married before made any difference in that area."

"Don't change the subject. What were you hmming about?" Becca glanced at the group of people Tuck had been looking at when he'd made the mistake of making his mysterious comment. Emma looked their way as well, but she didn't recognize the family as they stood and chatted while sipping what looked like iced tea.

Tucker drew in a deep breath and blew it out. "It's just—those folks over there are Jacqueline's parents. She was sitting with her family at the church, but I just noticed she's not here with them now." His gaze cut to Emma and then back to Becca.

Becca drew in a sharp breath and shot a glance at Emma. "Now, let's not jump to any conclusions. She probably just went to the bathroom or something."

Emma wondered why Becca and Tucker were both looking at her funny and bringing her into this conversation about some guests she'd never met. "Who's Jacqueline?"

And why did it matter if she were here or in the bathroom or wherever?

"Jacqueline is Jace's ex-girlfriend." Becca watched Emma as if she were waiting for a reaction. She got one.

Emma's mouth dropped open for a second before she recovered enough to slam it shut again. "Oh. I didn't realize she'd be here."

"I'm sorry, Em." Becca cringed. "I didn't even think about it when Tucker's parents put her and her family on the guest list. They're old friends. And she and Jace broke up over a year ago . . ."

"It's okay. You had no reason to remember to tell me. I wasn't even going with him as his date until he asked last night at the party." Emma let out a short laugh. "Though now that I know about this Jacqueline, certain things are starting to make much more sense."

Such as why Jace had seemed a nervous wreck while Emma was holding his arm at the church. Now, Jace was missing and so was his ex-girlfriend. It didn't take a rocket scientist to figure out what was happening here. It also proved that Emma might very well be one of those annoying, too-dumb-to-live heroines found in some of the romance novels she read when she was home alone in bed.

Alone. That's what she'd be if she continued to gravitate toward unavailable men. Guys who were obviously still involved with their exes. Giving Jace a second chance by agreeing to be his date to this wedding when he'd already proven to her he was still hung up on Jacqueline had been an insanely stupid move on Emma's part.

Fools like Emma ended up lonely, or worse, settling for bad relationships with bad men. She should count herself lucky she was the former and not the latter. If Emma were a glass-half-full kind of person, she might be glad she was alone rather than saddled with some loser. Unfortunately, her philosophy was glass-half-empty, all the way, and she found nothing to be happy about here.

She reverted to her maid of honor role as a distraction. "Listen, I'm going to go grab Tyler before he disappears, too. Then I'll tell the band we're ready for the introductions and the first dance. That way, you two can get on with enjoying yourselves."

Emma felt good with the plan, and felt even better that it gave her something to do. She needed to move, to get out from under Becca's intense and concerned scrutiny.

Time to get the official stuff over and done with. Then, with her duties behind her, Emma would be free to hit the bar. She'd feel better after a big glass of wine, although maybe wine wasn't going to do it tonight. Not in this situation. Maybe a vodka cranberry, light on the cranberry. A nice, strong one. Stupidity as great as hers required the hard stuff.

Chapter
Seven

"Mmm, I love dancing with you." Tara pressed against Logan, closer than was appropriate for two friends during the first dance at her older brother's wedding. Particularly since her parents and his were both present and watching. Not to mention the hundred or so additional guests, plus a photographer and a handful of caterers.

Tara's pelvis ground into his. Damn the girl for being so tall. They were aligned perfectly for her to rub his cock with every move she made. Long neglected, Logan Junior down there in his pants was happy to get some attention, not caring one bit if Logan cringed at even the idea of him and Tara together like that.

Logan pulled his hips back but she followed, as if some invisible force tethered them. She wasn't helping his situation at all as the whole length of her pressed against him while she clamped her arms tightly around his neck. He was trapped.

Jesus. He couldn't do this any longer. He had to get away from Tara, but he couldn't cause a scene on the dance floor. Not in the middle of Tuck and Becca's first dance as a married couple.

Knowing Tara, if he said anything about how the closeness was making him uncomfortable, or commented on how it wasn't proper here and now—or ever when it came to him and her—she'd either start an argument or storm off in a huff. With the entire tent full of people watching the three couples of the wedding party on the dance floor, people would be bound to notice.

Why wasn't Jace dancing with Tara? Logan would have been happy to be the odd man out since Tuck had one more groomsman than Becca had bridesmaids.

Logan surveyed the immediate vicinity, looking for his escape. He didn't see Jace anywhere, so there went any chance of handing Tara off to him under the guise of sharing the spotlight. He couldn't steal the bride from Tuck during the first dance, but, hell, he sure could take Emma away from Tyler. He'd enjoy doing it, too. Holding Emma close for a nice slow dance would be no hardship for Logan. Nope, not at all.

"Tara."

"Yes, Logan?" Tara gazed at him with puppy dog eyes.

Back in the old days, Logan could handle her hero-worship. But this weekend had proven that inside Tara an aggressive, single-minded wildcat had grown, and he wasn't prepared to deal with that.

He had to think. Concentrate and plan his escape. "Uh, the photographer just signaled me. She wants a picture of you and Tyler dancing together." After that whopper of a lie, Logan swept Tara closer to Tyler, trying to keep in time with the music to make his maneuver less obvious.

"What are you doing?" Tyler frowned as Logan artfully made the swap, fast, before Tara could argue.

"Cutting in." In seconds, Emma was in Logan's arms, where he'd wished she had been the entire time.

He steered her across the dance floor and away from the confused-looking Tara and Tyler. All before anyone, except for Logan himself, realized the smooth move he'd accomplished.

Once he was home free and it looked like the switch

was going to stick, Logan glanced down at Emma. "Sorry. I just needed to, uh . . ."

Words failed him. Shit. Why did he even try to explain? He should have just smiled, enjoyed having his hands on Emma, and left it at that.

"Needed to what?" Emma moved in closer. She raised one pretty brow above deep blue eyes a man could get lost in.

As they moved with the music, not so much dancing as rocking, she rested one hand on his chest. She gazed up at him expectantly, waiting for his answer, but all Logan could think about was how close she was, and how he wanted her to be so much closer. It was just Logan's luck that Emma wasn't grinding against him the way Tara had been trying to. Wrong girl at the wrong time—story of his life.

Just the thought of Emma pressed against him had Junior beginning to stir in Logan's pants, and he realized it was a damn good thing Emma wasn't any closer or she'd feel it.

He wrestled his mind back to the conversation. "Nothing."

Logan glanced at Tara and Tyler to confirm his dance with Emma wasn't about to be interrupted. He wasn't ready to let her go quite yet.

Emma followed his gaze as a smile twitched the corners of her mouth. "Looks like I'm not the only one having date issues at this wedding."

"Date issues?" Logan cocked a brow.

"Mmm, hmm." Emma nodded. "My date is missing and I noticed yours being a bit overly affectionate, shall we say?"

"Tara's *not* my date." He wanted that point made clear right up front. But more interesting to Logan than Emma assuming he was here with Tara as a couple, was what she'd said about Jace. "What do you mean yours is missing?"

"I haven't seen Jace since after taking the pictures at the church when he suggested I ride with my parents in their car to the reception rather than in his truck." She shrugged, which only drew his attention to her breasts, beautifully outlined beneath the material of the dress. He yanked his gaze back up.

"Really?" That was an interesting tidbit. Logan's gaze swept the crowd of guests again, but just as before, it didn't land on Jace anywhere.

"Don't bother looking. Jace isn't here. And apparently his ex-girlfriend is missing, too. Or so I've been told, since I don't know what she looks like. I've never had the pleasure of officially meeting the obviously irresistible Jacqueline face-to-face." The sarcasm was clear in Emma's tone.

Logan had trouble believing even an ass like Jace would abandon Emma at her own sister's wedding to go be with the girl who'd made his life miserable and dumped him over a year ago. The man was an absolute idiot, but for once, that worked in Logan's favor.

He looked down at the woman in his arms. "I have met her, more than once. Believe me, Emma, Jacqueline doesn't hold a candle to you."

"Hmm." Emma pursed her lips. "Thank you for that, but I'm not sure it makes me feel any better. Being ditched for her, I mean."

"Jace is a fool." Logan had no problem saying that with absolute conviction.

"I think I'm starting to realize that. Thanks for confirming it, though." She leaned closer, just a bit, as he felt her relax in his arms.

"Anytime." Logan adjusted his hold, pulling her a bit tighter against him until he could rest his head on the top of hers. "Emma?"

"Mmm, hmm." Her response was muffled since she'd laid her cheek against his chest. It felt damn good having her there. Natural. Comfortable. Almost as if they'd danced this way before, even though they'd just met.

"I want you to know that unlike Jace, I'm not a fool."

She lifted her head and looked up at him. "I never for one single moment thought that you might be."

The intimacy of her gaze holding his made Logan's heart begin to pound hard enough he wouldn't be surprised if Emma heard it.

He could feel the warmth of her body through the fabric beneath his hands. Her light floral perfume and the fruity scent of her hair filled his nose. She laid her cheek on his chest again and the sound of her sighing against him was nearly his undoing.

All these sensations enveloped him, making him feel as if they were completely alone, even while amid the crowd of guests who now joined them on the dance floor. If Logan could be sure of anything at all while his mind whirled along with the other couples surrounding them, it was that the song Becca had chosen for the first dance wasn't going to last forever. Neither was this magical moment. His time with Emma was limited. He needed to say something before it ended and he had no more excuse to hold her.

Emma obviously liked him. At least enough to let him hold her close here on the dance floor, moving in a motion so slow it could barely be considered dancing at this point. He swallowed hard, and then forged ahead. "So, since your date is missing and I came to this thing stag, do you think maybe you'd like to hang out with me for the rest of the night?"

Not his smoothest line, but Emma nodded anyway. She pulled back a bit and looked up at him. "I think I might like that. Very much. But can I ask you a question first?"

"Sure."

"You don't have an ex-girlfriend you're still hung up on lurking around town somewhere, or possibly on the guest list for tonight? Do you?"

"No. Definitely not."

"You sure?"

"As sure as I am of my own name." Logan laughed. "I've been married to the army for so long, no woman will have me."

"Then, yeah. I'd love to get to know you better. Much, much better." Her voice had dropped to a low, husky tone. It was sexy as hell.

He drew in a breath as pure need took over. "When do you leave for home?"

"Late tomorrow afternoon." She cringed. "Poor planning on my part I guess, but with Becca and Tucker leaving for their honeymoon right after the brunch in the morning, it didn't make sense for us to stay another night."

"I understand." Logan would happily spend a solid week alone with Emma getting to know everything about her, but she wouldn't be around that long. "We'll have to make the most of the time you are here."

Her gaze smoldered as it captured his. "I totally agree."

His eyes narrowed as he absorbed the signals she was broadcasting just as the song ended. They stood there, holding each other, not moving as the band kicked into a fast swing number.

"I guess I should go see if Becca needs me for anything." Emma looked as reluctant to end the dance as he felt.

"All right." Logan nodded. "I'm going to head to the bar and get myself a beer. Can I bring you anything?"

She shook her head. "No. The way I feel right now, I'm pretty sure alcohol is the last thing I need."

He didn't understand what that meant, but he had the

whole night to figure it out. "I'll meet you back at the head table then?"

Her smile seemed to light up the room. "It's a date."

Still in a daze, just from one damn dance and a smile from Emma, Logan made his way to the other side of the tent. No surprise, he found Tyler already there placing an order with the bartender stationed behind the rolling bar.

"Logan, my man. Shots?" Tyler sent him a grin.

"No. Definitely not." Logan held up both hands and shook his head. He turned toward the bartender. "I'll just have a beer. Thanks."

The last thing Logan wanted was to get drunk. He needed his wits about him now that the situation had changed. Jace was missing, Emma was currently dateless, and Logan was more than pleased about both.

"So, uh, don't think I didn't notice how you hijacked my dance partner out there." Tyler reached for the drink the bartender had just placed on the top of the bar in front of him.

"Did I?" Logan could play dumb with the best of them, only this time he was so damn happy about how the dance with Emma had gone, it was hard to keep the smile off his face.

"Yes, you did. Taking Emma and giving me my own sister? What the hell, dude?" Such a deep frown knit Tyler's brow, Logan couldn't help but laugh. Apparently, Tyler was unhappy with him, and Logan couldn't care less.

"Sorry, Ty. I thought you might want to dance with Tara, since she is your sister and this is your brother's wedding." Logan somehow managed to keep a straight face as the lie slipped off his tongue, smooth as silk.

"Yeah, right. You just wanted to get your hands on Emma and you know it. You two seemed to be getting cozy out there on the dance floor." Apparently Tyler was more observant than Logan had given him credit for. Not that it mattered. Logan was in too good a mood to care what Tyler thought.

"Do you blame me?" Logan lifted one shoulder in a shrug.

He might not be willing to spread it around that he hoped to spend more quality time with Emma tonight, hopefully alone, but Logan saw no reason he shouldn't admit his attraction to her to Tyler. He and Emma were both single, consenting adults, even if she was technically Jace's date for this wedding.

"Don't blame you one bit, my man. Not at all." Tyler chuckled. "I might have gone for it myself with Tuck's lovely new sister-in-law if I didn't already have my eye on someone else."

Logan had a feeling Tucker might have taken issue with a player like Tyler *going for it* with Emma, but he kept that opinion to himself. "Oh? Who's the lucky girl in your sights tonight?"

"The preacher's daughter over there." Tyler cocked his head in the direction of a nearby table. "She just turned eighteen and you know what they say about preachers' daughters."

Logan followed Tyler's gaze to where the preacher and his family were seated. "No, I don't. What do they say about preachers' daughters?"

"That they can be real wild and rebellious, doing things daddy wouldn't approve of, if you know what I mean." Tyler's crooked grin looked positively evil, making him appear more devilish than usual.

Since it already seemed to Logan that simply having this discussion could guarantee them both a one-way ticket to hell, he decided not to contribute to it any further. He pursed his lips and left his commentary at a nod, thankful when he noticed his beer on the bar top in front of him, placed there by the helpful bartender sometime during this surreal discussion.

Logan grabbed the bottle and took a swig as he scanned the room for Emma.

"She's at the head table." Tyler smirked.

He hadn't realized his looking for Emma was so obvious until Tyler answered the question he hadn't asked. Logan glanced in the direction of the bride and groom's table, and saw both Becca and Emma seated there. Sure enough, Tyler was right.

Apparently there was no hiding the extent of his attraction to her, so why bother trying?

"Then that's where I'm heading. See you later." Logan tipped his bottle to Tyler in a toast and aimed for the dais.

Emma reached for the champagne glass at her place at the head table and saw the tremor in her hand. One dance with Logan, a few moments in his arms, had her vibrating. She closed her fingers around the stem and glanced at Becca beside her to make sure she hadn't seen it, too.

Becca caught Emma looking in her direction and pinned her sister with her gaze. "Looked like you and Logan were having a nice time out there on the dance floor."

Luckily for Emma, Becca seemed too concerned with butting into Emma's business to notice that one dance had left her trembling like a teenager on a first date. "Mmm, hmm. He's a nice guy."

"Emma . . ."

"What?" She chose to play dumb in the face of Becca's prying.

Becca huffed out a breath. "Come on, Em. Spill. What did you two talk about?"

So much for Emma's assumption that Becca would

have too many other things to worry about after marrying Tuck and would stop butting into Emma's business. Emma shrugged. "I don't know. This and that."

Her sister leaned forward. "Details."

Emma drew in a bracing breath. "Well, first we talked about how my date ditched me for his ex-girlfriend. You know, the girl you invited to your wedding . . ."

That should have shut Becca up, but it didn't. "I already said I was sorry about that."

Emma switched gears and decided to shock Becca into silence. "Then we talked about having wild sex together. I'm not sure we want to wait until after the reception is over. Do you think the Jenkinses will mind if we use Tucker's bedroom?"

"Ha, ha. Very funny. Fine. Don't tell me what you two talked about. I don't care." Becca screwed her lips up into a pout and ignoring Emma, stood and headed for her new in-laws's table.

Okay, maybe what Emma had told Becca wasn't the truth, but she definitely wouldn't be opposed to it happening. Emma glanced up just as Logan appeared next to her, looking strong and tall and amazing in his tuxedo. Yup, a night with Logan sure would be nice.

He smiled. "Is this seat taken?"

She gazed up at him, marveling at how he could look so good even from this odd angle. "Nope. It's all yours."

If Jace ever did return, he could find his own damn seat elsewhere. Preferably out back by the garbage bins.

Logan pulled out the chair next to Emma and sat. "Glad to see you got us good seats."

"I'm glad to see you got away from your stalker." That definitely had come out sounding meaner than it should have. The bride's sister probably shouldn't call the groom's sister a stalker. True or not.

Why she was jealous over Tara, she didn't know. It wasn't as if Emma had any claim on Logan.

"She's sweet, but yeah, let's hope she's found someone else to occupy her tonight. So, did I miss anything important while I was at the bar?"

He raised his beer bottle to his lips just as Emma said, "Well, I told Becca that you and I were sneaking off to have wild sex in Tucker's bedroom."

As Logan coughed on the mouthful of beer he'd been swallowing, Emma decided her timing for that little joke had probably been a bit off.

"You did?" Logan recovered enough to be able to talk.

"Yeah. I kind of had to." Emma shrugged. "She was being nosy and annoying me. Don't worry. She didn't believe me."

"Wow. I'm going to be useless for the rest of the night now. I'm not sure I'll be able to think about anything else besides that image you put into my head."

Logan's gaze met hers. Emma felt it like an almost physical pull. The thought of them being together had affected Logan. Emma couldn't control a smile of pure female satisfaction. Knowing that he wanted her had her insides molten hot and her mouth dry.

"Eh, there's not too much left to do tonight anyway. You'll be fine." Trying to make light of what suddenly felt very serious, Emma patted the back of his hand where it rested on his knee. He turned his hand over and captured her fingers in his and she found it hard to breathe.

"Hey, darlin'." Jace's appearance in the tent had Logan pulling his hand away. Emma missed the contact immediately. It made her even angrier with Jace as he continued, "Sorry I disappeared. Something came up."

She'd bet something had come up. Something or rather *someone*. Thoughts of Jacqueline and how Jace had once again ditched Emma for her had her seething. Now, Jace thought he could waltz back in here, late and apologetic, and ruin a perfect moment between her and Logan?

She wrestled her anger into check. "Oh, Jace. Hi. Were you gone? I hadn't noticed."

In her peripheral vision, she caught Logan's smirk.

"So I guess this is where I'm supposed to sit." Jace glanced at the seating options.

The empty place next to Emma had clearly been taken. Becca had drunk some water and left a lipstick ring on the glass, and had put her bridal bouquet on the table in front of her chair. Jace's gaze moved to Logan, seated next to Emma. Jace wouldn't have the nerve to ask Logan to move. Even if he did, the stubborn set of Logan's jaw told Emma he had no intention of getting up.

"Leave the chair next to Becca's for Tucker, but there are a few empty spots down there." Emma pointed toward the far end of the table past Logan.

"A'right." Jace eyed Logan's seat again, looking a little wistful as he slunk off to the empty seat on the other side of Logan.

Jace had just pulled out the chair when Tara slid into it. "Thank you, Jace."

Logan appeared as unhappy to have Tara planted next to him for the duration of the reception as Jace did to be relegated to the very end seat on the far side of Tara. The last thing Emma wanted was Tara sitting next to Logan. Everyone was miserable with the seating arrangements, except for Tara. She positively beamed and leaned closer to Logan.

Emma caught Logan's gaze and smiled, hoping it told him everything she was thinking. That it didn't matter if Tara was wedged in next to him. Or that Jace was back after apparently having finished with Jacqueline for the moment. None of it mattered, because Emma and Logan had shared one magical dance together, hopefully the first of more to come. And they were together here at the table now. Emma could endure Jace and Tara, as long as Logan looked at her again the way he had before.

Logan treated Emma to a wink and her stomach did a little flip. The interaction, unseen by the two unwelcome guests behind him, was a private flirtation. Just between Emma and Logan. That made it all the more special.

When was the band, which was still rocking away on some quick country tune, going to switch up the music again? Emma could definitely stand another slow dance with Logan. With any luck, he felt the same.

Chapter
Eight

"So then the police came and tried to break up the party. But the neighboring house belonged to another fraternity so while the cops were at the front door, the guys snuck the keg out the back door and brought it over to the other house. Isn't that classic?"

Logan's eyes glazed over from Tara's frat house party story. He nodded while thinking this girl didn't know the meaning of classic. She was so young it hurt his head to try to think that far back in his own past. The caterers hadn't even opened the buffet yet and Logan was already ready to run and hide.

The first strains of Patsy Cline's "Crazy" filled the tent. Logan smiled when he heard it. Now that was a classic. He remembered his mother singing it in the kitchen when he was younger. Years before Tara had been born.

Logan stood and turned toward Emma. "Dance?"

Her bored expression was transformed as she treated him to a bright smile. "I'd love to."

She took the hand he'd extended to her and followed him out to the dance floor. Pulling her into his arms again was the highlight of his night. It made all the rest wash away.

"I'm glad you like dancing to this kind of music." He gazed down into the blue pools of her eyes.

One blond brow cocked up. "I'm glad you got away for long enough you could ask me to dance."

"So am I. You know, she means well. She's just so—"

"Young?"

"Yup. She is." Logan couldn't have come up with a better word.

"Most men like a nice firm young thing." Emma was baiting him, but if she was concerned that Logan was one of those men, she didn't have to worry.

"Most men are stupid. I like a woman who's lived life and knows what she wants."

"Interesting." Emma nodded.

"Why interesting?" He steered them around their little corner of the dance floor at a leisurely pace.

She shrugged. "I was just thinking that I've lived life and I definitely know what I want."

"And what do you want, Emma?"

"I'm not sure you can handle that answer." Both her eyes and her voice dropped, making the statement even more intriguing.

He lifted her chin with his thumb and forefinger so she had to look at him. "Try me."

She hesitated. "All right. I'll tell you, but keep in mind, the only way I could get through those college stories was by guzzling a giant vodka and cranberry."

Logan nodded. "Duly noted."

"After all of this is over and Tuck and Becca leave for their wedding night at the hotel, I don't want to be the sister of the bride or the maid of honor or anything else with responsibilities attached to it. I want to forget about everything and just have fun. Be. Feel. Live in the moment. And God, it's been so long since I've had sex." She stopped and looked up at his face. "Did I scare you yet?"

Scared, no. Speechless, yes, but only because all the blood in his body had rushed to his penis. Logan shook his head. "Nope, I'm definitely not scared. You, uh, have any candidates in mind for this night of reckless abandon?"

Emma brought her gaze up to meet his. "Do you have any plans?"

"No, I made no plans." Logan's heart pounded so hard, he could feel it vibrating his chest.

The way she looked at him, he couldn't think of anything except having breakfast with this incredible woman after a night spent working up a damn good appetite.

Emma glanced over her shoulder at her sister, then back to Logan, heat in her eyes. "Do you think we can sneak out of here early without anyone noticing?"

"I like how you think, Miss Hart." Sneaking out early to have sex. Logan felt like a schoolboy. He smiled. She returned his smile as he pictured kissing those tempting lips. The ones that kept saying shocking and tantalizing things. "And I'd like to say yes, but I'm afraid as much as we want to leave, we can't quite yet."

"Okay, so we'll stay and eat dinner. Then afterward, unfortunately, there are still official wedding things. Becca scheduled the best man's toast for right before the cake cutting. Then there is the bouquet toss." Emma bit her bottom lip as she plotted out the night. "I can't skip out on any of that. Becca would notice, and more importantly, she'd never let me hear the end of it. But afterward . . ."

Emma was a woman on a mission, and Logan was more than fine with that since the mission seemed to be getting alone—and naked—with him.

"Afterward," he continued her train of thought. "It's a date."

Logan couldn't ditch his groomsman responsibilities this early in the night any more than she could her maid of honor duties. Especially not since Jace had disappeared for the first dance. Logan had to be the better man. He wasn't about to sneak out on Tuck.

"All right. The second this reception is over, as soon as Tucker and Becca get in that giant truck of his and head for the honeymoon suite at the hotel I booked for them as a gift, you and I have got a date. Somewhere far away from all these people, where no one will bother us for the rest of the night." Emma's gaze followed her hand as she ran it over his tuxedo-covered chest, letting him know she wished they could leave now as much as he did.

The image of her doing that to him later, after he'd ditched the rented tux, when they were skin to skin, hit him hard. He pushed it aside and forced himself to concentrate on the conversation as she raised her heavy-lidded eyes back to focus on his face. Emma turned the full force of her crystal gaze back to him.

That, combined with the knowledge that he'd be alone with her later, was enough to make a strong man weak. God, how he loved a woman who didn't play games. But damn, it was going to be a long night until he had her all to himself. "So what do you suggest we do until then?"

"I guess we'll try to keep you away from your young and very touchy groupie over there so she stops pawing you." Emma cocked a brow and glanced at Tara, who was now watching them dance. "And I'll have to keep avoiding my date so I don't tell him what I think about him and his disappearing acts."

"You mean *former* date." Logan hated the way she referred to Jace. In light of their discussion and plans for later, that title should be reserved for him. But Logan was the one dancing with her now, and he would be the one holding her later, so he supposed he could get over the terminology.

Emma grinned. "Is somebody jealous?"

The toe of one of Logan's boots caught on a crack in the tent's rented dance floor. He recovered and began to rock again to the music as his own heated gaze met hers. Actions spoke louder than words, but he gave it a try and answered, "No. And do you want to know why?"

"Yes, please."

"Because any man who would walk away from you isn't worth your time or even a second thought."

"It's hard to believe that when it keeps happening." Emma latched on to her bottom lip with her teeth.

His eyes tracked the move. It made her look sexy as sin, but vulnerable at the same time. This was a side of Emma he hadn't witnessed before. A display of the insecurity she hid beneath a cocky, confident exterior.

"I have no problem proving it to you." Logan could reassure Emma in any number of ways. Many times.

"Hmm, are you sure? It could take all night." She raised a brow.

"Not a problem. I happen to have all night. All morning tomorrow, too."

"Good." The vixen was back as she eyed him from beneath her lids, her hands moving over his chest again.

He had a full-blown hard-on just as the song ended. Emma stepped closer, reducing what little distance remained between them to almost nothing. She wrapped her arms around his neck for a tight hug. Logan held his breath and froze, perfectly still. Pressed against him the way Emma was, there'd be no way she'd miss his arousal.

She stood on tiptoe, and groaned against his ear. "I'll look forward to *that* later. Thanks for the dance. See you back at the table."

The heat of her breath against his skin sent a shiver down his spine. She pulled back and, with a sly smile, turned and headed toward her seat.

"Damn." Logan watched her leave before he turned toward the bar. It was going to be a long, tense couple of hours waiting for the festivities to wrap up if his penis didn't get the memo that it had to wait until after the reception to be alone with Emma. But what awaited Logan on the other side of that agonizing delay—yeah, that would be well worth it.

He was about to order another beer when he turned just in time to see Emma walking outside toward the vicinity of the rose garden. A closer look told him why she hadn't gone back to the head table. Jace and Jacqueline stood just behind the chairs at the dais, apparently in a heated discussion.

Idiot.

Logan shook his head at Jace and abandoned the bar to follow Emma outside. He found her talking to Mark Ross, who was the head of the OSU English department, and his date, Carla, who was Tuck's assistant coach for the rodeo team.

Mark was a close friend, which was good. Hopefully he'd understand when Logan whisked Emma away from their conversation. He couldn't help himself. Mrs. Jenkins' garden was right there. Oh so tempting with lots of private places for him to sneak away and get lost with Emma for a few moments.

"Mark. Carla. Nice to see you both." Logan shook Mark's hand, delivered a quick peck to Carla's cheek, but didn't wait for any niceties in return. He launched right into his main goal. "Do you mind if I steal Emma for a second? Official bridal party business." He'd imbued his voice with a tinge of regret, which he didn't feel at all. Not one bit. Privacy and Emma were just around the corner, literally. Logan had his eye on the evergreens that separated the Jenkins' property from his parents'.

"No problem at all, Logan. Of course we don't mind." Mark pushed his eyeglasses up his nose. He glanced toward Emma. "We'll get to talk more later, I'm sure."

"Great. Thanks for understanding." Logan answered for Emma as he took her elbow and steered her away.

He didn't spare a glance for the beauty of the flowers in full bloom as he aimed past the rose beds and toward the row of hedges that separated his parents' property from the Jenkinses'.

"What bridal party business? Is everything okay? Does Becca need something?" Emma barely kept up with his pace as she asked her questions and tiptoed in her high heels through the grass.

With a quick backward glance, Logan made sure no one was watching, and then pulled Emma through the break in the hedges between the two yards. The same place he and his brother had used as a shortcut to get to Tuck's backyard for years. Once hidden from sight behind the hedge, Logan stopped and turned toward Emma.

"This is the important business." Logan stepped close and leaned low. Cupping her face with his hand, he pressed his lips to hers. The reality was better than the many times he'd fantasized about this moment.

It was meant to be a short kiss to remind Emma that it didn't matter if her former date's attention was focused on Jacqueline rather than her. Emma had Logan. He was all hers for the night, if she wanted him to be.

She drew in a sharp breath and reached her arms around his neck, pulling him closer.

Oh, yeah. It didn't take a mind reader to know she wanted him as much as he wanted her. The moan from deep in her throat broke through any reserve he'd managed to hold on to until now. He angled his head and slipped his tongue between her lips. She met his with her own. What had started out gentle began to turn wild. Logan felt like a teenage boy on a first date. Giddy. Needy. Crazed.

Not caring where they were or that someone could walk up on them at any moment, he reached down and grabbed her hips, holding her tight to him. The feel of her body against his had his cock at full tilt once again. She moaned and pressed closer, and he knew he was lost.

Logan took the kiss deeper. He thrust his tongue against hers, plunging into her mouth, just as he'd like to do to her body. All the while she ground her body into his. He fisted the fabric of her dress. In another moment, he'd be tempted to lift the skirt of that dress and take her, right there behind the bushes.

He broke the kiss and tried to regain his control and his breath. That was proving difficult with his hands still on her hips, pressing her close, but he wasn't ready to give up all of their contact quite yet. His gaze met hers. "I should apologize for that."

"Kiss me again and I'll consider forgiving you." She smiled, her hands making small circles on his chest. He didn't miss the raw need in her eyes. Or how right she felt beneath his hands.

She didn't make it easy for Logan to act like a gentleman. That was the excuse he held firmly in his mind when he groaned and leaned in to take possession of her lips one more time.

Crazy thoughts careened through his brain. Who would know if he reached down, slipped his hand beneath her dress, and tested her with his fingers? She'd be wet and ready for him. He knew that. She was as needy as he was right now. He could give her one quick, tiny little orgasm to hold her over until they could be alone.

No one would ever know. Then Logan would definitely have nothing to worry about. Jace could try to make amends with Emma all he wanted, but it wouldn't matter because she'd be satisfied and happy, and it would have been Logan that had made her that way.

"Maybe he went home to get something?" The sound of Tara's voice brought Logan's plans to a screeching halt.

He stepped back from Emma and closed his eyes, willing his erection to go down.

"I don't know. Just leave him alone, Tara. I'm sure he'll be back in a second. We should go back to the tent." Good old Tyler was trying to steer his sister away from where Logan and Emma hid.

Tyler had either seen Logan sneak off with Emma, or he suspected they had when both disappeared at the same time. The kid might be young, but he was already wise in the ways of the world when it came to women.

Logan opened his eyes again to find Emma looking horrified. Judging by the sounds of the footsteps, Tara and Tyler were getting closer. Logan and Emma were about to be caught behind the bushes with no excuse for being there alone together unless Logan did something quick.

"Stay here," he mouthed to Emma. After a bracing breath, Logan walked around the hedges and directly into Tara and Tyler's path. "Hey, what's up?"

Tara stopped dead. "Logan. We were just looking for you."

"*You* were looking for him. I, on the other hand, was enjoying a nice drink when you came bothering me about where he was." Tyler sent Logan a knowing look from behind his sister.

"Oh? Did Tuck or Becca need me for something?" Logan raised a brow, trying to look calm even as Emma hid just feet away.

"Well, no, but they just opened the buffet. I didn't want you to miss dinner. And then right after that is Tyler's best man's speech and the cake. I thought you'd want to be there for that. Where did you disappear to, anyway?" Tara frowned.

"I decided to use the bathroom in my parents' house instead of tying up the Jenkinses' while there are so many people here." Talk of bodily functions should shut down Tara's curiosity fast enough and prevent any further questions. Logan looped an arm around Tyler's neck and started toward the tent, knowing Tara would follow. "Come on, Ty. Let's get you inside so you can prepare for your big moment, and I know I'm ready for some of that tasty barbecue they're serving up."

"You owe me, dude," Tyler whispered once they were inside the tent and the sound of the music would prevent Tara from hearing him.

"For what?" Logan played dumb.

"For running interference with Tara so she didn't catch you two behind the bushes."

"Don't have a clue what you're talking about, Ty."

"Yeah, whatever. And by the way, there's a brand new box of condoms in the top drawer of the nightstand in my bedroom. Help yourself."

That had Logan stumbling over his own feet as his heart tripped, as well. He stored that bit of information away for later and changed the subject. "So, did you write down your toast or are you going to wing it?"

They'd arrived back at the head table, mostly empty since more than half of the wedding party had been outside.

"Yeah, like you really care." Tyler snorted. "Oh, look. There's your girl sneaking back in. Now if you'll excuse me, I'm going to get me that drink Tara dragged me away from."

As Tyler left him, Logan turned and saw that Emma was indeed sneaking back in through the other side of the tent. She made her way across the dance floor, red faced and looking freshly kissed. The sight made him smile, and had him rock hard again in seconds.

She reached his side, blushing prettily. Logan leaned in,

his mouth close to her ear so only she would hear his words. "Let's go get some food. You're going to need the energy for later."

The red hue coloring her face deepened. "Okay."

They moved to the buffet, clear of people now since they were late. "How much longer is this damn thing supposed to go on?" Logan asked, glancing sideways at her as he piled ribs onto his plate.

"They still have to cut the cake." Emma frowned at the remains of the whole pig in front of her, then moved on to the smoked brisket in the chafing dish.

"Then we leave?" He raised a brow, following her, and reaching for a scoop of coleslaw.

"Eager to go?" She smiled.

He let out a laugh at that understatement. "What do you think?"

She paused by the end of the table, where there was a small stack of napkins rolled around silverware. "Logan?"

"Yeah?" He stopped in his perusal of the culinary offerings to look at Emma.

"Thank you." Sincerity radiated through her words.

"For what?"

"Just for being there. Making me feel better. For everything." She shrugged.

With his body blocking the view of those in the room, he reached down and gave her fingers a squeeze. "You ain't seen nothing yet."

Chapter
Nine

"What did you tell your parents?" While walking, Logan glanced over his shoulder at the Jenkins house as he asked the question of Emma.

It felt as if they were fleeing the scene of a crime. So far, they'd gotten away unseen, but Tara was still at the house. So were both his and Emma's parents.

He'd smuggled their overnight bags into his truck about an hour ago when no one was looking because they were all busy eating cake. That had been right after he'd snuck into Tyler's bedroom and pilfered his drawer.

The presence of the strip of condoms in his bag had Logan red-faced, but he'd get over that. Now, all he had to do was slip Emma into the cab of his truck, get out of his parents' driveway without been spotted, and then they'd be scot-free.

"I told them I was going to hang out with some of the *young people* I met at the wedding and not to wait up for me. I'd get a ride back to the hotel later." Emma made air-quotes around the words *young people*. "They loved that I was making new friends."

She obviously knew how to handle her parents. Right now, he was more than grateful for that. Logan opened the passenger door. "And Becca? What did you say to her?"

"Ha. I didn't have to tell Becca anything. You saw

them. She and Tuck were so anxious to get to the hotel, she barely said good-bye to me. I'm a little concerned he's going to crash on the drive over." Emma hiked up her dress to climb in. He got a glimpse of bare leg and had to stop himself from staring.

"I know how they feel." He stifled a groan and moved around to the driver's side door.

Once he was settled inside, his hand poised on the key in the ignition, Emma turned to him from the passenger seat. "So, where are we going?"

"I got us a hotel room." He'd considered the options over the past couple of hours, ever since that amazing kiss in the bushes, and he'd realized there was no other choice. His bedroom in his parents' house was out of the question.

Emma's brow crinkled. "You didn't have to do that. I already have a hotel room. My parents have their own."

No way. That was too close for comfort. He didn't like the idea of going to the hotel where her parents were any better than he liked the idea of having sex in his own parents' house.

"Nuh, uh. I'm taking us to the hotel on the opposite side of town from where your parents are staying. I don't want either one of us to have to worry about being interrupted . . . or quiet." He turned the key in the ignition and the engine roared to life, sounding as anxious as he felt to get moving.

"Oh. Okay."

"You okay with that plan?" Glancing over, he saw Emma's cheeks had turned pink. Logan grinned at how adorable she was.

"Yes."

"Will your parents look for you if you don't come home tonight?" Logan wasn't bringing her back any earlier than he had to.

"No, I told them I'd come to their room tomorrow in time to leave for the brunch."

"Good." He definitely planned on keeping her with him at least until sunrise. One night with Emma before she left for New York wasn't going to be enough as it was. "Do you need to get anything at the hotel for tonight? We can swing by your room quick, before your parents get there."

"No. I got dressed for the wedding here with Becca this morning, so I have regular clothes and makeup in the bag I gave you before."

Perfect. A detour might just have killed him. "All right, then. That's it. Let's go."

She nodded as he fought the urge to reach out, grab the back of her head, and pull her toward him for a kiss. But the faster they got away from here, the less likely it was they'd be seen. There'd be plenty of time for kissing, and so much more, later.

Logan put the truck in reverse and backed into the street, feeling the urgency to get away. He threw the transmission into gear and peeled out, away from everyone still at the reception, heading toward one hell of a hot night in his very near future.

At the first stoplight, he glanced at Emma, who hadn't said a word since they'd left. "You okay?"

"Yes."

"You sure?"

She laughed. "I'm nervous. Isn't that crazy?"

"No, not at all." He didn't tell her his hands had been shaking when he'd packed the overnight bag for tonight. Instead he leaned over, wrapped a hand around the back of her head, and pulled her in for a kiss.

A car horn behind them told Logan the light had turned green. He pulled back and hit the gas, shooting a sideways glance at Emma. "Any better?"

She touched her fingertips to her lips and nodded.

"How many more red lights are there between here and the hotel?"

The answer to that deceivingly simple question was not enough lights if he got to kiss her at each stop, and entirely too many because they couldn't get to their destination fast enough.

He got them to the hotel, though it took every shred of will power he had to concentrate on the road. Somehow he navigated through the traffic in the center of town, and brought them safely to their destination. He swung the truck into a spot in the lot and cut the engine.

Striding like a man with a purpose, which he sure as hell was, he went to the passenger side of the vehicle and flung open the door. Finally, they were alone. Or at least not surrounded by relatives and friends. And they'd be alone soon enough.

Now, it was safe to kiss her. Logan did just that, cradling her face in his hands right there in the parking lot where there'd be no one to blow a horn and interrupt them. His lips crashed into hers and he let out a groan full of satisfaction.

She kissed him back with the enthusiasm he'd hoped for, and then pulled back. "Let's go inside."

Her eyes, heavy with need, had his gut twisting with anticipation. He needed to shuck this tuxedo, just as she needed to ditch her dress. As lovely as it was, he was certain there was something even more beautiful awaiting him beneath it.

"Good idea." He helped Emma out of the truck with one hand and then grabbed both of their overnight bags with the other. "I called the front desk during the reception to reserve the room and give them my credit card. They have our room all ready. The only thing we have to do is stop by and pick up the key."

Emma raised a brow. "A man who's organized. Wow."

More like a man who had sex on the brain, but he'd accept any compliment this incredible woman was willing to give him. In reality, Logan had figured he had better handle the details while he was still able to think. Because now, with Emma holding his hand, and the promise of a nice big, king-size mattress so close, he was having trouble putting one foot in front of the other.

Logan didn't tell her that. "Eh, logistical planning—just one of the many things the army has taught me."

"Lucky me. I get to see you in action." There was that suggestive tone again in her voice. Impossibly, Logan's cock grew harder. He'd show her action, all right. As soon as they were in the room.

He held open the door for Emma, and then led the way to the front desk. He forced his attention to the business at hand. Then he could concentrate on the more important business of getting his hands on her.

"Logan Hunt. I called a couple of hours ago and reserved a room. I requested an expedited check-in, if possible." The clerk nodded and reached beneath the desk. "Yes, sir. I have your keycards right here."

Logan glanced over and saw Emma's gaze cut to him as she smiled. If it was his efficiency at planning and logistics that got her hot, he was all set. The army had instilled that in him. He could also be very efficient in getting them both out of their clothing.

After a smooth and speedy check-in, Logan and Emma took one silent elevator ride to the second floor. With the adrenaline coursing through his veins, Logan could have sprinted the stairs in far less time, but instead he stood and held Emma's hand, trying to not let his own tremble with what he attributed to anticipation. He didn't want to believe it was nerves. In a few months he'd be forty years old. He shouldn't be shaking like a nervous teen, even if Emma made him feel like one.

The elevator came to a jolting stop and the doors opened. A quick glance at the sign on the wall told him which direction to go and moments later, they stood outside the door of their room for the night.

Their room. For the whole night. Damn.

Keycard poised and ready in his hand, Logan swallowed and glanced down at Emma. The look of heat in her eyes was all Logan needed to proceed as planned. He shoved the key into the slot, the light turned green, and the door handle moved beneath his fingers.

Logan dropped the two bags to the floor with a thud and was aware of the spring-loaded door clicking shut behind them. That was the last thing about his surroundings he was aware of as Emma became his sole focus.

Backing her against the wall, he tangled his hand in her hair and leaned low. He was about to kiss her when she braced her hand against his chest.

"Can we both turn off our cell phones?"

That out-of-the-blue request from Emma, right when things were about to get hot, gave Logan pause. The last thing on his mind when he'd been about to indulge in the pleasures of Emma's sweet mouth was his damn cell phone. Yet for some reason, it was on her mind. Enough for her to stop him to request he turn it off.

"Uh, sure. If that's what you want."

"It's just, I've been here before. In this situation." Emma laughed, and shook her head. "Almost exactly. This time, I don't want any interruptions."

"Of course." Logan took a step back. He slid his jacket off and reached into the pocket. Finding his phone, he pulled it out and hit the button to power the device off. "But I have to tell you, any man who would answer his phone while he was alone with you is a freaking idiot—"

Realization hit him the moment he said the word *idiot*.

Pieces of the puzzle began to fall into place. Emma's concern over being interrupted. Her insecurity at the wedding over Jacqueline. Jace was enough of an idiot that he might take a call from his ex-girlfriend while alone with a woman. Had Emma been with Jace like this?

Emma, kissing Jace, and maybe even about to do much more. Logan's stomach churned at the thought of Jace and Emma together in the same situation as he and Emma were in now. He hadn't thought things had gotten this far between her and Jace. Then again, now that he thought about it, Jace had been acting pretty cocky the night of the party, and he'd let plenty of hints drop about how he *knew* Emma. For the first time ever, Logan felt sincerely jealous of Jace.

Emma stepped forward. "Logan. Forget I said anything. Okay?"

"All right." With new enthusiasm, Logan tossed his phone on the nightstand. He'd make them both forget Jace even existed.

No matter what had, or hadn't happened between Emma and Jace, Logan was the one with her now. He'd show her what it meant to be with a man worthy of her. A man who wanted her and only her. The outside world, cell phones included, be damned.

Logan pinned her between his bulk and the wall, and crashed his mouth into hers. He kissed her with an intensity, an out-of-control ferocity, that belied his usual calm demeanor. Logan had remained collected during firefights. He'd stayed cool while being dressed-down by his superiors, and while reprimanding those in his command, but he couldn't seem to maintain his control now.

A caveman-like urge to dominate Emma, to claim her as his own, surged from deep within him. Logan took control, crushing her body and her mouth with his own, hoping to drive away the memory of every other man she'd ever been with. Every man she'd even thought about being with before him.

She somehow wiggled her hand between their tightly clenched bodies and fumbled with the closure on his tux pants. He'd ditched the black cowboy hat Tucker had requested the groomsmen all wear, as well as the tux jacket, but they were both still wearing too much.

"Emma." Her name on his lips was a growl, full of possession and need.

Logan pulled back to help her. He saw desire to match his own in her eyes as she unfastened the hook at his waistband and slid down the zipper. Struggling to toe off his boots, Logan discovered he couldn't do it. He was forced to back away from her and sit on the edge of the bed to yank them off because he couldn't take his eyes off Emma.

He dropped the boots to the floor one by one, then pulled off his tie as he planned how to divest her of her wedding clothes once he was out of his own.

"I'm just going into the bathroom to get out of this dress." She made a motion toward the door behind her.

"What? Why?" Logan paused after undoing the top two buttons of his shirt.

She didn't strike him as the overly shy type and more importantly, he'd been hoping to at least watch, if not help.

"Don't worry. I'm not going to make you shut off the lights so you can't see me or anything. It's just that dresses like this one require some heavy-duty undergarments that I'd rather you didn't see." Emma ran her hands over her torso. "These Spanx work great, but they're not real pretty to look at on their own."

"Spanx?" Logan raised a brow and followed the motion of her hand.

"It's a brand of shapewear. Women wear it under clingy

dresses and stuff . . . and I shouldn't have even brought it up." Emma looked embarrassed about the entire discussion.

Being a consummate bachelor, Logan didn't know what a Spanx was or what it looked like, but he didn't care. He did like the sound of the name, though. "It doesn't matter what you've got on under there, as long as it can come off. Go get undressed in the bathroom if you want to, but hurry back."

"Okay, but I'll be done much faster if you help me with the hook and the zipper in the back of my dress."

She didn't have to ask him twice. He was on his feet and moving behind her in seconds, ignoring that he was in his stocking feet and his tuxedo pants were hanging wide open.

The halter-top of the dress fastened at the back of her neck. The design left a good bit of her back exposed before the bottom half of the dress and the zipper that ran low, over her shapely ass. He gripped the tiny tab between thumb and forefinger.

Standing behind Emma and doing something as intimate as unzipping her dress had Logan breathing faster. He pulled the zipper down, tooth by tooth, as the motion ramped up his urge to strip her.

Logan reached up and brushed Emma's hair to the side. He felt for the three tiny metal hooks holding up the top of the dress. Emma waited motionless while he unfastened them, one by one. He was amazed at his own control as he maneuvered fingers much too bulky and not nearly steady enough for work as detailed as this.

After the release of the final hook the top fell. Emma clutched the fabric to her chest so it stayed mostly in place over her bra. He let her. He was fine with giving her the illusion of remaining covered for a bit longer since he no longer had any intention of letting her undress herself in the bathroom. Not now that he'd gotten a taste of the pleasure of doing it himself.

He dipped his head and pressed his lips to the top of her bare shoulder, then kissed a path to her throat. She tilted her head to the side and gave him greater access to the porcelain skin of her neck. Logan moved his hands to her bra, working by feel to release the strap from behind her neck. He moved to the lower band and found it crisscrossed in the back, then circled around her waist to hook in the front, all while remaining hidden beneath the low-backed dress.

Emma was no average woman. He'd known that already, but now he was learning that even the woman's undergarments were complicated. That was fine. Logan wasn't about to let anything stand in his way, tricky bras included. It would all be worth it in the end, and truth be told, he was enjoying undressing her. The process helped him get back some of the self-control he'd thought he'd lost completely in her presence.

While he stood behind her and latched on to her earlobe with his teeth, Logan slid his hands beneath the fabric of her dress. Running his palms along her ribcage, he felt the warmth of her skin. He slipped his fingers beneath hers where she still held the top of her dress up. He located and managed to unhook the remaining bra closure.

"You were supposed to let me get undressed in the bathroom," she said.

"You'll get over it." He spoke the words against her ear while palming her bare breasts.

A shiver ran through her. He felt it and smiled, before rolling her nipples between his fingers. They hardened beneath his touch, which only made him want to pull the pebbled peaks into his mouth. He'd get to that, but first,

there were other parts of Emma that needed to be undressed. He pushed her hands down, and the dress followed, falling to the floor with a swish of fabric.

"Don't worry. I'm not looking at your Spanx. I promise." He didn't promise not to touch her. Or possibly spank
her, now that she'd put that idea in his head.

Sliding his hand inside the front of what he assumed was
the undergarment she'd wanted to hide, he discovered the
fabric was thick, and tight, but Logan was nothing if not
determined. He continued a path down until his fingertip
parted her lower lips. Emma let out a sigh. He'd make her
more than sigh, if he had more room to work.

Time to get her naked. Logan hooked both thumbs inside the waistband of the garment restricting his freedom
and, bending his knees, pushed it all the way down her
legs until he encountered her high heels.

Okay, maybe being *completely* undressed was overrated,
because Logan would definitely like Emma to leave those
mile-high shoes on for a bit longer. He stood upright
again, running his hands back up her bare legs as he did.
From his position behind Emma, he pressed his palm to
her belly, and then slid lower. After stepping out of the undergarment, Emma widened her stance, and he took advantage of it.

He explored her damp folds with the fingers of his right
hand, while his left held her tight against him. Logan kept
his clothes on, knowing if he was naked as well it would
be too easy to slide into her. Oh, he would get to that.
Later. Now, he wanted—no, he needed—to feel Emma
come apart beneath his touch.

From where he stood behind her, his six-foot-two-
inches meant he towered over her even with her in heels.
Emma pressed her head back against his chest and he could
look down and see her face. Her eyes squeezed shut as her

lips parted. Her breath began to come faster, tinged with tiny sounds of pleasure that were tantalizing enough to make Logan fear he'd lose control.

He adjusted his hold on her and she gasped, "Don't stop."

Logan had no intention of stopping. Short of the room becoming engulfed in flames, there was nothing that could happen to make him stop now. He wanted this as much as she did. To prove it to her, Logan spun Emma around and lifted her onto the edge of the dresser. He spread her legs wide and groaned at the sight of her, bared to him, before he bent low.

Using hands and tongue, he worked her hard, inside and out, ignoring the tingle in his scalp as she clutched at his hair. Enjoying the taste of her as she pressed harder against his mouth.

She came loud with her head thrown back against the dresser's mirror. Her voice filled the room, and Logan loved every second of it. There was no one they knew nearby to hear them. Her muscles convulsed around the fingers that filled her. The need to be inside Emma overtook him.

Logan turned and located his bag on the floor. Leaving Emma still perched on top of the dresser, he strode to the bag and grabbed the condoms. Still mostly clothed, Logan shoved the waistband of his boxer briefs down, out of the way, and then covered his erection with the condom. He was ready and back to her long before Emma had regained her breath.

Good. He liked her breathless. With any luck, he'd keep her that way for quite a bit longer.

Looping her knees over his forearms, Logan supported her legs. He stepped between them and plunged inside her. He had to peer past the hem of his shirt to see as he drove into her wet heat, filling her. He forced himself to take his eyes off where they were joined and looked up to find Emma's gaze narrowed with desire as she watched him watching her. He could stare into those eyes all night while he made love to her. That was a definite possibility since Logan had swiped a strip of six condoms from Tyler's room.

At thirty-nine years old, it had been a very long time since Logan had made love to a woman even near that many times in one day, or hell, even in one week. But tonight, he had every intention of loving Emma until they both couldn't move, or she told him to stop.

He plunged into her, hard and fast. The small part of his brain that was still functioning took note that the mirror was bolted to the wall so at least his enthusiasm couldn't send it crashing to the ground. He wouldn't break the mirror, but that didn't mean the same was true of Emma as each stroke drove her back against the hard surface.

"You okay?" He asked the question between clenched teeth as he tried to hold on and not succumb to the urge to finish this sooner rather than later.

"I'm fine. Don't stop," she gasped.

Unfortunately, he already felt the telltale tingle building inside him. Logan knew he wouldn't be able to hold on for too much longer. He leaned in and took her lips, then moved to her throat. She bore down around him inside her, increasing both the friction and his need to come. Her muscles clenched tight as she let out a soft sexy moan that sent a shiver down his spine.

That clinched it. He was done. Logan held deep and came hard, his face and his fingers buried in the mass of Emma's hair. He felt every throb of his release, and every flutter of her body as it spasmed around him.

It wasn't until he'd finished pulsing inside her that he came back down to earth, and reality. It was then Logan realized he had Emma contorted between him and the mirror, her legs still over his arms as he fisted her hair in one hand.

Hissing in a breath, Logan took a step back and eased her legs down. "Sorry."

"It's okay."

He lifted her off the dresser and set her on the ground, leaving his arms around her when he saw her legs were still wobbly. No surprise, after the way he'd had her bent like a pretzel while he'd pounded into her. This time, they'd be on a nice soft bed. He led her there and watched her climb onto the mattress, naked and beautiful.

Which reminded Logan that he was overdressed. After disposing of the condom, he began tearing at buttons and cufflinks while she lay back and watched him. Finally he was free of the shirt, and soon made short work of his pants, underwear, and socks.

The look in her eyes as she watched him move toward her was enough to have Logan rising again as he crawled between her legs. He ran his hands up her thighs, loving how she'd spread them to make room for him. He wanted to touch, to worship, every inch of her.

Logan moved over her body. Drawing one nipple into his mouth, he scraped his teeth across the tender flesh and watched the gooseflesh rise on her skin. He was moving up farther, his final destination her mouth for a deep kiss, when he stopped dead at what he saw. He'd left a bruise on her throat. He must have latched on to the delicate skin with his mouth sometime during their lovemaking, though he'd be damned if he could remember when.

Leaning back on his knees, he scrubbed his face with his hands.

"What's wrong?" she asked.

"You're going to have to go to brunch tomorrow with your parents and your sister's new in-laws with a hickey on your neck because of me."

She smiled. "It's been a long time since I've had to camouflage a hickey with makeup, but I think I can still manage it."

"It's nothing to joke about, Emma. I acted like a crazy, irresponsible teenager." He shook his head at his own behavior one more time. "Biting you. I can't believe I did that."

"Stop worrying. I'm fine." Emma reached out, grabbed onto his biceps with each of her hands and pulled him closer. Logan allowed it, but remained braced above her, holding himself in check. "Want to know something?"

"What?" Logan was so ashamed of his behavior, he could barely look at her, or the deep purplish-red mark he'd left on her. It was darkening to become a nice bruise.

"I liked you being kinda rough." Her cheeks turned pink as she said it.

"Did you?" That stirred something deep inside Logan. Deep desires he never knew he had until now. The need to let loose, to allow himself to lose control for once. To take, mindlessly, until he was satisfied.

"Yes. It makes me feel"—she shrugged—"wanted."

He let out a low growl. "Emma. You're wanted. Believe me."

Logan silently cursed any man who'd made her feel unwanted. Though he knew if Jace hadn't treated her as second choice, Logan and Emma wouldn't be here together now. And while they were here now, Logan intended to take full advantage of it.

"Anyway. Don't you dare hold back." She touched a fingertip to her throat where he'd left the mark. "I felt when you did this and I didn't stop you because I liked it. I was about to come at the time. It pushed me right over the edge."

That was an intriguing piece of information. "Really."

"Mmm, hmm. You know, there are plenty of places you can bite me that my parents won't ever see."

After what she'd said, and the look in her eyes, he wouldn't be able to hold back even if he tried. He drew in a shaky breath and leaned down, stopping just shy of her lips. "You are amazing. Do you know that?"

"That a man as incredible as you are thinks so might just make me believe it. One day." She lifted one shoulder in a half shrug.

He'd do everything he could to make her believe it, to make today that day.

"So, are you done worrying about treating me like a china doll?" Emma asked.

He eyed her bruise again and thought about pounding into her on the dresser. "I haven't treated you like that at all, but yes, I'll try to stop worrying about it, if you want."

"Good, now give me some more to remember you by during those long lonely nights in New York when I have nothing but my vibrator for company. I want some really good memories."

A vibrator. Jeez. With that erotic image of Emma firmly planted in his mind, Logan leaned back and ran shaky hands down her body. He formulated a plan of where to begin.

"How *good* are we talking about here?" Logan asked.

It would be his pleasure to give her enough memories to last a very long time, but *good* was a relative term when it came to sex. There was sex that was kind of run of the mill but still made you feel good. Then there was sex that had you thinking *holy crap, did we really just do that?* Logan figured he should probably keep things somewhere in the middle of the two extremes.

"So good I'll never be able to tell another living soul about it, and I'm not the shy type."

He considered the many possibilities. "How long do we have? What time is that brunch tomorrow?"

"Noon."

"Perfect." Plenty of time, though he was certain they'd be tired for it, because he had no intention of getting much sleep tonight.

Logan was so hungry for more of Emma, it was hard to fathom he'd just had her. Of course, he wasn't eighteen anymore so he'd need a few minutes' recovery. But that didn't mean they couldn't keep busy in the meantime. He swung his feet to the floor and reached back to take her hand, pulling her from the bed.

"Where are you taking me?" Her eyes opened wider as he yanked her forward.

"The shower."

"The shower? Now? Why?"

"I want to explore each and every inch of your body. I'm going to run my hands all over you, and the shower is the perfect place for that. All that nice, slippery soap." Logan groaned and slid his hands down her bare skin. He laughed at her expression. "What's wrong? You said you wanted good memories. Would you like to take some things off the table?"

"No. Nothing is off the table. I just thought the *table* would be a nice, warm, dry bed."

"Trust me. I'll make it worth your while for you to get out of bed and get wet. Promise."

She smiled. "I believe you will."

Logan's mind spun with the possibilities of all he could do with her beneath the hot, pounding spray. How amazing she'd look with all that water sluicing off her wet skin. All the places he could slip into and explore. Maybe he didn't need recovery time after all. He was hard as a rock again just thinking about it.

He paused long enough to drop a kiss on her mouth, and then pulled Emma toward his ultimate destination—

the nice, big shower stall. He flipped on the water and stepped inside, turning to offer Emma a hand to help her in after him.

As the steam swirled through the air, Emma eyed him, looking wicked. She took him in from head to toe, and one part in particular—the hard-on that was aiming straight toward her like an arrow.

With the bar of soap in one of her hands, Emma reached between them and began to stroke Logan. The feel of her touch nearly took him off his feet.

He shouldn't be this affected considering he'd just had her. Apparently his body hadn't gotten the memo that it wasn't supposed to react like a pubescent teen. The very happy appendage seemed to know that for the first time in a while it was receiving attention from a hand other than Logan's, and it liked it. A lot.

Emma slid her closed fingers over his slick cock while Logan watched. When he raised his gaze, he found her focus was on his face. A sly smile bowing her lips, she stepped to the side. The stinging hot spray hit Logan, washing the suds off him, before she bent low and slipped his erection into her mouth.

His muscles clenched in reaction. The sensations as Emma engulfed him had Logan grabbing for the towel rack on the wall. Gripping it, he hoped it was good and sturdy. He needed something strong to hold on to as she slid him in and out of the heat of her mouth.

He tried to gather the will to tell her to stop what she was doing because he didn't want to come. At least not yet. He had too many plans for what he'd love to do with Emma.

As the water cascaded off her skin, Logan followed its path with one hand. So beautiful, every inch of her, and he had every intention of exploring all those many inches.

She scraped her teeth down his length and he hissed in

a breath. She liked to play rough. That was good. So did he. Tangling his hands in her hair, he took control of her motion. He held her head still until she looked up. Her crystalline gaze met his while his cock was buried between her lips. The sight was enough to make him weak in the knees.

Ever so slowly, he pulled out, then pushed back in while holding her head and her gaze. He repeated the action, sliding out and then in again. Her lids drifted closed.

He stopped moving and said, "Emma. Look at me."

She did, opening her eyes while reaching between his legs to palm him. He drew in a breath and the erotic slow motion dance continued. Taking her like this only ramped up his need to possess her again, but he couldn't bear to leave the warmth of her mouth. Their gazes remained locked while he continued to slide between her lips. He needed to pull out before he lost control, but he couldn't make himself break the intimacy of this connection.

Logan felt the tension in his body and tried to hold on longer. "Emma, I'm not going to last."

Fair warning of what was about to come only had her increasing the pressure of her mouth and hands on him. Logan gave up. He gave in to the overwhelming sensations and stopped fighting the inevitable. Clenching his jaw as a searing need traveled down his spine, Logan held on to her head tighter. He stroked faster, building toward release. It overtook him, bowing his body, bending his knees, even curling his toes as he tried to remain on his feet when what he felt threatened to take him off them.

Reality seeped back in. One by one, Logan regained control of his senses. Blowing out a slow breath, he realized how hard he'd gripped Emma's head and forced himself to let go.

She stood and let out a short laugh. "I guess you liked that."

Still shaking, Logan spun her around. He pulled Emma to him so her back rested against his chest.

"That's an understatement. Now, it's my turn. Hand me the soap." Nuzzling her hair, he spoke near her ear while he ran his hands down the front of her body.

"Oh really? And what are you going to do?" Angling her head, she peered over her shoulder at him while reaching for the soap.

"Don't sound so suspicious. I'm hoping to drive you as crazy as you drove me." He ran the bar over her skin, making sure to hit all the key areas. Logan was just massaging the lather into one breast when she pressed her head against him and sighed. Such a small sound but it cut straight through him. He wanted to hear it again. He moved lower, over her stomach until the hand holding the soap reached between her thighs.

She widened her stance without question, giving him more access to her most intimate area. Her submission and blind trust in him had Logan starting to get hard again. He worked up a lather over a spot that had Emma moaning against him. He loved how she reacted to every touch.

He brought the soap around and slid it between the globes of her ass. He felt her draw in a breath, before she bent from the waist and braced her palms against the tile.

That gave him quite a view of her generous hips and gorgeous heart-shaped ass. His body reacted, rising further. His hand faltered in its soapy path down her body, before he recovered his senses.

He put the soap back in the dish and took full advantage of the access she'd granted him, sliding his hands over her. Spreading her cheeks, he nuzzled his cock between her thighs, teasing, rubbing, but not entering her even when she pushed back against him and groaned.

The position was too tempting for him to resist her for very long. Logan pressed just the tip inside her warmth.

Emma rocked back and slid him all the way home. Logan's eyes closed at the sensation of being surrounded by her again. He had to hold on tight to his control. He couldn't come inside her. Not without a condom, and there was no way he was leaving her to get out of the shower to find one now. He needed a distraction. Something to keep him from giving in and finishing this too soon.

Picking up the bar again, Logan soaped up his hands. He ran both palms up Emma's spine, and then traced a path back down, continuing all the way to her ass. She must have liked it. She moved back, pushing him deeper into her. This position would have had him losing control in an instant if he hadn't just finished.

Logan wrapped both hands around her hips to hold her still while he worked his soap-slickened thumbs into the muscles of her lower back. In spite of his efforts, she managed to move again, sliding up his length.

This woman had a way of getting what she wanted. He should probably just give in and finish this, because she was too hard to resist.

She pushed back against him and Logan's grip on her slipped, as did his resolve. No use fighting fate. With one hand, Logan reached around front and connected with the spot sensitive enough to have Emma hissing in a breath. Then he set a pace that would take them on yet one more wild ride. They both obviously needed it to slake this overwhelming need.

Chapter
Ten

"Emma, sweetie, time to get up."

"Mmm. No." She snuggled deeper into the warmth of the covers.

He laughed, the sound warm and deep as he rolled on top of her. Having the warmth of Logan's body over her made Emma think of someplace warm she'd like to have him inside her.

"You have to. We have the brunch." Even Logan's silky voice didn't make that reality sound any better to her.

Stupid brunch. Emma should have talked her sister out of this plan. At least Becca hadn't set the time for too early. If their father had gotten his way, they would have all met for breakfast at six in the morning. Thank God the restaurant Becca chose didn't start serving until noon on Sundays.

Emma hated the whole concept of brunch. Whoever thought of combining the two meals should have been told it was stupid. There were far too many other things Emma would rather be doing this morning than getting dressed up to go and eat too much at some buffet consisting of a random assortment of breakfast and lunch foods.

Logan was one of those things she'd rather indulge in, and that wouldn't even require she get up or get dressed.

"One more kiss before we go." Reaching down, she grabbed the bare cheeks of his ass and held him close.

His chuckle vibrated through her as his weight pressed her into the bed. "Oh, all right. If you insist."

"You're so easily influenced." She smiled, enjoying his easy compliance, probably too much.

"By you, yes, I do seem to be." His mouth covered hers in a lazy, gentle kiss.

Kissing this man was addictive. Then again, so was everything else they'd done. Her body craved his. Even the tug of sore muscles didn't negate the need she felt. It was one that would be quenched by only him.

They'd enjoyed each other so many times last night that the frenzied need had cooled a bit, but not the deep down desire. At least, not on her part. Judging by the hard length pressed between them, not on his part either.

"You sure we can't just stay here?" She wasn't ready to have this time with him end.

"Not ready to face the family?" He nuzzled her neck, nipping at her earlobe.

"No." The dead last thing Emma wanted was to leave this warm bed and the embrace of Logan's naked body to be with a bunch of relatives. "Once we're with everyone, we'll have to pretend we barely know each other."

"That is going to be difficult, since I know you very well. For instance, I know you have this birthmark right here above your right breast." Logan kissed the spot, but didn't stop there as he moved down and drew her nipple between his teeth. As if an invisible tether connected her body to his, her hips rose toward him in reaction. He continued, "And I know how, when I touch you right here"—Emma drew in a sharp breath as his finger connected with her clit—"you make that exact sound. It cuts straight through me and makes me want to fuck you silly."

That sounded good to her. "Then what are you waiting for?"

"Not a damn thing." His dark eyes narrowed. "How much time do you need to get ready for the brunch?"

"Not too long. Half an hour?" Thank God she'd had the foresight to blow her hair dry last night after the shower sex. All she had to do this morning was throw on some makeup and the outfit she already had picked out.

"Mmm, that leaves us plenty of time. Don't forget to cover that hickey." Logan ran his lips over her throat. An uncontrollable smile crossed her lips at the word. "And please stop looking so happy about it. I'm still appalled with myself."

"I'm not."

"That is more than obvious." He shook his head, then rolled to the nightstand and reached for a condom.

"I know. I'm a bad girl. Maybe you'd better punish me." Emma smiled at the surprise that crossed his face in reaction to her suggestion.

"Careful what you wish for." Logan cocked one brow at her, before he tore into the foil packet.

"I always am." She watched as he rolled the latex over himself, and then rolled on top of her.

There was no substitute for the weight of a man over her body. All hard muscles and rough skin.

"Maybe my punishment for you could be denying you sex. Ever think of that?"

"You're welcome to try." Wrapping her legs around Logan's narrow hips, Emma put him in perfect alignment with the spot she wanted him to be.

He groaned and nudged at her entrance. She'd won this debate. Though as he slid all the way home, taking both of their breath, she knew there were no losers here.

★ ★ ★

Logan dropped Emma off at her hotel, where she would get ready and then catch a ride to the brunch with her parents. *After* she pretended she'd slept in her own room and not in Logan's, of course.

Since he was already dressed and ready, Logan killed some time getting coffee at the diner, and then drove to the restaurant. He'd arrive slightly ahead of schedule, but he figured Tuck and Becca might be there early, too.

Unfortunately, when Logan walked through the door, it was Tara who greeted him, and she didn't look happy.

"Where did you go yesterday?" A concerned frown creased her forehead.

Crap. He should have come up with a cover story. Emma had one, though not a good one. If anyone pinned Emma down as to which *young folks* she'd gone out with after the reception, he doubted she'd have a satisfying answer.

If nothing else, the army had taught Logan to think on his feet. Though lying wasn't part of his army training, he incorporated it into his other skills now. "One of my cadets lives not too far from here. He called and asked if we could meet."

"A cadet? Why would he want to meet with you?" Tara was relentless in her questioning.

"Because I'm his battalion commander, and I've got twenty years in the military. It makes perfect sense he'd turn to me." It made sense to Logan, at least.

"On a Saturday night in the summer?"

It was a damn good excuse, even if it was a lie. Logan was starting to get insulted Tara didn't seem to buy it.

"Tara, I shouldn't be talking about this with you. There's a confidentiality I have to respect." And a certain maid of honor just arriving out in the parking lot.

"Okay. Well, I saved you a seat at the table."

"That wasn't necessary. I'm sure Becca made sure there are plenty of seats for everyone." At her crestfallen expression, Logan stifled a sigh. "But thank you for thinking of me. Excuse me, I should go say hello to our hosts."

Taking his leave of Tara, Logan realized he was in for a long couple of hours.

The brunch progressed on schedule with the expected guests and food. What Logan hadn't anticipated was how hard it would be to mask his happiness every time he got a glimpse of Emma. Sitting so near her was torture. She was just across from him, but that seemed too far. He wanted to reach out and touch her. If they were next to each other, he'd be able to hold her hand under the table, but he couldn't do that from here, in the seat Tara had insisted he take. . . .

His gaze kept dropping to where the bite mark on Emma's neck was hidden beneath makeup. She'd done a good job of camouflaging it, but he knew it was there.

At least the guest list was limited for this shindig. Unlike the pre-party Friday night, which had a few dozen invitees, and the wedding, which topped one hundred, this brunch was just for the wedding party and the parents of the bride and groom. Logan had chatted with the Harts when they'd first arrived and pretended he hadn't been buried deep inside their daughter just a couple of hours ago. When that charade wore on him too much, he moved on to make small talk with Tuck's parents. All the while, he kept one eye on Emma and tried to control his temper when he saw Jace trying to suck up to her.

Honestly, did Jace think he still had a chance after his disappearing act during the reception? And why was Jace still flirting with Emma? She was about to board a plane in a few hours.

Emma was leaving. That realization sent Logan's mood

downhill faster than seeing her talking to Jace. A waitress reached in front of him and cleared his plate. That was fine. He didn't have an appetite.

"Hey, Logan." Tyler appeared at Logan's elbow. "Where's your tux? I'm driving over now to return 'em all."

Logan hadn't even noticed Tyler approach. He'd been too busy observing Jace's pursuit of Emma. Logan tore his gaze away from his visual stalking now and frowned at Tyler. "You're leaving?"

"Yeah, this thing's about to break up. Becca's family has a flight to catch and the manager here keeps giving us the stink eye like he wants us the hell out."

Logan glanced at the staff standing along the dining room wall watching them. The wait staff probably wanted to get out of there. The party, the weekend, and his time with Emma—it was all over. "My tux is hanging inside my truck. Doors are open if you want to grab it on your way out."

"Okay, will do." With a tip of his hat, Tyler headed for the exit.

Logan watched him go until movement on the other side of the table caught his attention. Emma and her parents had risen from their seats. Emma hugged Becca while their father shook Tuck's hand.

This was good-bye then. But Logan would be damned if he'd let her fly away to New York without a farewell kiss. Pushing his chair back from the table, Logan rose and moved to where Emma was standing.

"Leaving?" There was a feeling of dread in his gut.

"Yeah, we checked out of the hotel already so we just have to head to the airport and return the rental car."

He glanced at the time on his watch. "I thought your flight wasn't until later in the afternoon."

"Oh, it's not, but Dad likes to arrive a full two hours early for domestic flights. Three for international. Then of course he allowed extra time to drive to the airport and return the car."

"Ah, punctual. Man after my own heart."

"Emma. We need to go," the man in question called from the doorway of the restaurant.

"One second, Dad." She glanced at Logan and then back toward her father. "I just have to, ah, run to the restroom."

"Don't dilly dally. Your mom and I will be in the car."

"I'm sure you will." She smiled and then turned to Logan. "Maybe you'd be kind enough to escort me to the restroom? I do believe it's down the end of that very long secluded hallway."

Logan grinned. "It would be my pleasure."

Here was his chance for that private good-bye, which Emma apparently was keen for as well. Emma laid a hand on the bent arm Logan extended. He led her to the hallway off the dining room. When they reached the door to the coatroom, she glanced over her shoulder, and then pulled him inside.

Once in the privacy of the empty coatroom, Emma turned to face Logan. She rested her hands on the front of his shirt. The intimate gesture had him warming inside.

Logan covered her hands with his own, and gave her fingers a squeeze. "I had a really good time this weekend."

She raised her eyes to meet his gaze. "Me, too."

Emma hadn't offered him her phone number, and jackass that he was, Logan didn't ask for it. Maybe this was what they'd spoken about on the dance floor. Letting loose for a night. Scratching an itch.

Still, it couldn't hurt for him to hint to her to let her know he wouldn't be opposed to seeing her again. "So, I guess with Tuck and Becca living in Stillwater, you'll probably visit them there once in a while."

"I definitely plan to." She smiled and brightened his dimming hopes.

"Good. Good. I'll look forward to seeing you when you visit, then." He tried to sound a lot more casual than he felt. Emma hadn't even left yet, but he was already hoping for her return. "I hope you have a good flight."

"Thanks."

Good-bye loomed between them like a specter. In spite of knowing it was time for her to go, Logan didn't make a move to leave. Neither did Emma. Instead, she rose on tiptoes and paused near his mouth. The hesitation on both their parts seemed particularly ridiculous to Logan, given all they'd shared over the last eighteen hours.

Done with beating around the bush, Logan closed the distance and kissed her. If this was good-bye for he didn't know how long, he intended to make it count.

Sinking into the kiss, Logan drew in a sharp breath through his nose. He grasped Emma's face between his palms and kissed her deeper. He took complete possession of her mouth, angling his head as he plunged his tongue between her lips. Moaning, she kissed him back with a ferocity that matched the intensity of all they'd shared.

Logan pulled back. He knew very well her father was waiting for her so they could leave for the airport. With one last look at the face he was sure would haunt his dreams, he said, "You'd better go."

"Yeah." Emma nodded and took a step toward the door. "I'll be seeing you sometime." She turned and left Logan alone in the coatroom.

He certainly hoped that sometime would be sooner rather than later. While wiping a hand across his mouth to remove any lipstick, he realized he missed her kisses already.

Logan couldn't handle more of being social right now.

The brunch was breaking up anyway. No one would miss him. He strode directly for the exit and caught sight of Emma as she got into the backseat of the car and slammed the door.

After that one final glimpse of her, Logan turned toward his truck. Inside, he couldn't help but look at his empty passenger seat and remember how nice it had been having Emma in it, if only for a little while. He drove toward home feeling less jovial, knowing that with Emma on her way to the airport, that seat would likely remain empty for a long while—a very real reminder of the companionship lacking in his life.

Talk about symbolic.

Shaking off the depressing thoughts, Logan twisted the knob on the radio, turning up the volume to let Jason Aldean sing him out of this bad mood.

The restaurant, like everything else in this town, was only about a five-minute drive from home. Logan pulled in front of his parents' house and stopped. What he saw there had his heart stopping.

An ambulance idled in the driveway, lights blinking, and the back open.

A member of the emergency crew backed out of the front door, supporting one end of a stretcher held between him and another paramedic. Logan threw the truck into park and flung open the driver's side door. Eyes wide, he watched his mother follow the stretcher out of the house and realized that the prone figure on the stretcher was his father.

Chapter
Eleven

Three weeks. It had been three weeks since Becca's wedding and three weeks during which Emma hadn't had even one damn phone call from her sister.

After having talked on the phone every day—sometimes multiple times a day—since Becca's move to Oklahoma a year ago, the drought in communications was enough to drive Emma nuts. Sure, she hadn't expected a lot of contact—after all, Becca was on her honeymoon. But still, was one phone call too much to ask?

It had also been three weeks since she'd said good-bye to Logan, stealing a much too brief good-bye kiss in the coatroom before she left for the airport with her parents. Three weeks with no call from him, either.

For the entire week after the wedding, Emma had jumped every time the phone rang, hoping if it wasn't Becca, maybe it might be Logan. She'd been disappointed every single time.

She let out a huff and looked at the display on her cell phone one more time. She confirmed it was charged and had signal, and that she hadn't missed any calls or texts.

What the hell was wrong with her? She flung the phone at the throw pillow on the other end of the sofa. If Logan hadn't called yet, he wasn't going to. Proving beyond a shadow of a doubt that Emma's taste in men stank.

In spite of the fact they'd both gone in to that night together knowing it was just sex, she'd honestly thought he would call when he discovered she'd slipped her business card into the pocket of his tuxedo.

They'd connected on a level much deeper than sex. And Logan wasn't Jace, who had a history of ditching her. Of promising to call and then not following through.

This was Logan, the man who'd looked at her and made her feel as if she were the only woman in the world. He'd told her she was beautiful, both dripping wet from the shower, as well as when she was wearing her fancy dress at the wedding. They'd almost been late for the brunch because they couldn't keep their hands off each other. He didn't need to say all those sweet things to her, but he did. She hated to believe she was such a horrible judge of character, yet the proof was there in the phone that had never been more silent.

Logan was the man who'd never been married and hadn't had a serious girlfriend that Becca knew of. Emma needed to remember that. He obviously wasn't the kind of guy who wanted to settle down, not even for a casual, long-distance relationship.

Maybe he was incapable of giving more. A man didn't reach his age without ever having been married unless he had commitment issues. He'd blamed it on the army, but Tuck was a soldier, too, and he was married. Twice now.

As much as Emma had pretended to herself and to Logan that she only wanted a night of mindless sex, she wanted more. She'd hoped he had, too. Apparently, he didn't.

The fact that Becca was away and incommunicado wasn't helping Emma's sanity. The funny thing was, Emma hadn't even planned to tell Becca about the one wild night with Logan. Silly woman that she was, Emma had thought she would preserve that magic feeling of a new relationship and keep it to herself for a little while, before telling her sister. That was back when she still had hope he'd call, which he hadn't. Or that Becca would call, which she hadn't.

The gaping hole—make that holes—in Emma's life had never been more apparent. She had no life. She had a job that she used to love ten years ago when it was new and exciting but bored her to tears now. Work associates, but no close friends except for her sister. No boyfriend, and obviously no hope for one if recent experience with Jace and Logan was any indication.

Emma drew in a deep breath. She'd feel more settled once Becca was back in Oklahoma and calling her five times a day. Then, things would feel normal again.

She hoisted herself off the cushion. All this over-thinking was exhausting. She'd slept okay last night, but still felt as if she couldn't move her limbs now. She went to the fridge and looked inside, but that's all she allowed herself. The numbers on her digital scale this morning had been a very rude awakening.

One more reason to avoid men. They broke your heart, forced you to turn to food for comfort, and then you got fat. Now, Emma's favorite jeans were so tight she could barely zip them. At this point, she was ready to throw them away and live in sweatpants for the next—oh—ten years or so. Maybe then, she wouldn't care about men or Logan or her jeans not fitting her anymore.

Wandering back to the living room, Emma flopped onto the sofa again and grabbed the television remote. She flipped through the channels and found only crap. What else was new? It was fitting since her life was in the crapper, too.

"Sundays suck." She spoke aloud to no one at all. Maybe she should get a cat. At least then when she talked to herself, it wouldn't seem quite as crazy.

Monday through Friday, Emma kept busy at work. Usually at least one of her coworkers would be looking for something to do after work, and Emma would sometimes go along. Dinner. Drinks. Shopping. Whatever. She'd do anything to keep from having to go home alone. But weekends were the worst since Becca had moved from New York to Oklahoma. That's when Emma missed her sister's company the most.

The four walls seemed too close. Antsy, Emma flicked the TV off and stood. She needed to get out of here. She found her cell among the couch cushions and dialed as she headed for where she'd dumped her purse by the front door.

"Mom? Hi. Are you and Dad busy? I was thinking of driving over for a visit . . . Great. I'll see you in a bit."

Desperate times called for desperate measures. Even her parents' company would be preferable to the silence in her apartment. Then tonight when she got home, she'd take a look at the calendar and confirm what time Becca's flight was supposed to land tomorrow.

Finally, this eternally long honeymoon, and the hiatus in their communication, was about to come to an end. Becca might be Tucker's wife now, but Emma needed her bitching partner back. He had better understand that. Besides, it was Tucker's stupid boss Logan who hadn't called Emma despite the amazing sex they'd shared. Tuck should have to assume some of the responsibility for that. He could damn well share Becca to make up for it.

Emma locked her front door and got into her car. She'd just turned the key in the ignition when she realized she probably should have grabbed a bottle of wine from the rack to bring with her. Her mother could cook, but she had the worst taste in wine ever. If Emma didn't want to drink crappy wine, she had to bring her own.

Although, Emma's stomach hadn't been feeling quite

right lately. It was probably her Logan-induced stress man-
ifesting itself as an ulcer. She'd definitely lay off the wine
tonight and see if that helped.

Emma hoped that when Becca was back in Oklahoma
and in steady contact again, normalcy would return and
she would forget all about Logan. Then maybe the issues
with her belly would disappear.

With that plan in place, Emma steered the car to the entrance of the highway that led to her parents' house, but as
she drove, she realized Logan was going to be hard to
forget.

Logan glanced at the work still left to be done. Beside
him, his brother Layne opened the flaps of a box and
peered inside.

Blowing out a breath, Logan went back to his own box,
glancing at his brother. "Thanks for coming home. I know
I told you not to, but I'm glad you did."

"You gotta stop trying to be a martyr, Logan. I know
you're the older brother, but you can't handle everything
yourself."

Logan let out a snort. "I think I could have cleaned the
garage by myself. It's not hard."

Not hard. Just dirty and boring as shit. Logan was about
to lose his mind. Then again, at least while he was working out here in the garage, he wasn't at the rehabilitation
facility. He'd spent one too many days there already watching his mother feed soup to his formerly vibrant father.
Cheering him on for some small victory such as saying her
name, or something the speech therapist thought sounded
close enough to her name.

"You know damn well I'm not talking about us cleaning the garage." Layne stopped his work to shoot Logan a
glare. "I mean dealing with everything with Dad."

"It's not like there's a damn thing either one of us can

do to help him get better." Logan shrugged. "It's up to Dad, the doctors, and God."

That's what Logan had kept repeating to himself since the day after Tuck's wedding. He'd come home from the brunch to find his father being rushed to the hospital with a massive stroke.

That weekend had gone from the best one of his life to the worst in one fell swoop. It was almost as if the universe didn't want him to get too comfortable being happy. Logan had an amazing night with Emma, then *bam*! His father was a shell of his former self. No warning. Nothing.

"Well, even if that is the case, there was no frigging way I was going to stay in Japan after you called and told me that Dad had a stroke. Mom needed us here for support, even if Dad didn't really know we were there for those first couple of days."

Logan sighed and sat on the box he'd just filled and taped shut. "Do you think we're doing the right thing? Selling the business out from under him while he's like this? Unable to fully comprehend it all and give his opinion. I mean, that shop has always been in his life." For as long as Logan could remember, his father had been the face of Hunt's, and before that, it had been their grandfather.

"Logan, what do you want to do? Retire and sell cowboy boots and saddle blankets? Because you know Mom can't handle both the shop and taking care of Dad. The value is in the building, not in the retail business. We sell the property and Mom and Dad can live nicely just off the interest from what they'll make if they invest it well. Besides, people want to buy online nowadays, where they have more of a selection. Nobody's into going to little local stores that have only one brand of everything on the shelves anymore."

Logan's father had finally given in to pressure and had

begun to carry other brands of cowboy hats besides Stetson, but besides that, Layne was right. Small businesses were falling prey to the big mega stores and online shopping everywhere. It was only a matter of time. "I know, you're right. It's just—"

"It's the end of an era." Layne finished the thought. "I know and it sucks. I get it. I used to work there after school every day and all summer, just like you did. I shaped my share of cowboy hats, too. But things change, Logan. We chose the military, otherwise the sign would read Hunt and Sons by now instead of just Hunt's."

His little brother was right, and that was almost more than Logan could handle on top of everything else. "When the hell did you get so damn smart? I'm supposed to be the older, wiser brother. Remember?"

"Eh, you know." Layne shrugged. "Unlike the army, the marines make a man out of you."

"Yeah, yeah." Logan shook his head again and picked the next dusty cardboard box off the shelf. It looked like a case of fishing line. His father believed in carrying everything and anything the men and women of rural Oklahoma could possibly want. A weekend of fishing? He had you covered. Need a pair of horse clippers? Got those, too. Christmas cards with pictures of horses on them? Got 'em. Unfortunately, a lot of that stock ended up in the garage for lack of storage space at the shop.

Logan opened the top and looked inside, evaluating whether it should go with the inventory of the store, or whether he should just keep it for him and Tuck. Though how much fishing line could a man use in one lifetime? He sighed and shoved it back onto the shelf. Maybe he was becoming a packrat himself. It must be hereditary. "Let's just finish packing this stuff up. No matter what we end up doing—selling the business and the building together or selling off the stock separately—it doesn't make sense to have inventory from the store warehoused here at the house."

"Agreed." Layne shook his head and laughed. "Maybe Dad should have done a longer stint in the military instead of getting out after only a few years."

Logan shot his brother another sideways glance. "You're right. There's no way he'd be this unorganized if he'd been a career man."

"He sure is a packrat. Jeez. Look at this. I mean, what the hell is he going to use this thing for?" Layne held up a single bowling pin and laughed. It was a good sound. One Logan missed hearing on a daily basis.

"I'm gonna miss you, bro." In the past few weeks, Logan had gotten used to his brother being here. Layne had been around for long enough that saying good-bye again would be hard.

"I'll miss you, too, goofball, but Okinawa calls." Layne was scheduled to fly back to the USMC base in Japan in two days.

The military was generous about giving the troops time for emergency leave, but three weeks at home was the most anyone could expect to get in this kind of situation.

He'd lucked out with his own current billet at OSU that kept him close to home and his parents. But that didn't mean a Permanent Change of Station couldn't send him to the other side of the world, just as it had sent Layne to Okinawa.

Dreading his brother's departure, Logan sighed. "When are you going to PCS back to this continent, do you think?"

Layne let out a snort. "You know the answer to that well enough. Hopefully next year, but in reality, when Uncle Sam says so."

Logan did know. Too well. And for that reason, it

wasn't fair for Logan to pressure the family to keep the store, because neither of them could guarantee they'd be here to help out if his mom or dad needed it.

"Hey, hey, it's the Hunt brothers." Tyler walked through the open door, chipper as usual. "What's going on in here? And why aren't you drinking beer?"

"We're cleaning. And it's not even noon." Being in an exceptionally piss poor mood, Logan shot Tyler an annoyed look along with the answer to his questions. How could this kid be in such a good mood all the time?

"It's five o'clock somewhere." Layne glanced up hopefully. "Beer is an excellent idea, Ty. You bring any?"

"I could rustle some up, if need be. What's with the sudden cleaning bug?" Tyler glanced at the dusty items littering the floor of the garage.

"We're probably going to sell the shop, and half of this shit in here will go with it." It bothered Logan more than he'd anticipated to say that out loud.

"Sell the shop?" Tyler frowned. "But your family's owned Hunt's for like ever."

"I know, but what the hell else are we going to do?" Logan let out a breath and gave up on the box he was sorting through. He stood and stretched his back, sore from bending over.

"Why don't you just have someone else run it for your father?" Tyler leaned back against the cluttered workbench and crossed his arms.

Layne laughed. "You volunteering, Ty?"

"Yeah, maybe I am." Tyler cocked a brow.

"Yeah, right. You. A shopkeeper. Ha! That'll be the day." Layne let out a snort.

"Why not?" Tyler shrugged. "Maybe I've got some ideas for what I'd like to do."

"I thought you liked working at the ranch." Logan

frowned at Tyler. He was a cowboy at heart. Breaking horses, loading stock. Occasionally sporting a new limp or broken bone, but always with a smile because the injury was from doing what he loved. Standing inside a storefront all day rather than being out in the open air and sun would kill him.

"I do. I'm training cutting horses now. And we bought a few two-year-old bulls that are pretty good buckers. We have hopes to put them into competition, but it's not my ranch. I'm just a hand. I want to work at something that's *my* dream, not somebody else's."

"And running Dad's store would fulfill your lifelong dream?" Logan knew Tyler and his flighty nature well enough to take this new whim of his with a grain of salt.

"Maybe." He shrugged. "I've been doing a lot of leatherwork. Making belts and stuff for the other guys at the ranch. I'm pretty good at it. It would be nice to have a shop to sell it at."

Tyler making belts and wanting to be a shopkeeper. Layne giving Logan life advice. Tuck getting remarried. It seemed Logan's whole world had turned upside down.

"I don't want to talk about this anymore. We're not gonna decide anything today. Everything's still up in the air. Either way, keep it or sell it, we're organizing this damn mess of a garage. Got it?" Logan shot both of the younger guys a look, feeling every bit of his thirty-nine years.

"Got it." Layne nodded. Going back to work on his box of crap, he glanced at Tyler. "So, when's that crazy brother of yours coming home from his honeymoon?"

"Tomorrow," Tyler answered.

"Good. I mean I'd like to see him once before I leave for Japan. Who the hell goes on a three-week honeymoon, anyway?"

"A guy who has a ton of leave saved up because he never takes it," Logan answered, jealous of Tuck for being away and free of all the problems that had surrounded Logan for weeks now.

Lucky for Logan, he was the same way as Tuck was about taking leave. He had plenty of days stored up, and it looked as if he'd need them all to straighten out this situation with the shop and the building. Thank God his father's stroke had happened in the summer. It was easier for him to take time off between semesters. He didn't have to transfer his duties as battalion commander to someone else. If there was such a thing as a good time for this to have happened, it was now.

"And don't forget Tuck now has a hot new wife," Tyler added. "I don't blame him for wanting to hide out and keep her to himself for a month."

Logan couldn't help but remember that Becca also had a very hot sister. One he thought about much too often, considering he didn't know if or when he'd see her again.

Layne laughed. "Yeah, I'd like to meet her, too, since she managed to do the impossible and get a wedding ring onto Tuck's finger again."

"You ain't kidding." Tyler laughed. "I never thought that was gonna happen. But anyway, the happy newlyweds land late tomorrow. I'm picking them up at the airport. So, you'll still be around?"

"Yes, sir. I don't leave until the day after tomorrow." Layne smiled. "Damn, it'll be nice to see Tuck again. I haven't seen him since before I left for Okinawa. I definitely think this reunion will require that beer you were talking about."

"I'm on it, dude. No worries. The adult beverages will be there. And wait until Tuck sees that new ink you got in Japan. Man, is he gonna be jealous." Tyler bobbed his head at one of Layne's arms. Exposed by the short sleeves of his T-shirt was a dancing girl, inked in all the colors of the rainbow.

"Yeah, I'm happy with how this one turned out. Think the new wife will ever let Tuck get another tattoo?" Layne asked.

Tyler laughed. "That's currently up for debate, my friend. We'll all have to wait and see."

As Tyler and Layne went on to compare tattoos, Logan couldn't help but think this could be exactly what he needed. A night spent out—or in—drinking and kicking back with the guys. Maybe that would help him put the worries about his dad and the decision about the store out of his mind for a while.

And perhaps, while they were hanging out, Tuck would let some news about Emma slip out . . .

Chapter
Twelve

Emma glanced at the caller ID and then answered her ringing cell phone. "About time you called me."

Becca let out a humph. "Hello to you, too. And yes, my loving sister, I had a lovely honeymoon. Thank you so much for asking."

"Don't get snippy with me. I don't think it's too much to expect a phone call." Emma sighed, feeling bad. "But I'm glad you and Tuck had a good time. Really. I am."

"What's wrong? You don't sound good. Did something happen while I was away?"

Besides Emma cursing and hating the whole world one moment, and feeling as if she could cry the next?

"No, not really." Nothing had happened. That was the problem. Becca hadn't called. Logan hadn't called. Emma's boring life was the same as it had always been. All while her sister was off having the time of her life with her new husband. "But really, Becs. It would have been nice if you'd called once or twice during the entire month you were away."

"It was three weeks, not a month, and I called you the moment I stepped foot here in Tuck's parents' house. Look, I'm sorry, but when Tuck and I landed in Hawaii, we made a deal. No cell phones. No Facebook or Twitter or anything to do with the Internet or technology or the outside world. Just the two of us."

"Must be nice." Emma let out a snort. "But you could have let us loved ones left at home know that."

"Tuck's mom had the name of our hotel in case there was an emergency and they needed to get in touch with us. Why are you in such a bitchy mood? Are you PMSing?"

"Maybe." Emma sighed.

That would be good actually. If hormones were to blame for Emma's persistent moodiness, at least that meant it would pass. Emma was tired of feeling like this. Crying over the sappy, B-star, made-for-cable TV movies she couldn't seem to stop watching. Then getting angry over something tiny the next. This morning she'd yelled at the coffeemaker for beeping at her when she forgot to put the filter basket back in. Not that the machine could hear her, and it had been her own fault, but irrational as she'd been lately, she'd yelled at the innocent appliance anyway.

"I took so many pictures. I can't wait for you see them. Hawaii was so gorgeous, I can't even begin to tell you." As Becca launched into a story about the beaches she and Tuck had gone to, Emma walked to the calendar hanging on the wall of her kitchen.

She half listened to her sister while searching the numbered boxes, looking for the one marked in pen with an X. She frowned. Had she forgotten to mark when to expect her period this month? Cradling the phone on one shoulder, Emma took the calendar off the hook and flipped back to the prior month. There it was. The big X marked on a date last week.

Last week? She was late. Emma drew in a sharp breath.

Becca paused in her honeymoon tale. "What's wrong? Emma?"

"Uh, nothing. Sorry. I just realized I forgot to pay my credit card bill and I, uh, thought for a second it might be late."

Late. Oh my God, she was late.

"Is it?"

"Uh, no. I have time. Go on with your story." Holy shit. Three days late. She was never even a day late. Looking back at the date of the last time she'd had her period, she counted forward. She'd landed in Oklahoma thirteen days into her cycle. Unlucky thirteen. During her most fertile time of the month, she had been in a hotel room in Oklahoma having sex with Logan for about twelve hours straight.

But they'd used protection every time. Hadn't they? He had that whole strip of condoms. He'd worn one every time they'd had sex during that night—and the next morning. Hadn't he?

The shower.

Emma held back another gasp at that realization. In his haste to get her into the shower, Logan hadn't brought any condoms with them into the bathroom. She remembered the taste of him as he slid in and out of her mouth. His whole body shaking as he tried not to come. How he finally had, and then had spun her around and taken her again.

They were both dripping wet, so rather than get out and run to the bedroom to get a condom, they'd counted on alternative means of birth control. She remembered the feel of his hands, gripping her hips from behind her as she bent at the waist and braced against the wall. His groan as he thrust inside her. His curse as he yanked himself out and came.

How many children were born every year because the guy thought he could pull out in time? Emma would bet quite a few. Crap. She was thirty-one years old. She should know better.

Her heart pounding, she tried to grasp for any other explanation. Anything that would make her not pregnant with Logan's baby, because this was not by any stretch of the imagination a good situation.

He lived in Oklahoma. Her home was New York. He was a career soldier and apparently a lifetime bachelor. She had a job here, and boring or not, it paid well. And like it or not, they weren't dating. They had shared nothing but a one-night stand. No plans for the future. No promises of more. Just two single attractive adults enjoying some good times. Since he'd never contacted her again after their one night together, he obviously didn't want anything more.

Maybe it was stress causing her to be late. She needed to buy a test. And that test needed to come back negative, because this was an impossible scenario. She didn't think she could stand living a life with a man who was only with her because she'd gotten pregnant.

Emma had a feeling that's exactly what Logan would do—the right thing. Marry her and give the baby his name, whether he wanted to be with Emma or not. She didn't want that. Emma wanted the fairy tale. What Becca had found with Tucker. A man who would drop down on one knee and ask her to spend her life with him. Sweep her off her feet so they could ride off into the sunset together.

The sheer number of clichés spinning through Emma's head made her realize she wasn't thinking clearly right now. She was a modern woman with a good job. She'd been supporting herself for many years now. She didn't need Prince Charming to rescue her from a life of servitude to her evil stepmother. That didn't mean she didn't want a man to charm her. But she wanted a man to want to be with her because he couldn't stand to be without her, not because he felt obligated.

With Becca still babbling in her ear, Emma grabbed her purse and headed for the door. She needed a drugstore test, and she needed it now. Then, and only then, would she let herself worry about the future. About Logan. About her own happy ending. She only hoped there was one.

Not worry. Ha! Easier said than done.

"Em?"

"Uh, yeah?"

"If you're too busy there to talk to me, you can just say so. I'll understand." Becca's tone said the exact opposite of her words, but Emma couldn't coddle her sister right now.

"I'm sorry. I'm listening."

Becca sighed. "It's okay. I should get off anyway. I have to go next door and see Logan."

That caught her attention. "Logan? He's there?"

Emma would have thought he'd have gone back to Stillwater by now. Maybe he had, and was just in town visiting his parents.

"Mmm, hmm. We came home to find out his father had a massive stroke the day after our wedding. Can you believe it?"

Emma stopped with her hand on the door of her car. Possibly her heart stopped, too, at Becca's revelation. That's why Logan hadn't called. His father had had a stroke. "Wow. That's crazy. I had no idea."

"Yeah, it's pretty horrible. According to Tuck's mom, Logan's not handling it all that well. His brother even flew home from Okinawa."

The news couldn't overshadow her discovery that her period was late, but it might make the possibility of her being pregnant slightly less horrifying. Logan had a very good reason for not contacting her over the past month.

What should Emma do with this new information? Her mind churned. "Maybe I should call him. Uh, you know, just to offer him my sympathies."

"I'm not sure if you should offer sympathy, exactly. His dad isn't dead, though I heard he is debilitated. Empathy is the word you were looking for." There Becca went, being all literal and professor-like again. It was a trait that sometimes made Emma want to smack her sister and tell her to stop being a word geek. "But this opens up another question. Why would you call Logan? You barely know him."

"You know we spent a lot of time talking at your wedding. We did sit next to each other at the reception. Remember?"

"Uh-huh. And?" Becca was baiting Emma, looking for information. It wasn't going to work.

"And what?"

"And did you two exchange numbers? Did you speak about keeping in touch? Did he friend you on Facebook?"

"Logan doesn't strike me as the Facebook type, so no." Emma slipping her business card into the pocket of Logan's tuxedo jacket before they left the hotel didn't exactly qualify as exchanging phone numbers.

The tux. The next realization hit her as hard as the first. The groomsmen's tuxedos were all rentals. What if he'd never checked his pockets before turning it back in?

Emma tried to grasp all the revelations this phone call with Becca had brought to light. It was as if Emma had lived in some sort of daze the past three weeks, only to wake up to reality now that Becca was back.

The details fell into place and formed a new reality for Emma. Logan hadn't contacted her, but it most likely wasn't because he didn't want to. It could be because he'd never found her card in the rental tux's pocket, and he was too busy dealing with a family crisis.

Newly armed with these facts, Emma now needed a plan. She'd take the drugstore test. If it was positive, she'd take another one, just to make sure. But whether she was pregnant or not, she was going to call Logan to let him know she was thinking of him. She'd bet his parents' house number was listed. She could try looking it up online first to avoid asking Becca. She'd feel him out during the call.

Baby or not, the past few weeks had convinced Emma that she couldn't stop thinking about Logan or their weekend together. Sure, she'd been in Oklahoma for what amounted to not much more than forty-eight whirlwind hours, but it had been enough for her to know she was interested in much more with Logan. Maybe not *this* much more . . . but she'd deal with that possibility once she took the test. Hopefully, he was interested in more with her, too.

"Em. Stop being stubborn. You're obviously into Logan, whether you want to admit it to me or not." Even Becca saw what Emma was finally ready to admit to herself. Might as well stop denying it.

With her new plan in place, Emma would deal with her sister, and whatever else fate threw her way.

"You're right." Silence greeted her. "Becs?"

"Did you just say I'm right?" Becca asked.

"Yes, I did." Emma loved nothing more than shocking her sister. She couldn't help but think about what would be the shock of a lifetime if the test came back positive.

"You'd better go to the doctor."

That tripped up Emma. "What? Why?" How could her sister know she was late? Was Becca psychic now?

"I think there's something wrong with you. You said I'm right without being sarcastic."

"Oh, yeah." Emma forced out a short laugh. "I suggest

you enjoy it and stop being a smart ass. Look. I have to run out for an errand. I'll call you later."

The need to know one way or another overwhelmed her. For better or worse, the drugstore and a pregnancy test awaited.

"No." The single word was delivered with a hefty dose of determination.

"No?" Emma repeated.

"No, I'm not letting you go. I'm your sister. I've known you my entire life, and you're not acting right, so tell me. What's happening?"

Emma laughed. "Just because I agreed with you and said you're right?"

"No. It's not just that. There's something else up with you. I can tell. You don't sound like it's nothing, so spill." Becca's voice softened. "No judgment, Emma. Whatever's bothering you, I want to be here to help. Okay?"

Emma switched the phone to speaker, got into the car and started the engine. "Let me go run this errand and I'll call you back right after. Okay?"

If the test was positive, Emma might need Becca. But she wasn't going to share anything until she knew the answer.

The machine shot out a steady stream of hot, moist air. Logan stood to the side of it and marveled at how much things had changed, and how much they'd remained the same. When his father had first taught him to use the steamer to shape the cowboy hats they sold in the store, Logan had been so young, he'd had to stand on a stool to reach.

Now, even though he towered over it, he might as well have been that kid again. Uncertain. Confused.

With Layne heading back to Japan tomorrow, and his mother so consumed with his father's recovery, the weight of the decisions to be made sat firmly on Logan's shoulders. They'd both told him to do what he thought best.

How could he sell the shop that was his dad's life? But then, how could he not? He had a life and a job to get back to in Stillwater. He was a career army man. Yet, here he stood, steaming the brim of a felt cowboy hat so he could shape it for the customer who'd special ordered it.

He couldn't think clearly anymore. The options swirled in his brain until they got all mixed up, like the colors of a kaleidoscope. He turned the hat in his hand, the mindless task helping settle his reeling mind, even if he still couldn't resolve anything.

The bell above the front door tinkled, a sound that used to be so familiar to him in his youth when he'd spent every afternoon between the end of school and dinnertime here. So long ago, though it felt like yesterday. Only now, his father wasn't out front to greet the customer. Since Logan had decided to go into the shop to take care of the long neglected special order, today greeting this customer was his job. He should have remembered to lock the front door behind him.

Sighing, he set the hat down and headed through the door of the workroom to the front.

"Tuck." Logan smiled, for what felt like the first time in a long while.

"Hey, buddy." Tuck drew him into a one-armed hug. "You doing okay?"

Logan let out a snort. "I've been better."

Tuck nodded. "I hear ya. I'm sorry we didn't come home sooner to be with you. We kept our cell phones off. I didn't know about your dad until we got to the airport and Tyler told us."

"No, don't be crazy. Your parents offered to call your hotel, but I told them not to. Nothing you could have done, so why ruin your honeymoon?" There was nothing anyone could do now, including Logan.

Nothing except wait . . . and get Mr. Royce his new hat before he left yet another message on the store's already full answering machine.

"Well, now that I'm back, I'm here for you. Whatever you need."

Logan dismissed Tuck's offer with a wave of his hand. "Really, we're fine. Layne's been here to help. Your mother has been great. She's dropped off meals for us at the house every day for weeks now. Your father mowed our lawn the other day while we were out visiting Dad. It's all more help than any of us ever expected."

"That's what neighbors are for." Tuck glanced around the shop. "You keeping the store open by yourself?"

"Not really. It's been closed since . . ." Logan hesitated. He couldn't bring himself to say since his father had collapsed and become an invalid, so instead he said, "Since your wedding. I only came in today to handle a few things."

Logan could see the question on Tuck's face as he glanced around the shop. He figured he might as well answer before his friend had to ask. "No, I don't know what I'm doing with it yet. Layne and Mom have left the decision up to me."

Tuck's brows rose. "That doesn't seem fair to lay it all on you."

Logan let out a short laugh. "Tell me about it."

"You could get somebody to run it for you for a while." Tuck's gaze met Logan's. "Just until you know more."

Such as whether his father would ever recover enough to be able to walk and talk and resume a normal life? "I thought about hiring a few high school kids who are off on summer break, but I don't know if they'd be responsible enough to work without supervision. If I'd have to be here to watch them, I might as well work here myself."

"Work here yourself? As in retire from the military?"

"No. Of course not. Just temporarily." Logan blew out a breath. "Hell, I don't know."

"You know, I bet some of the old guys from the veterans' association would love to play shopkeeper a few days a week. They run that VFW like a tight ship. I'd trust them with the store. And your dad's a member. They'd want to help a fellow vet, I'm sure."

"Hmm. I hadn't thought of that. Maybe I'll stop by there later." It was a good suggestion, and one Logan never would have come up with himself. It could buy them enough time to make the right decision.

A few pounds lifted from the weight that had settled on his shoulders that day almost a month ago when his father was taken to the hospital.

"Uh, there's something else I wanted to just mention." Logan raised a brow. "Yeah?"

"Right before I left the house to come here, I walked in on Becca while she was on the cell phone with Emma."

"Oh?" Logan's heart rate sped just hearing Emma's name again.

"They were talking about you."

"Oh." Logan swallowed hard. Jeez, that had sounded guilty.

"Know of any reason why Becca and her sister would be discussing you long distance when they haven't spoken to each other about anything at all for weeks?"

"Uh, maybe." Logan met Tuck's gaze. He was torn between being thrilled Emma had been talking about him, and feeling like a crappy friend for having had sex with Tuck's new sister-in-law hours after the man's wedding.

"Oh, really? I'm listening." Tuck leaned back against the table, displaying cowboy boots and folded arms.

"You're going to be mad at me." Logan ran his hand over the stubble on his chin and glanced back at Tuck.

"Madder than I was at Jace for disappearing with Jacqueline after he'd asked Emma to be his date?"

"Uh, no. Probably not. Who knows?" Logan leaned back against the counter by the cash register, settling in. This might be a long conversation. "You sure you want to hear this?"

Tuck shook his head. "I don't know. Do I?"

"I'm thinking probably not." Logan wasn't one to brag about conquests, but he owed Tuck some sort of explanation.

"All right, then. Let me say this, whatever happened or didn't happen, I would hope you treated her the way I'd expect you to."

A wave of guilt hit him. They hadn't discussed contacting each other. In fact, they'd both gone into that night knowing it was just that, one night. Then she'd fly away. But it had been a really good night, and he should have called. He would have if she'd given him her number. "To be honest, she and I haven't talked since she left. I've been so consumed with Dad. And I don't have her phone number."

Tuck hoisted himself away from the table and ambled toward Logan. As Logan prepared himself for pretty much anything, including a punch in the face, Tuck reached past him and grabbed a sales slip and a pen off the register. He pulled out his phone, scrolled through a few screens, and then scribbled a number on the paper. "Here. Now you have it."

"Thank you." Logan took the paper and glanced down at the number that would lead to his hearing Emma's sweet voice.

"You have any idea what you're going to do with that?" Tuck nodded toward the paper in Logan's hand.

"Yup." Logan nodded. "I'm going to call her the minute you leave."

"Because you think that's what I want?" Tuck eyed Logan from beneath the brim of his hat.

"No. Because I like her and want to talk to her again. Not because I'm afraid of you, if that's what you're insinuating."

Tuck snorted out a laugh. "If Jace isn't afraid of me, you sure as hell ain't gonna be."

Logan felt the scowl settle on his face just at the mention of Emma's would-be date. "Jace always has been a fool."

"Agreed." Tuck dipped his head. "So, you need me to do anything here to help out?"

Logan laughed. "Not unless you have any experience shaping a cowboy hat."

A frown knit Tuck's brow beneath his own well-worn hat. "Can't say I do. Though I could sure use some. This old thing is starting to get a little out of shape."

"Give it here. I've got the steamer running. I can have that fixed up in a few minutes." Logan reached out one hand.

"Really? Hmm, I never knew you were so handy." Tuck lifted the hat off his head by the crown, then handed it to Logan.

"That's because you and Layne were busy playing while I was here slaving away on the steamer after school every day."

"We were only seven."

"No excuse." Logan took a closer look at Tuck's hat. "Jeez, man. Don't you have a brush for this thing?"

"Yeah, I had one. I can't find it."

Logan shook his head. "They're over there on the shelf. Go grab one."

Tuck glanced at the brush display. "You sure are good to have around. Maybe I'll have Becca talk Emma into marrying you—that way my hats will always look good."

"I can keep your hats looking good, but I don't need to be married to do it. Jeez, just 'cause *you're* married, we all have to be?" Logan joked, but being married didn't sound so bad to him.

"You should try it. You might like it."

"Yeah, yeah. And misery also loves company." Logan turned for the back room, Tuck's hat in his hand. "Come on back here and bring your big head with you. What the hell size is this hat anyway? Seven and three-quarters?"

The tinkling of the bell above the door announced another arrival. Logan turned in time to see Tyler coming into the store.

"I thought that I recognized those two trucks out front." Tyler glanced around him. "Jeez, this feels like the old days when we were kids. Remember how we'd all come in here after school and look at the new hats we wanted but couldn't afford on our allowance?"

"What allowance?" Tuck screwed up his face. "You and Tara may have gotten an allowance, but the minute I was old enough to work for other people, that shit stopped for me."

"Aw, it's good to have you home, bro. I missed your bubbly personality for that month you disappeared after the wedding. Which reminds me." Tyler handed a small white card to Logan. "The rental place checked the pockets when I returned the tuxes after the brunch. That was in the pocket of yours. With all the stuff happening with your dad and all, I kept forgetting to give it to you. I've had it stuck in the console of my truck all this time."

The smug look Tyler delivered along with the card had

Logan wondering what the hell it was. Then he glanced down and saw Emma's name and contact information on it.

Emma had given him her number. She'd slipped her card into the pocket of his tux and he'd totally missed it. It could have been lost and he might never have known. Yet here it was, in his hand, by way of the bridal rental shop and Tyler.

If this wasn't fate telling Logan to call Emma, he didn't know what the hell it was.

"Thanks for this." He pocketed the card, and hoped Tyler wasn't in the mood to interrogate him about Emma, especially since Tuck was here.

Logan eyed Tuck and saw he was so busy checking out one of the hats on display, he hadn't taken much notice of the exchange. Good. It was another stroke of good luck working in Logan's favor. He decided to move the Jenkins brothers' attention elsewhere and avoid any talk of him and Emma or what might have happened between them.

Still holding Tuck's hat, Logan glanced at Tyler's. "Give me your hat, Ty. I'm fixing Tuck's. I might as well do yours while the steamer's hot."

"Who am I to argue with an offer like that?" Tyler surrendered the brown hat.

Logan spun it in his hand. "The brim's all fucked up. What the hell did you do to it?"

"A bull may or may not have stepped on it a little bit." Tyler grinned.

"I thought you were gonna start wearing a helmet to ride." Tuck shook his head at his brother.

"You don't." Tyler frowned.

"That's not the point." Tucker raised one brow. "You should."

"Do as I say, not as I do? Real nice, bro." Tyler scowled.

Leaving the two brothers to argue, Logan headed to the

workroom. This was good. Distraction was just what he needed right now. Then, when the distractions who were two of his closest friends left, there was a woman he was long overdue in calling.

Chapter
Thirteen

Much as a watched pot never boiled, a watched clock didn't move. At least that's how it seemed to Emma as she stood in the bathroom holding in one hand the stick she'd just peed on, and her cell phone in the other, waiting for three eternally long minutes to tick by on the cell's time display.

The phone vibrated and she jumped, nearly losing her hold on both.

"Oh my God." Emma tried to calm her racing heart as she shoved the stick onto the edge of the sink—better hold the phone in both hands before she ended up dropping it from her shaking fingers into the toilet.

She needed to calm down. Flipping the seat lid shut, Emma sat and drew in a deep breath. With the cell safe from the threat of death by toilet, she looked at the caller ID as the phone continued to vibrate.

It was a call from a Stillwater, Oklahoma, phone. She'd dialed Becca's apartment phone enough to recognize the area code, but she didn't know this particular number. Maybe Becca was calling from someone else's phone.

She hit the button and said, "Hello."

"Emma?" A very deep, very male voice stopped her just as she'd drawn in a breath to lay into Becca for not being able to wait for Emma to call her back.

It wasn't Tuck. She'd spoken to him on the phone enough to recognize his voice. Could it be . . . "Logan?"

"Yeah, it's me."

She shot a sideways glance at the white plastic stick on the edge of the sink. A hell of a coincidence he'd be calling now. "Hi. I, uh, heard about your dad. Becca told me. I'm so sorry."

"Thanks. That's why I wanted to call. I've wanted to talk to you, but with the whole thing with my father, that's why I haven't contacted you since . . . you know."

"The wedding?" Memories of their time together, both at the wedding and after, had Emma's pulse pounding.

He let out a short laugh. "Yeah, since the wedding."

"I know you couldn't call. You had to be there for your family, Logan."

"I'm glad you understand." He sighed into the phone. "It's good to hear your voice."

"It's good to hear yours, too." Emma couldn't begin to tell him how much.

She glanced at the stick again. Nothing yet. No plus or minus. Or pink or blue, or whatever the hell it was supposed to show. Maybe she had better fish the box out of the garbage and see what she should be looking for. Later.

Now what she'd hoped for had happened. Logan was on the phone. She forced her gaze away from the little white plastic stick that would decide her fate.

"So how have you been?" he asked.

"Oh, you know. Busy at work." *Possibly pregnant.* "The usual. Tucker and Becca are finally home from their honeymoon."

"Yeah, I know. Tuck just stopped by. It's pretty funny, actually. Tuck had just given me your number when Tyler walked in and handed me your business card. The bridal shop had found it in the pocket of my tux."

"That is funny. I'm glad you have my number now, and that you called. I've been thinking about you."

"You have?"

"Yes. Are you surprised?"

"Yeah, I guess I am." He laughed.

Emma's brows drew down in a frown. "You shouldn't be. I had a great time at the wedding . . . and after."

"I did, too. A really great time." He drew in a deep breath and blew it out. "Emma, if things ever get back to normal again, I'm hoping we can keep in touch, you and I."

"I'd like that. And even if things don't get back to normal for a while, Logan, I want you to know you can call me anytime. Just to talk. To vent. To escape from reality for a little while. Whatever. I'm here." Emma hadn't meant that last part to come out sounding like an invitation for phone sex but she feared it had.

Oh well, she wouldn't be opposed to that, either. Logan had the best voice. All deep and gruff . . . She eyed the pee stick again and reality crept back in. Would she ever enjoy sex with Logan again, phone or other, if it was positive?

"I'll take you up on that." His voice dropped low now, all deep and sexy. It made her chest tighten.

Damn, she needed to know what was happening with this test.

"Crap. Emma, I've got a customer."

"A customer? Uh, what?" Emma wasn't exactly on top of things in the midst of all that was happening in her life right now, but still, there was no scenario she could come up with as to why Logan would be servicing customers.

He chuckled. "Sorry. I'm at my father's shop. I should have locked the door after Tuck left but I forgot and now someone's come in. Can I call you again sometime?"

"Of course. Go do what you have to. Call anytime. I'll be here." *Waiting.*

"Great. Thanks. We'll talk again soon." The low promise in his voice had her cradling the phone closer.

"All right. Bye." Emma disconnected the call and was about to exchange the cell phone for the pee stick in her sweaty grasp when the phone rang again.

Jeez, why was she so popular all of a sudden? She looked at the caller ID and punched the button to answer. "Becca, I told you I'd call you when I was done with my errands."

"I know, but I have something to tell you. Tucker just got back from seeing Logan and apparently things are tough for the family right now."

"I imagine they would be." Emma kept the fact she'd just hung up with Logan to herself.

"Logan's brother is leaving to go back to Okinawa tomorrow and Logan's got his dad and his dad's store to worry about, so Tucker and I decided we're going to help him out. Even Tyler is on board."

"That's nice. He'll appreciate it, I'm sure."

"He'd do the same for Tuck if the situation were reversed. So anyway, we're staying here for at least a few more weeks instead of going back to Stillwater."

"Really. Can you do that?"

"Sure. As long as we're both back in time for the start of the new semester. I already called my boss and he said it's fine. He's a friend of Logan's so he understands. And Tucker doesn't mind using the rest of his leave to help out a friend."

Of course he wouldn't mind, because Becca had found herself the perfect man. Emma might have, too, in Logan if he weren't the quintessential bachelor. She'd like to explore the possibility of changing Logan's mind on his bachelor status. She could only hope there wasn't a big old complication on the horizon that would get in the way.

Three minutes must be up by now, but she was afraid to look at the stick and find out what it said. Emma swallowed hard and avoided it for just a moment more, long enough to make some plans. Once she looked at the results, Emma had a suspicion she wouldn't be able to think.

"You know what, Becs? I have a bunch of vacation time stored up myself. Would it be okay if I flew out for a visit?"

"Oh my God, could you do that? We didn't get any time together, just the two of us, over the wedding weekend."

Wasn't that the truth. And all that free time might have gotten Emma into a whole heap of trouble. "Would Tuck's parents mind if I stayed there at the house with you?"

"I'll ask but I'm sure it won't be a problem. Tuck and I are sleeping in his old bedroom. You can stay in the room with the sleeper sofa."

"Is Tara still there?" Emma cringed and waited for the answer.

"No. She went back to take some summer classes at her college, so there's one less person in the house. I'm sure Tuck's parents won't mind if you stay here with us."

One more obstacle gone. "Great. I'll take a look at flights. Just please double check with them and make sure it's okay?"

"I will. I'm so excited. It'll be so nice to have you here. I miss having you near me. Believe it or not, even if I am married now, I still need my big sister."

Emma glanced at the stick and saw a symbol had formed. She drew in a deep breath. "I need you, too, Becs."

"Hey there, cowboy. I'm looking for Logan Hunt. Any idea where I might be able to find him?"

The sexy feminine voice had Logan's hand slipping. The brush skipped across the brim of the hat, slipped out of his hand and skittered to the floor. He looked up and had trouble believing who he saw.

"Emma?"

"Hi." She smiled, looking a little tentative as she hovered in the doorway.

Happiness warred with confusion as he took a step forward. "What in the world . . . What are you doing here? Is Becca okay?"

Surely Tuck would have called him if there were something wrong.

"Yeah, she's fine. Just a social call." She looked so sweet, so good, it was all he could do not to stalk to where she stood and plant a big kiss on those tempting lips.

What the hell? Why couldn't he? There wasn't anyone around, and it could be just a friendly kiss. They were friends, kind of. Weren't they?

"It's nice to see you." As his pulse roared in his ears, Logan moved toward her and bent low. He pressed his lips to hers in a quick, chaste kiss, and fought the need to go further.

"It's nice to see you, too." Emma's gaze traveled from his cowboy hat, to his pearl-snap plaid shirt and worn denim jeans, to end at the leather of his boots. "I know Tucker had you wear the hat and boots for the wedding, but when did you turn full-time cowboy?"

Logan knocked the brim of his hat back to get a better look at her and shrugged. "I guess it's an easy habit to fall back into. There was a day, before the army, when I was in a cowboy hat and boots from sun up 'til sundown. That's what happens when your dad owns a store that specializes in western sporting goods . . . and other assorted sundries."

He glanced around, remembering the packed boxes of

inventory and the decision he'd put off making regarding what to do with all of it.

Emma looked closer at the displays of stock surrounding them. "I love it. It's got charm. Like the old country store on *Little House on the Prairie*. Remember that TV show?"

"Yeah, I do. My mom never missed an episode." Logan smiled. Good memories from a time when he didn't have a care in the world save for keeping up with his homework in addition to his chores, which in hindsight, was a pretty good deal compared to adulthood.

"Where I live in New York, stores like this are usually tourist traps. They're in quaint little towns within driving distance from Manhattan so they can grab the folks who want to get away to the country for the weekend."

"Tourists?" Logan let out a snort. "No tourists are coming here, and if they do, it's not to buy any of this stuff."

"You'd be surprised. The places I've seen are designed to look like charming old-fashioned shops to lure in the city people, then they hike up the prices and make a killing." Emma crossed the short distance toward the register and picked up an item sitting there. She raised one brow. "You're definitely not pricing this stuff high enough."

He laughed. "For a store in a small town in Oklahoma, I am. You can't get much more than that around here. Maybe I should consider packing all this stuff up and driving it to New York where I can get top dollar." The plan seemed pretty good to Logan since Emma lived there.

"Well, don't do that right away, because I'm here for a long visit."

"Really?" This news was as good as it was unexpected, just like Emma's sudden appearance in the shop.

"Yup. I'll be here visiting with Becca. Hanging out. Soaking up the Oklahoma summer sun. I was hoping I'd get to see you, too." She turned and caught him in that gaze that never failed to draw him to her.

For the first time in what seemed like a very long time, Logan felt happy about something. "I think that can be arranged."

"Are you sure? I know you're busy with your dad and the store." A strange expression clouded her features. "And if you'd rather not . . ."

"Emma, I'd love to spend more time with you while you're here." Logan remembered his time wasn't his own right now. "As much as I'm able to with all that's going on."

It was enough to make a man weary to the bone, thinking about everything he had to deal with right now, when it would be so easy to forget about it all and escape into Emma.

"Good." Her gaze intensified as she watched him. "How are you doing, Logan? Are you okay?"

"Sure, I'm fine. Dad's making progress. I'm getting my land legs back here at the shop." He shrugged. "It's not now I'm worried about so much. It's when I have to go back to Stillwater for the fall semester that I'm most concerned with."

Then, he didn't know what the hell was going to happen, and delaying the decision regarding the future of the shop hadn't helped his unease.

"Yeah, I bet. Well, for now, I'm here to help you in any way I can. Need some shelves dusted, or something?" Emma smiled.

"No." Logan shook his head. "You're not going to help me while you're on your vacation, and I'm sure as hell not going to let you do any dirty work around here."

"Then maybe I can do something else. I am a graphic designer, after all. And some of your signs could use a good makeover. Maybe a punchy slogan. Some nice graphics." She raised a brow and glanced in his direction.

Some of these signs had been here since he was in high school. Nostalgia aside, they did look pretty old, and not in a charming way. A small change like that might freshen up the store. It wouldn't hurt, even if they did decide to sell it.

Smart and sexy as hell—Emma had it all. It was good to see her again.

Logan smiled. "Okay. *That* I might let you do. If you insist."

"I do. And maybe you'll let me rearrange a few things? Change some of the displays a bit?" She eyed the display of work-boot laces hanging by the cash register.

"You are bound and determined to help, aren't you?" He crossed his arms and tried not to think about wrapping them around her.

"Yeah. I'm sorry. That's horrible of me to even ask, but it's kind of been a dream of mine. When most little girls wanted to play house, I used to play store." She shrugged.

Logan laughed at that revelation. "Far be it from me to deny a woman her lifelong dream. If that's what you want, go for it. Rearrange anything you want."

A smile lit Emma's face as she moved a step closer until they were inches apart. "Thank you."

"Anytime." If this was all it took to make her happy, Logan would let Emma play store all she wanted.

As she stood on tiptoe and planted a kiss near the corner of his mouth, Logan realized there were so many other ideas he had that he hoped would make Emma happy. The least of which would be allowing her to move the shoelace display.

After her kiss, Logan gave in to the urge he'd been fighting. He wrapped his arms around Emma and held tight. She snaked her hands around him and squeezed him back. Dropping his chin to rest on the top of her head, Logan realized something. On the outside, he'd been holding himself together for everyone else, but deep down he was ready to snap. It wasn't until he held Emma, leaned on her, literally, that he realized he needed someone to lean on.

She remained quiet. Neither of them spoke as they just stood, holding each other. He felt her breathing as her back rose and fell beneath his hands. He smelled her perfume and her shampoo. It all took him back to a time when he was carefree and happy. Back to the night of Tuck's wedding when the biggest thing Logan had to worry about was getting Emma alone.

The memories of their time together, the ones he hadn't had time to revisit lately, surfaced and his body reacted. Emma pressed against his growing length. His erection was wedged between them and making his jeans really uncomfortable.

She glanced up, her eyes heavily lidded with what he hoped was need for him. "How bad would it be if you locked that front door and put an *Out to Lunch* sign up? Just for a few minutes."

"I can definitely do that." Though he hoped whatever they did together would take more than a few minutes.

His heart pounded as he strode to the front door and turned the lock. Looking back at Emma, he couldn't believe what a welcome sight she was. He wanted her. Needed her. How much he hadn't realized while they'd been apart. Now, together again, it was clear.

Grasping her hand in his, Logan pulled Emma to the back room before someone saw them. Once they were out of sight of the front windows, Logan's resolve broke. His mouth punished hers with a rough kiss he couldn't control.

He stopped kissing her to yank his belt buckle open, and then it hit him. "Shit. I don't have a condom."

The last thing he'd thought about this morning, or hell, even over the past month, was having sex. He sure as hell didn't keep a condom stashed in his jeans, and birth control was the one random thing his father didn't sell here.

Emma touched his forearm. "Logan, it's okay. We don't need one."

She must have gone on the pill since he'd seen her last, and he couldn't be happier.

"That's good to hear." His voice seemed almost feral to him, as he finished opening his pants and crowded her between his body and the workbench.

Logan went to work on her clothes, not stopping until he'd stripped off her black knee-length shorts and her lace underwear so she was naked from the waist down. He hoisted her onto the workbench.

It was high, built by his grandfather to accommodate the tall men in the Hunt family. It helped prevent back-aches when working at it. The height put Emma in the perfect position for Logan to appreciate what he'd been missing. He ran his hands from her waist down to her thighs. He spread them wide and took in the view.

Reaching between her glorious legs, he spread her lips and drew in a breath when he saw the tender, pink flesh hidden there exposed. All the while, she watched him with those eyes, so deep, like pools of cool spring water. He'd missed her.

He slid one finger inside. It was going to feel so good to bury himself in that tight heat. The thought stirred some-thing deep inside him. Brushing a thumb over the hidden bundle of nerves, he watched her eyes drift shut and her mouth open. She drew in a shaky breath.

Here on the workbench next to the saddle he was supposed to be working on for a customer, Logan had every intention of working Emma to orgasm.

Determined, he used both hands and mouth until she began to shudder beneath his touch. Her muscles clamped down and began pulsing around his fingers inside her. He held himself in check as long as he could, until the spasms began to slow, and then he couldn't wait any longer. He pushed the elastic of his underwear out of the way and thrust deep into Emma. While her bare feet were braced on the edge of the table, he clung onto Emma's hips and rocked into her, hard and fast.

The wooden workbench groaned from his motion. Logan spared a brief moment to hope the legs would hold under the stress. He looked up to meet Emma's gaze as she watched him. It made him want to kiss her.

While still buried inside her, he did just that. Logan pulled her upright and took possession of her lips. She gasped for breath as his mouth covered hers.

The table was the perfect height as he pounded into her. How had he never noticed that? All those years he'd worked here as a teenager, thinking of nothing except the clock and when he could go home, he'd never considered how convenient this big bench would be for certain activities. He appreciated it now, as Emma perched on the edge, clinging to him. He ran his hands over her back and felt her heart thundering beneath her ribcage.

Having her in his arms again so unexpectedly made him want to hold on and make this last. Breaking the kiss, he moved to bite on one earlobe before he pressed his mouth against her ear and said, "God, I missed you."

"I missed you, too." She sounded breathless.

"How long are you staying?" It was crazy to ask while he made love to her, but he needed to know. Logan held her tight and thrust inside one more time.

Her mouth opened on a gasp and her muscles clenched around him. "Two weeks."

As their eyes locked, he knew that two weeks of stolen moments with this woman wasn't going to be long enough.

Chapter
Fourteen

"I'm so happy you're here." Becca wrapped her arms around Emma and squeezed. All the air whooshed out of Emma's lungs from her sister's enthusiastic stranglehold on her.

Emma let out a breathless laugh and extricated herself from Becca's grasp. "I'm happy to see you, too."

"Did your plane land late? I expected you over an hour ago."

What could Emma say to that? Maybe she should lie. If Becca had already checked the airline's website, she wouldn't be asking because she'd know the flight had landed early. The last thing Emma wanted to do was admit she'd picked up the rental car and driven directly to Logan's shop.

Her web skills had come in handy, as did the fact Logan's hometown was as small as they came. It had been easy enough to find. A few searches had yielded the store conveniently named after the family. The rental car's GPS had led Emma to him.

She'd thought she could drop in and see Logan, then come straight to Becca without anyone noticing. What Emma hadn't counted on was she and Logan not being able to keep their hands off each other. Her attraction to him hadn't changed or lessened over time. Not one bit.

Since her heart had started pounding the moment she saw his truck parked outside the shop, Emma should have realized how strongly she'd react to the man himself. He acted like a drug on her system. She felt so good when she was with him, and so bad when she wasn't.

And it wasn't just knowing she carried a piece of him inside her. She hadn't been able to stop thinking of him even before she'd realized she was late and had taken the test.

One more time, Emma found her hand covering her stomach. She moved it before her sister noticed and somehow guessed the secret Emma hid from her. She wouldn't be able to hide it forever. Emma would have to figure everything out soon.

Becca narrowed her gaze, acting a little too observant for Emma's liking. "Emma, what's going on?"

Apparently, she'd taken too long answering Becca's question.

Emma used to be a champion liar. A trait she seemed to have lost thanks to her current situation. Just when she needed it most. Now what? She channeled her inner bad girl and remembered that the best deceptions contained a tiny bit of the truth.

"All right, I'm going to tell you something, but you have to promise not to tell your husband." Emma kept her voice low to add to the illusion she was about to confide the complete truth.

"Okay. I promise." Becca's eyes grew wide as she nodded.

"I stopped by to see Logan at his father's store on my way here."

Becca drew in a sharp breath. "Oh my God. You did? Was he there? How did you know where it was? Wait, have you two been talking this entire time? Are you dating? Why didn't you tell me?"

That had worked out nicely. Becca had hit her with a string of questions, but that was fine with Emma. Not one of them had anything to do with the real secret she wanted to hide.

Emma distilled Becca's inquisition down, choosing what to answer to best suit her purposes.

"No, we're not dating or talking. I googled the store because I think Logan's cute and I wanted to see him again while I'm here visiting you, but I knew if I asked you about him, I'd get a hundred questions." Emma delivered that last bit in hopes the guilt would keep any further questioning from Becca at bay.

"We can definitely make sure you two get together while you're here. It's perfect timing. I mean, it's terrible what happened to his dad, but with Logan right next door, and Tuck and I already planning on helping him out, we'll see a lot of Logan." Becca couldn't have looked happier. Her matchmaking instincts had kicked in and for once, Emma wasn't upset about that.

"That's what I thought, too. I'm glad you're not angry. I missed you, but I also had an ulterior motive for visiting."

The confession had Becca throwing her arms around Emma one more time. "Of course, I'm not angry. I'm thrilled." She pulled back. "Imagine if you and Logan got married? Tuck and Logan are like brothers to each other. We'd be almost like sisters-in-law."

Emma laughed at Becca's crazy logic. "Uh, we're already sisters, but yeah, it would be cool."

From Becca's mouth to God's ears. The best-case scenario would be for Logan to fall in love with Emma without knowing about the baby. That was the only way she could accept a marriage proposal from him with confidence.

"I'm even happier you're into Logan than I was when I thought you liked Jace." Becca truly did look happy.

"And why is that?" Emma cocked a brow. "Because he and his ex-girlfriend disappeared for half your wedding?"

"It wasn't half—" At the look Emma shot her, Becca cut off her own remark. "Anyway, if you marry Logan, we could be army wives together."

"Will you stop taking about Logan and me being married, please? You're going to jinx us. I'm not even sure Logan's interested. I mean we get along well enough." Envisioning herself half naked on the workbench beneath Logan made Emma realize what a vast understatement that was. "I'm just afraid he's not the commitment type."

"Why would you say that?" Becca frowned. "He's very responsible. He's an officer in the army and the head of his department. He's in charge of lots of soldiers and cadets."

"That doesn't mean he wants a wife. Or even a serious girlfriend. He told me at your wedding that he's married to the army."

"Hmm, I don't know." Becca pursed her lips together. "I wonder . . . what if something happened in his past that I don't know about? Maybe an old girlfriend broke his heart. I could ask Tuck—"

"No! You will not say a word to Tucker. Rebecca, do you hear me?"

"Yes, fine. You don't have to pull a Mom and use my full name. I won't tell him."

The faraway look that appeared in Becca's eyes put Emma on immediate alert. "Becca. Stop plotting."

"I'm not. But what if I could unearth some information about Logan's romantic past on my own, without Tucker getting suspicious?"

Knowing Becca and her inability to keep a secret, Emma drew in a breath in frustration. "See, this is why I don't tell you anything."

"Stop. I would never betray your trust. You know that."

"Mmm, hmm. I also know you can't seem to keep your nose out of my love life."

"I seem to be married to a cowboy and living in Oklahoma because you couldn't keep your nose out of my life or your hands off my laptop keyboard." Becca raised a brow in challenge. "Remember?"

"Yes." Emma couldn't deny she'd been the one to secretly send Becca's résumé to OSU for the teaching position, but she could remind her sister that it was all for the best. "You've never been happier. You're welcome."

"Whatever. Now where did Tuck's mom put the wine? I went to the store and stocked up when I heard you were coming. Ah, there it is." Becca headed for the kitchen counter where at least half a case of wine bottles were lined up in orderly rows, like little glass soldiers.

As much as Emma needed a drink about now, she couldn't drink. Not for many more months. "Wait, Bec. You know what? No wine for me. I think I'll just have some water."

"What?" Her sister spun to face her, the bottle in one hand and a corkscrew in the other. "What do you mean you don't want wine?"

Uh, oh. This could be the thing that outed her. Emma had never said no to a glass of wine, and after all these years, Becca damn well knew that. Emma pressed one hand to her belly. "My stomach isn't feeling that great."

Becca's frown deepened. "You always said wine was good for an upset stomach."

"Not this time." She crinkled her nose as if in pain. "I think I might be getting that acid reflux thing. Wine seems to make it worse."

Her sister's eyes opened wider. "You'd better go to the doctor. Fix it before it becomes a real problem."

"I will, but I bet he'll just tell me to lay off the wine."

"Probably." With a scowl, Becca put the bottle back.

"You can still have a glass."

"No. It's no fun without someone to drink it with." Becca's lips formed a definite pout.

"Sorry, Becs. Want to have a cup of herbal tea with me instead? You like that." Emma counted on how well she knew her sister to get her out of this jam. It was the ritual of sitting down together that Becca enjoyed most. It didn't matter if it was wine in a crystal glass or tea in a porcelain mug.

Looking moderately happier at that suggestion, Becca turned toward the stove and reached for the kettle on the burner. "Okay. That sounds good."

Crisis averted. Emma breathed in relief.

"Hey there, darlin'. What're you doing here?"

Or maybe not . . . What more could the universe drop on her shoulders?

Emma turned to see Jace striding across the kitchen, his end goal obviously her. After knocking his ever-present cowboy hat back a few degrees, Jace wrapped his arms around Emma in a big hug, followed by a kiss planted dead on her lips.

Now he wanted to get romantic with her? Of course. Given Emma's luck it was expected, really. Why wouldn't Jace be all over her now that she was carrying Logan's baby? His ex-girlfriend must be busy elsewhere. Emma stifled a sigh.

"Hello, Jace. I'm visiting my sister." *And my baby-daddy.* God, how in the world had her life gotten so complicated? "What are you doing here? Don't you live in Stillwater near Tucker and Becca?"

"I do, but it's rodeo season. I'm here to steal my compadre away from his new bride and take him to Elk City for a competition."

"Ah." As if Emma knew where Elk City was. "Got a lot of elk there, do they?"

He grinned. "Can't say I ever saw one there myself."

"Tuck's just out back, Jace." Becca glanced over her shoulder as she stood on tiptoe and stretched toward the shelf in a cabinet far above her head.

"Thanks." Jace reached past Becca to grab one of the mugs that were just an inch out of her arm's length on the second shelf. "This what you want?"

"Yes, two please."

Jace took down two as Emma watched, baffled. His persistent gentlemanly behavior had been one of the things about Jace that had gotten to Emma in the first place. Back before she knew it also extended to being a doormat for his ex's every whim, no matter how inappropriate.

The irony wasn't lost on her that the problem with Jace had been his past long-term relationship, and the current issue she had with Logan was his lack of one. Having a very Goldilocks moment, Emma had to wonder if maybe there was no man alive who was *just right*.

"Anything else you need here? Stepstool?" Jace grinned as he joked with Becca.

"No, thank you. Go get Tuck. He's expecting you. He's got his overnight tote all packed and ready."

"Overnight tote?" Jace's brow drew comically low. "Jeez, woman. It's a *gear bag*. You make it sound like he's got, I don't know, silk pajamas and an eye mask in there or something."

Becca rolled her eyes. "All right. I stand corrected. His *gear bag* is in the truck, packed full of extra manly, bull rider things, I'm sure."

"Damn right, it is." Jace gave a single enthusiastic nod as he put one hand on the doorknob. "And we won't be gone overnight. We should be back late tonight, unless we're both too tired or broken up to drive."

"Too broken up. Great. Good to know." Becca looked less than thrilled with that information. As Jace opened the back door, she said, "Hey, Jace? Please tell Tucker he'd better come inside and kiss me good-bye before you two leave."

"As if he'd ever give up a chance to kiss you. But yes, ma'am. I'll tell him." Jace turned and winked at Emma. "I'll see you when we get back. Maybe you'll save a kiss for the winner?"

"Okay, I will. Just make sure to bring him home with you." Emma smiled at her own wit as Jace grinned and, after a tip of his hat, was out the back door and out of sight.

"I don't understand this thing between you and Jace at all." Becca shook her head. "You two seem to get along so well."

"I thought you already had me married off to Logan." Emma's brows shot high. "What happened to you and me being army wives together? Now you're back on Jace? What the hell, Becca? Fickle much?"

Emma joked with Jace. She could even joke with Becca about being with Logan, but secretly, she never forgot how serious her situation was.

"You need to go to the doctor, Em. I can see your stomach is bothering you." Becca's focus dropped to where Emma had once again pressed her hand to her belly without realizing it.

"I will." Emma swallowed hard. She had to stop acting pregnant. At least the upset stomach story was holding. "And you really have to stop pushing me at Jace."

"I will." Becca sighed. "I know he was a jerk to you at the wedding."

Emma held her hands in the air. "Finally. Thank you."

For the first time, Emma felt vindicated. Becca had admitted the truth about that night and didn't act as if Emma had exaggerated the whole thing with Jace and Jacqueline.

Standing next to the kettle on the stove, which was taking its time boiling, Becca drummed her fingernails on the countertop. "I bet Tucker's mom knows about Logan's past. I mean their parents are good friends."

And now it seemed Becca was back on the subject of Logan, and back to her meddling. Trying to follow her train of thought was enough to give a person mental whiplash. Emma eyed the bottles of wine on the counter, wishing she could have some. She'd never needed it more.

For the first time in the past month, Logan walked into the rehabilitation facility that had become his father's home with a spring in his step. He knew it wasn't from the old cowboy boots he'd taken to wearing again now that he wasn't at campus and in combat boots every day.

His energetic pace was all due to Emma showing up out of the blue. That was as unexpected and as welcome as a cool breeze on a hot summer day.

Logan pushed through the doorway of his father's room and stopped dead mid-step. His father was standing. One shaky hand was braced on the back of the wheelchair supporting his weight, but he was standing on his own two feet nonetheless.

"Dad?"

His father turned at the sound of Logan's voice, and that upset his delicate balance. He pitched forward, grasping for the chair with the hand on the side most affected by the stroke. It was useless in preventing his fall, and Logan felt just as useless as he reached for his father.

"No. I can do it." The older man tried to push Logan away.

With a hand beneath each of his father's arms bearing all his weight, Logan had to disagree with his father. "Not right now, you can't. You've done enough. You have to rest."

The only reason the man wasn't lying flat on the floor, with a few less teeth, was because Logan supported him.

His mother walked through the door just as Logan attempted to single-handedly get his father into the wheelchair. How did the nurses make it look so easy? Some of them weighed far less than Logan did and yet they moved patients bigger than his father all day long and made it look almost effortless.

"What happened?" She rushed into the room, putting the water pitcher down on the bed tray as she passed it.

"I found him in here standing up." Logan glanced at his mother. "Since when can he stand on his own?"

"Since yesterday." She unlocked the wheels of the chair and moved it to behind his father. "He walked a few steps with his physical therapist on those parallel bar things."

"That's great." Logan meant what he said, but it didn't relieve his main concern. "But that doesn't mean he's able to walk, alone, on his own with no bars or nurse for support."

He'd said the last while looking at his father. Logan knew him well enough to know the man would push his body so hard and fast, he'd end up doing harm.

"Have to get better." His father's speech had improved dramatically. Another good sign.

Logan would be happy if he stuck to just practicing speaking for now. *That* he could practice all day long without risk of doing bodily damage.

"You will get better, dear. It takes time." His mother smiled. "But you're improving every day."

"No. Now." His father's zeroed in on Logan.

The look was so intense, Logan got the feeling there was more going on here than just the older man's stubborn willfulness. "Dad, I'm staying here to help you and Mom for the summer. I don't have to go back to Stillwater until right before the fall semester starts."

"Then sell?" The words were stilted from the stroke, but not the meaning or the concern behind them.

That was it. His father didn't want the store sold. Through all of this, Logan had never sat down with his father to discuss the future of Hunt's. Sure, he'd talked about it with Layne and their mother. Hell, it seemed as if he'd had the discussions with everyone, including Tuck and Tyler. Everyone except his father.

In Logan's defense, that had been to protect the man. He needed to concentrate on recovering, not worry about the shop. But meanwhile, worry had been eating him up inside. That was obvious now.

Logan pulled a chair over close to the wheelchair. He sat so they could talk eye-to-eye. "Maybe not, Dad."

His speech might be affected, but his father still managed a derogatory snort.

Logan's mom rested one hand on the back of the wheelchair. "I can help. I did used to work there too sometimes, you know."

"I know, Mom. I remember. Tuck had an idea. I haven't acted on it yet, but I think it's a good one. He thinks some of your friends at the VFW would help us out. He might be right. Most of the time, they sit around the bar and complain how their wives drive them nuts at home." Logan shrugged. "Maybe they'd enjoy a day or two a week at the shop."

A slow nod from his father told Logan he liked the idea, though he wasn't so sure of the reaction to this next part. His father hated change. "And Becca's sister is in town. Remember Becca, Dad? Tuck's new wife? Well, her sister, Emma, works in advertising or something in New York, and she's offered to design a few new signs for us to help spruce up the shop. It can't hurt, right?"

Another nod followed. Logan breathed a sigh of relief. His mother squatted next to the chair and took his father's good hand in both of hers. "See, honey. We'll make it work somehow. The store will be there, waiting for you when you're recovered."

Logan only hoped his father would recover enough to be able to enjoy it. But as he watched the scene before him, his mom's devotion, his father using what little strength he had to cling to her hands, it hit Logan how hugely important they were to each other.

His father, as debilitated as he was right now, had something Logan didn't have—a wife who'd been totally dedicated to him for forty-five years. Yes, he had two sons here to help when he needed them most, but just as Layne had left to go back to his responsibilities, so would Logan soon.

Logan had let forty years pass him by without finding the kind of love his parents had. He'd been so focused on his career, he never bothered looking too hard for it, always thinking there'd be time later. He should know better. Military or civilian, no one knew when his or her time would run out. His father was the perfect example of that.

It was past time for Logan to correct the situation. And maybe he wouldn't have to look very far, either. It was possible his love was right there—at least for the next two weeks.

Would Emma consider a serious relationship with a man half a country away? Could they get serious enough that maybe she wouldn't want it to be long-distance anymore? It would have to be Emma who moved. Logan couldn't relocate right now. Not only was he stationed in Oklahoma, but his family was here, and they needed him close now more than ever.

It was a lot to ask her, to move to Oklahoma for him, but her sister was here. That was a point in his favor . . . And what the hell was he doing, jumping to all these conclusions? Talk about putting the cart before the horse.

He had two weeks to determine if the reason he shook like a schoolboy every time he saw Emma was love or lust. Two weeks for them both to get to know each other a whole lot better, and not just in bed. It was all he had. It would have to be long enough.

Wars had been won and lost in less time. Hearts, too. Logan knew he was well on the way to losing his already. He had been since that one fateful weekend when life had stepped in, knocked the happiness he'd found with Emma aside, and demanded all he had.

It was time to take it back.

Chapter
Fifteen

The air inside the dimly lit VFW swirled with thick smoke. It took Logan aback when he walked in. No wonder his mother always knew when his father had stopped by here on his way home from the store. His clothing would have reeked of smoke.

Logan guessed that even if no one was smoking inside, the building itself would still retain the odor. The wood paneled walls would probably ooze the combined remnants of all the cigarettes, pipes, and cigars smoked inside it for over fifty years. Good thing it was a warm night and someone had propped the door open so there would be some fresh air coming in.

The moment Logan walked through that open door, Mack the bartender spotted him. "Logan Hunt! About damn time you came and joined us old guys here."

Grumbling by the older members about how today's servicemen didn't bother with veterans' organizations and how things were different in the old days was a constant. Looking around, Logan had to admit the old guys probably had a point. The age of the patrons made Logan the youngest in the room by at least thirty years.

"It's a bit of a haul to drive here from Stillwater just for a beer." Logan pulled out an empty barstool and took a seat between two vets he'd known for years.

"Yeah, well, while you're here visiting your parents, I expect to see you around once in a while." Mack continued to wipe down the ancient wooden bar top with his rag.

Harry O'Neil swiveled on his barstool toward Logan. "How's your dad doing?"

Logan turned to the old man to his right and shrugged. "Good days and bad, but we're hopeful. He's progressing in the right direction, so that's positive."

Harry adjusted the baseball hat he wore. The embroidered insignia named the vessel he'd served on in Korea. "Good to hear. Send him my best."

"Will do." Logan nodded. "That's what I came to talk to you all about. My dad. More specifically, his store . . ."

As Mack poured him a beer, and the rest of the men seated at the bar listened, Logan explained what he hoped would be a viable plan to keep the store up and running after he left for Stillwater, and while his father continued to recuperate.

When he'd finished, Harry leaned in to slap Logan on the shoulder. "Of course, we'll help you out in the store. Your father has been a member here for as long as I can remember."

"And since Harry's been here since at least the Civil War, that's saying something." Rod, a Vietnam-era air force veteran, snorted at his own joke, then pushed his empty beer mug across the bar. "Another one here, Mack."

"You need another?" Mack eyed Logan's mug as his hand grabbed the empty one from Rod.

"I shouldn't. I wanted to get back to the shop and finish up some stuff tonight."

Harry let out a wheeze sounding like half laugh, half cough, and Logan began to fear for his health thanks to all this second-hand smoke. "Whatever it is will wait. Do it tomorrow. Have a drink with us tonight. You young kids never come in here. Act like we're just a bunch of dinosaurs. Well, I'll tell you something, kid. You could learn a lot from us old-timers."

Logan was sure he could. And it didn't hurt to be called a kid, since lately Logan had been feeling every bit of his thirty-nine and three-quarters years.

"All right. One more. But then I'm going." Logan could walk home from here if he felt he needed to after drinking the beer.

It would be a hike, but that was fine. He'd been real lax in his PT since he'd been here. He could use the exercise. It wouldn't be the first time someone had left their vehicle in the parking lot overnight and came back to get it in the morning.

That was the beauty of living in a small town—places were close. People, too. He realized that as the night progressed. Rod demanded he buy Logan's beer for him. Then Harry insisted Logan tell them all about Layne's visit home, and Mack wanted to hear more about Logan's position at OSU.

It seemed Logan's dad spent the majority of his time at the VFW talking about him and Layne. Or maybe boasting was a better way to describe it. Either way, his dad had told the old guys all about Logan and Layne—their military service and their lives while they were away from their hometown. The man was obviously very proud of his two sons. It was something Logan hadn't realized, but something he wouldn't soon forget.

It was late by the time Logan navigated his truck through the dark deserted streets to his parents' house. He'd drunk a couple of beers. Then stayed even longer, sipping on pop and listening to the vets tell war stories from their own eras. Before Logan knew it, it was past his usual bedtime. Who knew the old guys had such staying power?

He'd always assumed they'd all be in bed by the end of the evening news, when here it was after eleven and he had just left them.

He put on his signal, about to pull into the driveway, when the truck parked next door in the Jenkins driveway had him slamming on the brakes.

"Son of a bitch." Logan stared at it, not believing what he saw. But there it was, as living proof. Jace was there. In the house where Emma was staying. In the middle of the damn night.

What the hell was Jace doing at the Jenkins house so late?

Moving in on Emma while Logan wasn't looking was the most likely answer. Jealousy hit Logan like a fist in the gut. Emma had been with Logan today. Had made love to him. He tried to remember that fact as it felt as if a vise was being clamped around his chest.

What could he do? It was too late to go over and knock on the door. That was for sure. But it was also late enough, and dark enough, for some reconnaissance.

Realizing that having his truck idling in the middle of the road was not the best way to be invisible, he pulled into the driveway. He cut the lights and engine, and got out, closing the door as silently as he could manage.

Logan cursed his cowboy boots for making his footsteps sound even louder as he tried to move, quickly and quietly, across the driveway and to the back door of the Jenkins' house.

What he was looking to find, he wasn't quite sure. As long as it wasn't Emma and Jace snuggled up together, necking like a couple of teenagers, he'd be good. Just the thought twisted his gut.

Like a ninja, Logan crouched low and crept toward the back of the house. There was one light on inside, and it was in the kitchen. It was crazy, but he had to look. Had to see what was happening, even if what he saw might make him ill.

At six-foot-two, Logan figured he'd be able to see inside while standing on the ground if he stretched. He moved closer to the window, giving himself a pep talk as his heart thundered. He'd deal with whatever he discovered, even if Jace and Emma were together in there.

Logan would fight for her. Jace had been his competition for Emma's attention from the day he'd met her, but Logan had been the one she'd left with after the wedding.

With that resolve made, Logan put one hand on the windowsill and rose onto his toes . . . and saw an empty room. The illumination had come from a small light inside the hood above the stove. Mrs. Jenkins must have left it on as a nightlight in case her houseguests got up in the middle of the night and wanted something from the kitchen.

Logan blew out a breath and tried to calm the pounding in his chest. Emma was probably snug in bed, sound asleep. That still didn't explain the presence of Jace's truck in the drive at this late hour, but Logan would have to find out the answer to that in the morning. He turned, about to head home and to bed himself when a dark shape blocked his path.

"Logan?" Tuck's voice came through the darkness. "What the hell? You okay? Your dad okay?"

"Yeah, fine." Crap. How could he explain being here? "Where are you coming from?"

"Elk City. Rodeo with Jace." As Tuck moved closer, Logan could see the gear bag in his hand.

They'd been at a rodeo. Of course. Logan should have thought of that. Jace hadn't been here with Emma at all. That revelation was an unbelievable relief.

The sound of a truck starting in the driveway caught Logan's attention. "That Jace leaving now?"

"Yeah, he's got a job to do early in the morning in Stillwater. Besides, he's so wired from all the energy drinks he downed tonight, he'll have no trouble driving the couple of hours back."

Another relief added to Logan's growing list. Jace was leaving, not crashing here for the night where he would wake up to Emma at the breakfast table.

"So, what are you doing creeping around in the dark outside my house at this hour? You're usually not such a night owl."

"Actually, I just got home from the VFW. You were right. The guys are willing to help us out." Logan motioned toward the window, hoping his diversionary tactic worked. "When I saw the light on, I thought you might be up. I came by so I could tell you thanks for the suggestion."

"That's good to hear. I'm glad." Tuck delivered a nod, and shifted his bag from one hand to the other.

So far, so good. Maybe Tuck did believe Logan's bull-shit excuse.

"And I'm sure your interest in thanking me in the middle of the night has nothing to do with the fact my new sister-in-law is here for a visit."

Or maybe not.

Speechless, Logan considered how to sidestep that accusation.

"It's okay, Logan. I get it. I started acting like a fool the minute I saw Becca. Must be something in that New York water. Makes the women from there irresistible to us guys here in the Midwest."

Logan laughed and gave up his attempt to deny Tuck was right. "Could be."

"So how about you come over bright and early in the morning for breakfast? You can pass on the good news about the old guys helping out at the shop. I'm sure my parents and Becca and Emma would all love to see you."

"I don't want to intrude—"

"Jesus, Logan." Tuck interrupted Logan's halfhearted protest. "We were in each other's houses as much as we were in our own growing up. Emma's being here doesn't change that, and I know you want to see her, so just cut the crap and come over."

"All right." Logan couldn't fight it. Tuck was right, so Logan gave in and tried to preserve what was left of his dignity. "Thanks."

Tuck shook his head. "No problem. Can I go in and shower now, so I can get to bed? I smell like bull and there's a sweet thing inside waiting on me."

"Of course. Go." Words couldn't express how envious Logan was of Tuck, though it was the other Hart sister Logan wished was in his own bed waiting on him. Tomorrow, he'd see what he could do about making that happen.

Emma stifled the guilt as she reached for a coffee mug, knowing that according to some experts, she shouldn't have any caffeine at all. She had cut down to one cup a day and she wasn't giving that up. It was one small concession, a last vestige of normalcy. She'd given up alcohol, and she'd weaned herself off her usual pot of coffee a day, but she could only do so much for this baby. It would just have to get used to one little tiny cup of caffeine.

"Good morning." Logan's voice at the back door had Emma's hand pausing on the handle of the coffee pot.

As the screen door slammed closed, Mrs. Jenkins said, "Good morning, Logan. Come on in. Have a seat. Coffee's made and bacon is on the way."

"Thank you, ma'am. That sounds wonderful." Logan

moved across the room, the coffee pot Emma held obviously his objective. He stopped so close, he had her pinned between his body and the counter. "Morning, Emma."

Her pulse beat faster at the heat she saw in his eyes. "Good morning. Coffee?"

"Definitely. Thanks." He reached into the cabinet above her head to grab a mug, and all she could think about was him lifting her up, setting her on top of the counter, and doing inappropriate things to her.

"Sure. No problem." It took all she had to not shake when she poured the steaming black liquid into his cup.

"So what are your plans for the day?" He raised a brow and sipped at his black coffee.

She concentrated on stirring cream and sugar into her own cup. Another concession to the pregnancy—she'd switched back to real sugar instead of the fake stuff. If Becca didn't notice all these sudden changes in Emma's behavior, she must be blind.

But Emma couldn't worry about that now. She had to keep the words *I'm pregnant with your baby* from showing on her face as she tried to act casual with Logan.

"No plans so far. Are you working at the store today? I could help if you'd like."

His lips turned up in a smile. "I'd like that very much. I figured I'd drive over around ten. I could give you a ride. Or you can take your own car in case you want to leave early. I'll be there a while—"

"No, that's fine. I can ride with you and stay for however long you do."

His smile broadened. "That will be nice. Having the company, I mean."

Emma's cheeks heated as she remembered yesterday and their encounter on the worktable. From his expression, and the way his voice dipped low and intimate as he spoke to her, she knew Logan was remembering, too. Maybe even envisioning what could happen today.

"You working on that saddle today?" Oklahoma had obviously gotten into her blood. She'd fallen asleep last night fantasizing about what she and Logan could do with the sturdy piece of leather equipment as their prop.

"I am."

"Good. I wouldn't mind being there for that. You know, getting a closer look at the kind of work you could accomplish on a saddle like that." She kept her voice low and her words generic, but hopefully Logan would get the deeper meaning.

His brows rose a bit. Logan nodded. "I think I can arrange for you to be there to witness that."

"I look forward to it." With one last smoldering look, Emma carried her coffee mug to where the family sat.

Taking her seat at the breakfast table, Emma was in such a good mood she could even ignore the openly interested expression Becca wore. That was in direct opposition to how Tuck kept his head down while he studied the front page of the morning newspaper as if his life depended on it. Good man. He was giving them privacy. Or he was really into the local news. Either way, it worked for Emma.

Thank goodness Tyler had already left for work, Mr. Jenkins was busy with the sports section of the paper, and Mrs. Jenkins was too busy frying bacon to care. Otherwise the entire Jenkins family might have seen her and Logan flirting over the coffeemaker.

Emma glanced up and saw him coming across the kitchen. He took the empty chair next to her at the wooden table. "So, you got to see our good old friend Jace yesterday, huh?" Logan eyed her over the rim of his mug as he took a sip.

Wasn't this interesting? If Emma wasn't totally off base, Logan was jealous. This could play right into her plans. "Yes, I did." Emma looked at Tuck, enjoying this game she was playing with Logan. "In fact, Tucker, I think I promised to kiss last night's winner. Who won?"

Tuck glanced up, wide-eyed and looking less than happy to be included in Emma's game of cat and mouse with Logan. "Uh, not me."

"Then who?"

"Jace," Becca answered for her husband.

"Really? Wow." Hmm. She hadn't counted on him winning. Emma shot Logan a sideways glance and noticed the expression he wore. It looked as if his coffee had gotten very bitter. Making him a little jealous was one thing, but she didn't want to drive him away by making him think she was slutting around Oklahoma. Especially not now. Emma swallowed hard. "So, where is Jace?"

"Stillwater," Tuck answered in seemingly as few words as possible.

"Oh, well. That offer had an expiration date so he'll miss out." She turned her attention to her sister. Time to change the subject. "Becca, what are you and Tuck doing today?"

"I'm fixin' to mow our lawn and the Hunts's yard right after breakfast."

"No, Tuck—" Logan began to protest.

"Quit." Tucker cut off his friend. "I stayed in town to help your parents out, so let me help."

Logan drew in a deep breath, looking uncomfortable. "Thanks."

Tuck nodded his acceptance and went back to reading the paper, though he never did turn the page.

"And I thought I'd need to spend the day keeping you busy, but it seems I don't have to. Logan's willing to do it for me." Becca smiled.

"Becca, you should spend the day with your sister."
Again, Logan appeared uncomfortable.

"No, really, Logan, you'd be doing me a favor. I still
have to write and address all the thank you cards for the
wedding. It'll probably take me all day. It'll help me knowing Emma is being taken care of." Becca was playing
matchmaker again, but this time, it was fine with Emma.

Logan looked at Emma. "You sure you won't mind being stuck with me all day?"

Emma met his dark gaze. "Not at all." She couldn't
think of a better way to spend a day . . . or a night.

Chapter
Sixteen

"My grandfather owned the shop first. Then my father ran it. I know he hopes Layne and I will take it over one day." Logan rubbed the leather of the saddle with a rag as he spoke.

Emma paused in the midst of tearing into a cardboard box in the store's back room and looked up. Logan wore a wistful expression when he spoke about the family history of his shop. "Logan, I hadn't realized. This store's a real family tradition."

He sniffed out a short laugh. "And how could I have even contemplated selling it, knowing how much it means to my father?"

"No." She shook her head. "That's not what I was saying at all."

"I know." Logan sighed like the weight of the world rested on his shoulders. "You don't have to say it. I've said it to myself at least a hundred times."

"And in this conversation with yourself, what do you say back to you?" Emma cocked a brow.

He let out another humorless laugh. "That depends on the day, and time . . . and my mood. Then I ask myself the other big question haunting me. How can we keep it? Mom's busy taking care of Dad. Layne's in Japan. I'll have to go back to Stillwater. Even with the guys from the VFW helping out, it's a lot of work."

"I know, Logan. I don't think anyone will blame you if you decide you need to sell it."

His expression told her he didn't believe that. "I keep putting off doing anything. I guess I was hoping something would change. And you know what? I think it just might. Something changed yesterday."

"What changed?"

"I walked into my father's room at the rehab facility and he was standing. Before this, he's always been in bed or in the wheelchair when I visited."

"Logan, that's wonderful."

"Eh, not quite. He fell right after that, but he had been standing, so that's something. His speech is improving, too."

"That's great. He's getting better. See, there's a light at the end of the tunnel."

"His improvements might be a double-edged sword. You know? If he were totally disabled, permanently, there'd be no question what I needed to do. We'd have to sell. And if he makes a complete recovery, there's no question he'll want to keep working here. But what if his condition stalls somewhere in the middle? Then what?" Logan sighed.

"I understand. We have to have faith that this is the start of that complete recovery. I'm glad he's making progress."

"Me, too. And I'm *really* glad that when Mom was so distraught over Dad and told me and Layne to decide by ourselves if we wanted to sell, we didn't rush and do it. With my luck, we'd sell, he'd be as good as new, and never talk to me again."

"I doubt he'd feel that way, but I'm happy you didn't sell, too. Because, you know, I have a fond place in my heart for that workbench. I'd hate to think of a stranger getting it." She grinned.

He let out a burst of a laugh. "My grandfather built that bench. If he ever knew what we'd used it for."

"He was a married man. I think he'd understand."

"I don't know." Still chuckling, Logan stopped working the conditioner into the saddle and turned to face Emma where she sat on the floor surrounded by cardboard boxes. He frowned. "What are you doing?"

"Seeing what's inside all of these."

"I can tell you what's in them. Dusty old crap from my parents' garage."

"No. There's some great stuff in here." She glanced toward the floor next to her at pile of treasures she'd unearthed so far.

"Oh really. Like what?"

"Like these deer antlers I found. And this kerosene lamp. And over there, covered in dust, is a nice old trunk. I just have to clean it up a little."

He looked in the direction she pointed. "Actually, that's a tack box."

"Okay, tack box. Whatever." Emma dismissed his correction with a wave of one hand as her mind spun with possibilities. "It will look great with that wool throw for sale out in the store."

"Wool throw?" Logan frowned.

"Yeah." Emma nodded. "The one with kind of a Native American-style print."

"It's a saddle blanket not a throw. Just like the tack box, it's for horses, not people." He smiled.

"Fine. That's even better. I can put together a whole horse theme." She conceded his point so she could make her own. "What I'm saying is, when I pull all these things together in one corner of the store, it will create a scene.

It's going to look like you stepped into the Ralph Lauren store on Madison Avenue."

"Oh, really." Logan cocked one brow. "And that's a good thing?"

"Yes, it is. A very good thing. It will draw the customers farther inside, back to the stuff you want them to buy. The big ticket items like the saddles and cowboy hats."

"Sounds good. Don't let me stop you. If it'll move more stock, keep pawing through this dusty old stuff." Logan came over and squatted down next to her. He brushed a thumb across her cheek, and then glanced at his fingers as he rubbed them together. "But don't blame me when you get filthy."

"I've never been opposed to getting a little dirty." That came out sounding very suggestive, just as Emma intended it.

The nuance wasn't lost on Logan. He smiled and shook his head. Standing, he said, "You keep talking like that and my work here will never get done."

The way the heat radiated off him and into her, just from the smallest touch, that was a very good possibility. "How about I offer an incentive for both of us? I get my displays done. You get your work done. Then we can take a little break."

"And do what?"

She shrugged. "I don't know. Maybe figure out a creative way to test out that saddle you're working on?"

"That certainly is an incentive to finish it." He grinned. "I think I can make that work."

"Excellent, but you have to help me move my trunk first, before you go back to your saddle."

He reached down and gave her a hand up. "Tack box."

"Whatever." Standing, she brushed the dust off her jeans.

He shook his head and let out a laugh. Grabbing the handle at one end of the box, he waited for her to get into position at the other end. "Emma?"

"Yeah?" She glanced up as she bent to reach for the dust-covered handle.

"I'm glad you're here." The depth of sincerity in his voice had Emma pausing before she got herself together and took hold of the other handle.

"Me, too." She tried to keep her response light, but inside her heart thundered.

Eventually, this thing between them would either go somewhere or it wouldn't. It was the latter option that worried Emma, because eventually she'd also have to confess her secret. They couldn't just keep having casual sex.

She'd worry about that later. Maybe it would all work out, just like Logan's problems with his father and the store hopefully would.

Emma focused on her work, rather than on the secret she was keeping from him. It was safer while she was feeling so vulnerable and squishy around him. Getting into designer mode, she directed him to where she wanted the trunk set down and brushed her hands together.

"Now get going and finish the saddle so I can work on my display."

"Yes, ma'am." He tipped the cowboy hat he'd taken to wearing again. "Call me if you need anything else heavy moved. I don't want you hurting yourself."

His concern for her well-being made her heart do a little flip. That was bad. It made her want to confess everything. She couldn't do that. Not yet.

Maybe she should say to hell with their work for the day and get to the incentive part right away. Sex would be a good distraction to take her mind off her hopes and fears about their future. Hell, sex was good for lots of things.

Who was she kidding? Sex wasn't a safe distraction.

Somewhere along the way, sex and love had gotten all mixed up when it came to Logan.

Emma restrained herself. For now. "Yes, sir. Will do. Now get."

"All right." Walking away, he left her to her work, but she couldn't get to it as long as he treated her to the enticing view of his jean-clad butt and cowboy boot swagger.

She watched him until he disappeared into the workroom. Only then did she try to focus on anything other than Logan.

Somehow Logan kept his mind on his work, though it wasn't easy. Not when he was hyper-aware of Emma's presence. He could hear her out there, moving things around, occasionally humming along with the radio station. She even laughed at one particularly funny line in a song. That had him smiling as he finished up the saddle.

The pleasure having her close gave him made up for all the times she had his mind wandering to her rather than remaining on his task. The job was simple enough, but made difficult thanks to the lovely Miss Hart's proximity and Logan's visceral reaction to her. One of his father's customers had brought in the saddle to have a few leather straps and some old hardware replaced.

Logan's work ethic and training, instilled in him at a young age by his father, wouldn't allow Logan to send it back to the owner without cleaning and conditioning it first. It was little things like that—taking the time to clean and polish the saddle until it looked as good as new—that kept customers coming back to Hunt's all these years. He only hoped his father would be able to keep serving his loyal clientele for many years to come. His father got as much out of this business as he put in.

Glancing at his cell phone, Logan realized how late it had gotten. The noise from the front of the store told him

Emma was still working hard. With a smile, he went out front to see what she'd done.

What he saw stopped him in his tracks.

"Holy shit. Emma, this doesn't even look like the same place." He turned in a circle and took in all the changes she'd made, all on her own and in an amazingly short period of time.

She cringed. "I know. I kind of got out of control. Is it okay? Will your father be mad?"

"Mad. Are you crazy? It looks amazing." Logan walked to one corner, to where she'd set up a display with the tack box and a saddle. She followed him over.

"I made this the equestrian area, so I tried to move everything horse or riding related over to this corner of the store." She spun to the opposite corner. "Over there I put all the outdoor sportsman-type stuff."

Logan turned and saw the deer antlers and a fishing creel on top of an old metal cooler that must have dated back to his grandfather's day. He shook his head. It made sense. It would be easy for the customers to find what they needed. And it made the whole place ooze with a homey charm it had never had before.

"I just started on a home corner. I love that old kerosene lamp. I thought I'd set it on top of that wood table you have stashed behind the cash register counter. If you don't mind me moving it out to the floor."

"Uh, no. I'll do it for you though. It's heavy." He shook his head again. "Emma, this really is incredible."

"Thanks, but I'm not done yet. I was thinking I could paint wooden signs for each section. Any chance you have some old, weathered wood lying around? The rougher the better."

"I'll take a look behind the garage at home. Or there might be something at the hunting cabin."

"Ooo, a hunting cabin?" Emma's eyes lit with interest. "I'd love to see that."

"I'm sure it's not what you're picturing, but I can take you to see it, if you really want." He smiled. His city girl sure was a surprise. "You're amazing. You know that? And the customers are going to flip when they see all the changes."

A frown furrowed her brow. "Yeah, that's something I wanted to ask you about. We didn't have any customers today. Is business always this slow?"

"No." Logan laughed. "Didn't you see? I have the *Closed* sign on the door."

Her eyes widened. "Why?"

"I was working in the back and you were busy moving things around out here. It would have been too much to be open, too. Everyone in town knows my father isn't able to work right now. They don't expect us to be open for regular business. The custom orders I've been getting done were just a courtesy."

She planted her hands on her hips. "Well, that has to stop. I didn't do all this so no one can see it. Tomorrow, we open for regular business hours. I'll print up a paper sign at Tuck's house tonight announcing it."

Logan raised one brow. "*We* open for business?"

"Sure. I want to be here. I'd like to hear what people say about the changes. I had fun today." She grinned wide, then held a hand to her stomach and swallowed hard. "Can we take a break to eat?"

"Oh my God, Emma. I'm sorry. I got so distracted I worked you right through lunch."

"*You* didn't work me through lunch. I got distracted, too, but I could use something in my stomach."

"Of course. There's not a lot around here, but we can go eat at the diner down the block."

"I'm kinda dirty." She glanced down at her shirt and jeans. She was a little grungy. He tried not to feel guilty about that. He'd never assumed she'd be pawing through all the old crap that nobody had touched in years.

"I can run over and bring us back something. How's that sound?"

"Wonderful. That way I can finish up the new home section. And there are a few more details I thought of while I was rearranging things. *And* I didn't get through all those boxes in the back yet—"

"Emma, you're supposed to be on vacation."

"And you're supposed to be getting me lunch. A bowl of soup and some packages of saltine crackers would be perfect."

His heart did a little flip at how amazing this woman was. He tamped it down and nodded. "All right. You've got it. I'll be right back. Lock yourself in when I leave."

"Against what? The crime spree in this horribly dangerous part of town?" She rolled her eyes at him. "I'm a New Yorker, remember?"

"And I'm your boss while you're here, remember? So please, do as I ask and lock yourself in."

"Humph. Yes, boss. And I'll be thinking of what sort of compensation and fringe benefit package I want while you're gone."

Knowing Emma, and seeing the heated look she shot him as she followed him to the door, Logan was sure he'd enjoy delivering on all of her demands.

Chapter
Seventeen

"So what do you want to do tonight?" Becca glanced over her shoulder while standing at the sink. "Tuck's parents have Scrabble. The real kind with the tiles and everything. Not just the iPad app."

"Old school, huh? Sounds good." Emma smiled.

She was too bone deep tired to be up for anything too exciting. After hauling stuff around the store all day, her energy was at a low. And forgetting to eat lunch until her stomach was queasy didn't help.

Crap, she hadn't taken her pregnancy vitamins since she'd been here. Forgetting those wouldn't help her energy level any. The only time the horse-sized pill didn't make Emma sick to her stomach was when she took it after a big meal, so right now would be a perfect time. Her belly was full of Mrs. Jenkins' homemade macaroni salad and charcoal-grilled burgers.

Eating dinners big enough to satisfy a bull rider wasn't going to help her waistline any, but she supposed it was a moot point. That area was only going to grow as time ticked on, but both she and the reason for her weight gain needed the proper nutrition. Emma had to remember to take her vitamins.

While Becca was drying dishes, Tuck was who knew where, and his parents were already settled in the living room watching television, Emma reached into her purse on the kitchen counter. She blindly felt around until she found the prescription bottle.

With one eye on Becca to make sure her sister was still occupied, Emma pulled out the bottle and tried the lid. She smothered a curse when she couldn't get it open. Damn childproof cap. Emma flattened her palm and tried to press down on the top while turning, like the directions said. The bottle shot out of her grasp and fell to the tile floor with a sound that resonated throughout the room.

That figured. The one time it was crucial she be inconspicuous, she'd proceeded to drop it. And loudly, too. Of all the things no one had ever told her about being pregnant, that she'd become a klutz and start dropping every damn thing she tried to pick up would have been a nice piece of information to have.

Becca glanced over her shoulder. "What was that?"

"Just my vitamins." Emma started in pursuit of the bottle as it rolled across the floor, hoping to grab it before Becca noticed it looked more like a doctor's prescription than a brand of vitamins available in the store, when Tucker walked into the room.

Emma watched in horror as he bent to pick it up. He frowned at the label. "Prenatal vitamins?" His eyes grew large as his gaze shot to his new bride. "Becca? Are you—"

Becca put the dish she'd been drying down and turned to stare at Emma. "Um, no."

Tuck's focus moved back to the bottle. He spun it in his hand and drew in an audible breath when he got to the portion of the label where the patient's name had been typed. "Emma? These are yours?"

This wasn't how Emma had envisioned telling anyone, but what could she do? She supposed she could make up some story that she was anemic or something, and the doctor thought the prenatal vitamins would help, but it was only a matter of time before everyone would know anyway. No hiding this for long.

"They're mine. I'm knocked up." She forced a laugh. "Surprise."

"By who? Someone from New York?" Tuck's eyes moved back and forth between Becca and her.

Tuck obviously thought Becca already knew. Not a surprise. Becca looked as guilty as if she had known. Emma could only guess that was because, after their conversations about Logan, Becca suspected who the father might be.

When neither Becca nor Emma answered, Tuck let out a frustrated huff. "Why won't you tell—Oh my God. Is it Jace's? Is that why you don't want to tell me? Because you know I'll kill him if he did this to you?"

"No." Emma let out a short laugh. "Not Jace's." Jace hadn't left Jacqueline's side for long enough to get anyone else pregnant.

"Then who?" His frown changed as Tucker drew in a sharp breath. "It's Logan's."

That had been a statement, not a question, as realization dawned on Tuck's face. He looked at Emma for confirmation. When she didn't deny it, and most likely the expression on her face only confirmed his suspicions, he knocked his cowboy hat back a half inch and blew out a puff of air. "Holy crap. When? Where? During the reception?"

"Yes, Tucker. At the reception in your parents' backyard. Right there under the buffet table. Good thing the caterers chose such long table cloths." Emma rolled her eyes at his ridiculous assumption.

"I just can't believe I was so blind I didn't notice something going on that day."

"You were focused on me—your bride. Remember?" Becca moved to stand between her husband and her sister.

Tucker frowned at his new wife. "Did you know about this?"

Becca's gaze cut to Emma before she answered Tuck. "I guessed something was going on between them, but I didn't know it was this."

Emma had known her sister would figure it out eventually anyway. There were too many clues not to.

Tucker continued to look dazed "Holy cow. Logan. A father. Have you told him?"

Emma grabbed the prescription bottle Tuck still held. She didn't want any evidence lying around for any more family members to find. "No, and you can't either. He has enough to deal with right now with his dad and the shop."

His gaze dropped down her body and she knew what he was thinking. You couldn't hide something like this for very long. Theoretically, Emma shouldn't be showing any outward signs of pregnancy so early, but thanks to her stress-induced weight gain, she was. Her boobs felt huge and heavy. There was a small bump in her belly where there didn't used to be. Granted, that was likely the result of too many pints of Ben & Jerry's ice cream rather than the seed Logan had planted that fateful wedding weekend, but Tuck didn't know that as he zeroed in on the changes in Emma's body.

He shook his head. "You have to tell him, Emma."

"Tucker, don't get involved." Becca laid a hand on his arm. "Emma will tell him when and if she wants to."

"If?" His eyes flew open. "Emma—"

"Stop. Both of you. I'll tell him. Just in my own time."

"And when will that be?" Tuck cocked a brow.

"I don't know." When she realized she'd pressed her hand over her belly, she dropped it down to her side.

Tuck's gaze followed the action. "Emma, Logan's like a brother—"

"And Emma is my sister." Becca crossed her arms over her chest.

Emma's heart swelled with love for her. She had one person on her side in this. "Tuck, please. This whole thing is devastating enough. Don't rush me."

"There's no need for it to be devastating. He's the most responsible guy I've ever known. He'll do the right thing. He'll marry you, Emma. He'll take care of you and the baby. You have to know that."

"That's the problem." Tears filled her eyes. "Oh, crap. I'm crying again. Stupid hormones. I hate this." She squeezed her eyes shut and willed her emotions to settle down.

Becca was by Emma's side in an instant. "Tucker. Please go away and leave me and Emma for a little while."

"I didn't make her cry." Tuck looked horrified as he protested.

"Yes, you did." Becca shot a scathing look at him.

"Jeez." Tuck ran a hand over his face. "Emma, I'm sorry."

Emma dismissed Tuck's apology with a wave of her hand, before she swiped at her eyes. "It's okay. Everything makes me cry now."

"I guess I'll go trim the bushes outside."

"Good idea." Becca rubbed Emma's back as she effectively dismissed Tuck.

After a moment of hesitation, Tucker backed toward the door, and then left.

"Wow. A baby. And here I thought I'd be the one pregnant first." Becca smiled.

"Then we're even, because I thought I'd be the one married first." Emma let out a tearful laugh. "Or at least married before I got pregnant."

Tyler came through the door and halted. "Pregnant? Uh, what are we talking about in here?"

The damn man walked too quietly considering he was as tall as Tuck and was wearing cowboy boots. Maybe Emma just wasn't all that observant lately.

Becca stepped forward. "Uh, nobody. See I thought I might be but I wasn't so don't tell anybody, okay?"

Good try on Becca's part, but Tyler's gaze fixed on Emma. He wasn't buying it.

"Crap." Emma dropped her chin. "This is impossible. I have to tell him. Whether I'm ready or not."

"Emma, it's okay." Tyler sounded sincere. "I won't tell Logan if you don't want me to."

"How do you know it's Logan's?" Becca's question just confirmed it, even if Tyler hadn't been sure.

Emma shook her head. Good thing Becca's career didn't require she be deceptive, or she'd be sunk.

"Who do you think Logan got the condoms from at the wedding? Guess you didn't use 'em." The corner of Tyler's mouth lifted as he looked at Emma. "Unless you ran out."

Emma was definitely not going to supply the intimate details to Tucker's little brother and her own sister. "I'd appreciate it if you gave me a little time to tell him myself."

"All right. Don't wait too long though." Tyler shook his head as his gaze dropped. "Your tits are already getting huge."

"Tyler!" Becca's eyes popped open wider.

"What? The man's gonna notice, Becca. He's not blind. Jeez." Tyler walked to Emma and dropped a kiss on her cheek. "Congrats, Em. Grow him big and strong. I look forward to teaching the little rug rat how to ride."

Emma let out a sigh. No use fighting it. This baby was going to happen, and the secret was out. Might as well start to embrace that reality. "Thanks, Tyler."

Tyler treated Emma to a wink, which she was sure, along with his good looks and charm, had divested many a cowgirl of her panties over the years. Then he walked out the same door Tuck had disappeared through earlier.

"I'm sorry." Becca shook her head.

"It's okay. But can we stop talking about this here, please? I don't need the parents hearing, too."

"All right. Tyler was right though."

"About what?"

Becca's gaze dropped to where Emma's breasts were straining the fabric of her blouse. "He's going to notice soon."

This was her sister's idea of not talking about it anymore? "I'll deal with that when the time comes."

Emma insured the conversation was over by leaving. She headed for the guest room, where she intended to bury the bottle of vitamins so deep in her suitcase no one would ever find them again.

She was still hiding away in the room just off the Jenkins living room when Logan's voice had her ears perking up. Emma couldn't get used to having him so nearby he could pop in any time of day or night, but she'd like to. She made her way to the kitchen and found him there.

He smiled when she walked in. "Hey. All cleaned up from today, I see."

"Yeah, I am."

He hooked a thumb toward the door. "I was thinking about heading to the cabin to look for some wood for the signs you wanted. It's on a lake and there should be a nice sunset tonight. We can make it there before dark."

A lakeside cabin at sunset. Logan didn't need to ramp up the romance because Emma was already smitten, but the setting would have been enough to snag her even if she hadn't been. "Sounds beautiful. Let's go."

Logan glanced at Becca and hesitated. "You don't mind if I steal your sister away from you again, do you?"

"Not at all. I uh, still have to finish those thank you notes." She looked pointedly at Emma. "I'll talk to you later."

"Later. Don't wait up." Emma was sure Becca would anyway.

Logan led the way to his truck, which was parked in his parents' driveway next door, striding to the passenger door so he could open it for Emma. He waited for her to get settled in her seat, before he closed the door and walked around to climb into the driver's side.

As he turned the key in the ignition, he glanced to Emma. "I think she's started to figure out that we're not just casual acquaintances."

Casual acquaintances. No. Not quite. More like two people who happened to be having a baby even though only one of them knew it.

"Are you okay with that? With Becca assuming we're—" Emma hesitated. What the hell were they in his mind?

"Involved?" Logan raised a brow.

Involved was as good a word as any, Emma supposed. She nodded. "Yeah."

"Sure." Logan dipped his head. "It's fine with me. Is it okay with you?"

"Yup. I can handle my sister and her being nosy." Emma had had plenty of practice with that over the years.

He grinned. "I guess it's easier having a brother than a sister. Especially a brother who's on the other side of the world."

"You have no idea." Emma let out a snort at the truth of that and then moved them on to a more pleasant topic of conversation. "So tell me more about this cabin."

"Not much to tell. My grandfather built it years and years ago. He always said a man needed a place to call his own, but it was never like he went there to escape from the family or anything because he usually ended up bringing the kids with him." Logan talked as he drove. "I can't count how much time I spent there as a kid, fishing with my dad and grandfather. Hunting. Just sitting around a campfire eating something out of a can."

Emma could picture the scene as Logan described it. Three generations of Hunt men, bonding over eating beans out of a can. She couldn't help but wonder whether she had the first of the fourth male generation inside her. A boy with dark hair and eyes who would grow to be tall and strong like his father. Or if she carried a little blue-eyed girl who'd turn out petite and blond with a smart mouth like the Hart side of the family.

She glanced at Logan as he navigated a turn off the highway and onto a country road. "I would've loved to have met this grandfather of yours. He sounds like quite a guy."

"He was." Logan glanced at her before focusing back on the road. "I wish you could have met him. But you can get to know my dad. If you want to, that is."

The offer made Emma warm inside. "I'd love to. Do you think he's up to seeing people yet?"

"You're not *people*. And yes, I think he'd love to visit with you."

Because she was important to Logan? Emma wanted so badly to ask Logan that, to make him expand on his comment, but she didn't want to push.

"I'll look forward to it." A thought hit her and she cringed. "He's going to be okay with the changes I made to the store, isn't he?"

"I think so. Why wouldn't he be?"

"I don't know. It just looks so different from the way he had it arranged. I'm not sure he'd be okay with it." What if she alienated her baby's grandfather before she even gave birth?

"Emma, it looks better, not just different. Besides, nothing you did can't be undone again by moving a few things back. But really, I think he'll love it." Logan shot her a sideways glance again. "I know I do."

Hearing the word *love* from Logan's lips, even if it wasn't said in quite the way she longed for, still made her feel all squishy inside. "Thanks. I'm glad."

"You're welcome. And thank you for all the work you've done. And for being here for me. It means a lot."

"I wouldn't want to be anywhere else."

He reached over and squeezed Emma's hand before releasing her. She missed his touch immediately, but she soon understood why he'd let go as he slowed the truck and made a sharp turn onto a dirt road. "Here we are."

She recovered enough from the effects of that brief moment of intimacy to glance at their surroundings. As the truck crept along the unpaved path, a small cabin sitting next to a lake framed by trees came into view.

Emma drew in a breath. "Logan, it's beautiful."

He shifted the truck into park and turned to smile at Emma. "I'm glad you like it. Come on. Let's go look around."

She'd just reached to open the door herself, when Logan jogged around the truck and leapt for the handle. Emma lowered her hand and waited for him to open the door for her. He held out his hand to help her down. Having a man opening doors for her was something she'd have to get used to. At least, Emma hoped Logan would be around long enough for her to get used to it once she revealed what she'd been hiding.

"Thank you." Once standing on the ground, Emma was glad she'd worn flat, comfortable shoes with her knee-length walking shorts. Guided by Logan, she picked her steps carefully across the uneven dirt of the driveway, until they were walking through ankle deep grass.

"Sorry about the condition of the property. I'll have to make time to get over here and cut the grass."

"Logan, give yourself a break. You've had a few other things on your mind."

"Yeah, I guess." Logan stopped their progress and stood gazing at the still water. "Anyway, this is it. The lake where my grandfather taught me and Layne to swim, and my father taught us to fish. Hell, not just us. Tuck and Tyler would sometimes come, too."

That raised a question in Emma's mind regarding a subject she'd managed to steer clear of since she'd arrived. "Tara didn't come?"

"Yeah, she tagged along once or twice." Logan laughed. "That girl wanted to do everything and anything her brothers did. I think it was more on principle than because she wanted to bait a hook. She looked pretty bored and miserable the whole time we were fishing."

"Humph. Poor thing. That's a shame." The statement came out sounding bitchier than she had intended.

Logan turned toward Emma, took one look at the expression on her face and smiled. "Are you jealous of Tara?"

"No." She felt the frown settle on her brow. When he looked doubtful, Emma sighed. "Okay, yes. I hate that you two have a lifetime of history together. And I hate that she has a crush on you."

"The crush I can't do much about, but our history is that I changed the girl's diapers while babysitting her, for God's sake." He brought his hands up and laid one on each of her shoulders. "There is *nothing* for you to be jealous about."

She looked up into his eyes and knew what he said was true. Sometimes it was just too easy to let jealousy get the better of her. "All right."

"You don't look convinced." He took a step forward, closing the small distance between them. "I'd be happy to prove it to you, if you need me to."

"I think I might." Emma had a good idea how Logan could go about proving it, if they were somewhere private.

He kissed her like he meant it, before pulling back with a groan. As the sun began to dip lower toward the horizon, he glanced back at the cabin. "There's a blanket inside. Wait here."

"Wait, Logan. Outside?"

He grinned. "Yup. I'll be right back."

When he jogged back with the blanket, Emma knew he was serious. They were actually going to do it out here in the open. With a snap of his wrists, he opened the folded blanket. It drifted down to cover the grass.

He sat and glanced up at Emma. "What's wrong? Where's my adventurous New Yorker?"

"Indoors, that's where." She sat next to him, still not sure about this.

"Trust me. No one is coming up here." Logan leaned closer as he spoke, his eyes focused on her. "It's a private road. There's no reason for them to. Besides, you've never really made love until you've experienced it outdoors, under the sky. Maybe even in the water."

"In the lake?" She eyed the water, the water getting darker by the moment as the sun dipped behind a tree. "With the fish? Do they bite?"

"There's only one thing around here that's going to bite you." Logan slid the neckline of her shirt over, to expose her throat. He latched on to her flesh with his teeth as he tumbled her onto her back.

She couldn't control the soft moan that slipped from her. He stopped torturing her long enough to ask, "Is that a yes?"

"To which part?" She wasn't sure if she was ready for complete immersion in the great outdoors—or the lake.

"How about we start slow here on dry land and see how it goes?" Logan didn't give her a chance to answer. He was already running one hand down her side. Then he stopped, and propped his head on one elbow next to her.

Emma lifted her head. "What's wrong?"

He rested one palm low on her belly, causing her stomach to tense. "Emma, I want you to know something. You and me? It's not just about sex. Not that I don't enjoy that, but it's more, too."

Relief and hope had her heating clear through her body. "I wasn't sure what you wanted."

"Maybe for a while, before I met you and before Dad's stroke, I wasn't sure what I wanted either. But now I am."

This could be the perfect time for a confession. With Becca, Tuck, and Tyler all knowing, Emma was going to have to tell Logan sooner rather than later. Then again, news like this could be enough to send Logan into a full out retreat. Talk about going from zero to sixty.

This was all too complicated. As Logan continued to watch her, Emma said, "I'm glad, because it's not just sex for me, either."

"Good. We're on the same page, then. Real good." He seemed nervous for the first time since she'd known him.

"Mmm, hmm. Real good," she echoed.

Logan leaned down and kissed her, a chaste brush of his lips over hers before he pulled back again. She wrapped her arms around his waist, snuggling in for more. Logan pressed another kiss against her hair. "Emma?"

"Yes?"

"There's one more thing." He sure was in a talkative mood tonight.

"All right."

"You're not the only one who gets jealous. If I have to listen to you talk about even the possibility of kissing Jace, I may haul off and punch him the next time I see him."

That was quite a confession. Emma couldn't help her smile. Logan was jealous.

"You don't have to worry about Jace, or my kissing him."

"Good." It was obvious he'd dropped the subject of Jace as Logan walked his fingers down to the waist of Emma's shorts, where he popped open the button.

She gave in and let him take control. Gazing at the sky, she marveled at the peace and beauty of their surroundings as he slid her shorts, then her underwear, down her legs. Then all Emma could think about was Logan and what he did to her every time he touched her.

On the ground next to the lake, Logan loved her, lavishing his attention over every part of her body. It was different from the first night they'd been together, which had been a frenzy of lust too long denied. It was different, too, from their reunion in the shop, where the naughtiness of doing what they'd done there on the workbench had overcome both of them, and overshadowed all else.

Today, their loving was slow and gentle. He took his time. There was no sense of urgency; no rushing in his movements. Logan spent time just lying next to her and watching her face as he trailed his touch from one part of Emma's body to another.

He ran his mouth over her skin. When he reached one particularly sensitive spot behind her ear, she felt him smile as she reacted. He stayed there and teased her with his lips for a while, before moving on to explore the next area.

Finally, he snaked a fingertip between her thighs and found the spot that made her writhe beneath his touch. His eyes never left her face, though they did turn dark. He waited until her body stopped twitching from the orgasm and then rolled on top of her. His gaze met hers as he pushed inside her and set a slow pace.

The intimacy of his gaze holding hers while he loved her had Emma falling deeper in love with this man with every stroke of his body into hers. Each thrust tightened the ties binding her to him.

She watched his brow draw down over his eyes as he came inside her. She felt him shudder to completion, and saw in his eyes what she knew was affection, but hoped could be love.

This was it. She couldn't continue to hide her secret from him. Emma swallowed hard. "Logan?"

His name on her lips seemed to snap him out of his trance. He let out a short laugh and rolled off her. "I know. We need to get moving. Stay here. I'll get some paper napkins from the truck so we can get cleaned up, and then we'll find your boards."

Before she could protest, he was up and headed for the truck.

Emma sighed, as much relieved at the reprieve as she was disappointed the moment had passed. Tomorrow. She'd tell him tomorrow.

Maybe.

Chapter
Eighteen

Emma turned to Logan after he'd pulled the truck to a stop in his parents' driveway. They'd spent most of the day together, yet she didn't want to say good night. "Thank you for tonight."

Logan laughed. "You're welcome, but you don't have to thank me. All I did was take you crawling around an old shed looking for barn boards so you can paint signs for my father's shop. I should be thanking you."

Emma shrugged. "It must have been the company then that made it so special, because I had a wonderful time."

"Definitely the company. I had a wonderful time, too." Logan leaned across the cab of the truck and cupped her face. He hovered just shy of her lips. "If I start to kiss you now, there's a very good chance I'm not going to be able to stop."

She wrinkled her nose. "Eh, go ahead and risk it. Take a chance."

He smiled. "You're so bad."

"You like me that way."

"Yes, I do." Logan closed the remaining distance between them, pressing his lips against hers.

Emma sank into his kiss. Logan had been right that it would be much too easy to slide down the slippery slope from kissing to doing so much more—if they weren't sitting in a parked truck in his parents' driveway next door to her sister's new family. Any number of people could see them through the vehicle's windows.

Finally, he pulled back. Good thing, because Emma didn't have the willpower to. She'd take any time together knowing that the moment she told him about her pregnancy everything would change. And there was no guarantee the change would be for the better.

"Time to get you back inside before Becca starts looking for you." Logan opened his door and walked around the truck to open hers. He helped her step down onto the driveway. "I'll walk you over."

"Don't be silly. I can get next door on my own. Go on in. I'm sure your mother is wondering what's taking you so long to come inside as it is."

"You sure? I can just—"

"Logan. Yes, I'm sure. I'll see you tomorrow?"

"Yes, ma'am. You will. I'll stop over first thing. Promise."

"Good. I'd like that." Emma was starting to get used to having breakfast with Logan every day.

He smiled at her. "Night, Emma."

"Night, Logan."

He hesitated, as if he might kiss her again, then didn't. She understood why. If he had, they might have ended up making out in the driveway, this time without the small bit of privacy the truck interior had provided.

This time, she was the strong one. With a small good-bye wave, Emma turned away from Logan. She even made her way to the back door of the house after looking back at him only once.

Inside, she found Becca waiting for her in the kitchen.

"Emma. Thank God you're home."

"Why? What happened?"

"I was talking to Tuck's mother and one thing led to another and before we knew it the subject of Logan being almost forty and still single came up."

"Oh, Becca. You didn't ask her, did you?" Emma felt the blood drain from her face.

"No, she kind of volunteered the information. Anyway, stop being angry with me because I found out something pretty important about Logan's past."

"And. What is it?" Emma couldn't possibly imagine how important it could be since she'd been spending lots of time with him and nothing had come up.

"Tuck's mom told me that Logan was engaged. Years ago before he joined the army."

"Okay." Emma considered this good news. It meant at least at one point in his life he'd thought about being married. "That must have been like twenty years ago. Did she say what happened?"

Becca ran a hand over her face. "That's the bad part. *He* apparently broke off the engagement."

"Did she say why?"

"No one knows. Neither Logan or the girl explained why."

"Something must have happened." The Logan Emma knew needed a good reason to do just about anything. Breaking off an engagement would require a huge one. "Who knows? Maybe she cheated on him."

Her sister's brow rose. "Maybe he cheated on her."

"Becca!"

"Just exploring all the options."

"Well, stop. You're not helping." Emma knew Logan well enough to know he wasn't a cheater. "Did you talk to Tuck about this?"

"No. He doesn't like when I pry. He's going to yell at me."

"Oh, stop. There's no way he'd ever get mad or yell at you, so suck it up. I need to know. Go ask your husband or I will."

Becca hesitated, and then let out a breath. "All right. Did you say anything to Logan tonight?"

"No." Judgment—make that disapproval—was clearly written in Becca's expression. Emma hated that she felt the need to explain. "I was planning on maybe telling him tomorrow, but now you've got me all turned around with this news. I'm not telling him until I find out some answers."

Becca's eyes widened. "No, Em. Don't change your plans. You have to tell him. What are you going to do? Wait until the day before you leave for home?"

"No. Stop pressuring me. I still have time before I go back." Emma shot her sister a frown. "Go find your husband."

"I can't. He took the truck to the store to buy lumber before they close."

"Lumber? What for?"

"He and Tyler are going to build a wheelchair ramp next door for Logan's dad. He's coming home tomorrow."

"Tomorrow. Wow. I wonder why Logan didn't tell me." Maybe Logan wasn't as forthcoming as Emma thought he was.

"Emma, don't look like that. He probably didn't know. The doctors just told his mom tonight. She came over on her way home from visiting his dad."

"Okay, that makes sense." It still didn't ease Emma's racing mind about the mysterious broken engagement. "But the minute Tuck is back, you have to ask."

"Fine. And as soon as you know the answer, you need to tell Logan." Becca waited, looking expectant. "Em, promise."

Emma blew out a big breath. "All right, I will."

Maybe.

★ ★ ★

"Hey, Mom. What's going on here?" Logan glanced around at the chaos in what was usually a quiet house. It was after dark, yet his mom was wide awake and as busy as if it was nine in the morning rather than nine at night.

She paused, a batch of sheets in the laundry basket held in her hand. "They're releasing your father tomorrow. I have to get the house ready for him."

"Really? They think he's ready?"

"Yeah. The docs say he can come home. There will still be a lot of rehabilitation, but they said he could do it here. He hates being in that place. They think his being at home will help his state of mind and make the recovery go faster. The physical therapist will come once a day to work with him."

"That's wonderful." Surprising, but good news.

"There's so much to do. All the furniture needs to be moved so he has a clear path for the wheelchair. The physical therapist said we needed to install bars in the bathroom, both next to the toilet and in the shower. I still have to measure the bathroom doorway to make sure the chair is even going to fit through it." Pressing her lips together, his mother shook her head and looked overwhelmed.

He wrapped an arm around her shoulders. "Mom, we'll get it all done. Don't worry."

"I know. Thank you. You're such a comfort. And the Jenkins family, too. I don't know what I can ever do to repay their kindness."

"Not necessary." Tuck walked through the door at just that moment.

"Well now, Tuck. Let's not be too hasty." Tyler followed his brother into the room. "I do remember some cookies you make every Christmas. They have some sort of raspberry jam in the middle."

"Tyler, the woman more than has her hands full right now. Don't you dare hint she should bake you cookies." Tuck frowned.

"You're talking about my thumbprint cookies," Logan's mother said, and smiled. "And they're Mr. Hunt's favorite, too. As soon as he's home and settled, I'll happily make a big batch for both of you. He'd love some, I'm sure."

"See." Tyler sent Tucker an' *I told you so* look.

Tuck rolled his eyes and then turned to Logan. "We've got all the supplies we need to build the wheelchair ramp. We laid it all out on the grass. Do you want to come and take a look? See how steep an angle it's going to be to get from the ground to the top step."

Logan glanced outside and saw how dark it had become. "It's late. You sure you want to do this now?"

"Sure." Tuck dipped his head in a nod. "If you all don't mind, we'll lay it out now. That way we can get right to work on it at first light."

"I don't mind a bit. I have a dozen things to do before bed tonight anyway." Logan's mother glanced at the overflowing laundry basket.

Logan hadn't seen his mother this excited in a while. She was happy to have his father coming home, while he was getting a little worried thinking about installing ramps and grab bars. Caring for a man recuperating from a stroke at home was going to be challenging, but he wasn't about to burst his mother's bubble. Instead Logan agreed. "All right. Let's go on out and take a look."

They'd just cleared the front door when Tuck asked, "How'd the date with Emma go?"

"It wasn't a date. We just drove over to the lake. I showed her around the place. We grabbed some of the old barn boards from the shed, then we came home."

"Mmm, hmm. Sure." Tyler's comment earned him an elbow in the gut from Tucker. "Ow. Stop that."

"Stop being a smart ass." Tuck returned the dirty look Tyler had given him for the elbow.

"Sorry. I was just saying—"

"Well, stop." Tuck cut off Tyler and turned back to Logan. "So, how are you two getting along?"

"He means, are you in love yet?" Tyler stretched the word *love* out like he was a kid teasing his friend in the schoolyard.

Tuck spun on his brother so fast, Tyler had to jump out of striking range. He stayed a safe distance away with his hands up in surrender. "Okay. I'll be quiet."

Even with all the excitement, Tuck still turned his focus back to Logan. Confused, Logan asked, "What?"

Tuck knocked his hat back and glared at Logan. "You and Emma? What's going on?"

Logan laughed. "The better question is what's going on with you? You've never given a shit who I'm seeing. Is this because Emma is Becca's sister?"

Tyler stayed uncharacteristically quiet, watching and waiting for Tuck's answer. That was Logan's first clue that maybe something was going on. The second was Tuck's hesitation, and the expression of pure agony on his face. "I . . . It's just I'm stuck in the middle here, Logan."

"Is Becca bothering you about my intentions toward her sister?"

Tuck ran a hand over his forehead. "Something like that."

"Tell your wife she doesn't have to worry. I'm into Emma."

At Logan's comment, Tyler let out a snort and laughed. "I bet you are into her a lot."

Logan reevaluated how to word what he was trying to say. He sent a warning glance in Tyler's direction and then continued, "*Meaning* I like her. A lot. I'm not going to do anything to hurt her, Tuck."

That didn't seem to appease Tuck, who kicked the toe of his cowboy boot into the grass at his feet. "You, uh, see yourself maybe getting serious with her?"

Something was definitely going on here. Becca must really be putting the pressure on Tuck for some answers.

Logan had always been a private person. He didn't tell tales about the few serious relationships he'd had in his life. Which was what made it doubly strange when he felt compelled to confess the truth. "Yeah, I think I can."

Tyler's wide grin caught his eye. Logan turned to him. "What's making you so happy? What do you care?"

"Hey, I like that I can say I was there from the very start. Like cupid but instead of using arrows, I hook up lovers with condoms at wedding receptions."

"Jeez, Tyler." Logan felt his face heat. He couldn't bring himself to look at Tuck.

"Relax, Logan. It's okay. Tuck already knows." Tyler's statement didn't make Logan feel much better.

"How?"

"I told him." Tyler shrugged.

"You're nothing like cupid, dumbass." Tuck shook his head at his brother and then glanced at Logan. "It's okay, Logan. I'm not one to judge anyone on his or her behavior. I'm just glad you and Emma are getting along. You know I love you like a brother. Sometimes more—"

"Hey." Tyler frowned, looking insulted.

Tuck continued, "So you know nothing would make me happier than to have you as a brother-in-law."

Logan laughed. "Let's not get ahead of ourselves. Emma and I are still getting to know each other. I don't want to rush things."

"Dude, we're way past worrying about that. Believe me." Tyler slapped Logan on the back and then bent to grab one of the boards. "Tuck. Grab the other end of this for me?"

"Sure." With one final glance at Logan, Tuck dipped his head and moved to take the board. No yelling at Tyler to shut up. No comment at all about Tyler's strange statement, leaving Logan to wonder what the hell they knew that he didn't. It was a feeling he didn't like. Not one bit.

Chapter
Nineteen

The atmosphere at the Jenkins breakfast table was the strangest Logan had felt in a long time. It was as if everyone seated at the table was watching him and Emma, waiting for something. What that something was, he didn't have a clue. Still Tuck, Tyler, and Becca all kept shooting him looks.

He glanced sideways at Emma, trying to see if maybe during yesterday's encounter by the lake he might have unconsciously given her another hickey and that's what they were all intrigued by. There were no marks on Emma that Logan could see. At least, not from this angle. Then again, he couldn't get a good look at her from the other side.

This was too crazy. To be dealing with this shit at this point in his life felt ridiculous.

Mrs. Jenkins stood at the stove in her usual position, flipping pancakes today instead of bacon. She seemed normal. Happy. Chatty. Mr. Jenkins had already left for work. Whatever this involved, it was limited to the younger members of the family.

Maybe Emma had confessed to Becca what had been happening between them? That would explain Becca and Tuck's strange behavior, but not Tyler's. And honestly, Logan and Emma were two single consenting adults. They could choose to engage in a physical relationship if they wanted to. Hell, it was allowed, unlike Tuck and Becca's relationship had been when they were blatantly breaking OSU's faculty non-fraternization rule by dating last year.

Damn. He was dying to get Emma alone and ask her what was going on. But his father was coming home today and there were still things to do . . . And that was the perfect topic of conversation to break the tension hanging in the air.

"So right after we eat, we'll finish up that ramp? It shouldn't take too long, right?" Logan glanced from Tyler to Tucker.

"Shouldn't take more than an hour or so." Tyler nodded. "After we're done, I'm gonna have to leave and get to the ranch. We're moving some bulls today."

Tuck eyed Logan. "What are your plans for the rest of the day?"

Why did Logan feel as if he was being interrogated? "I guess I'll check in with my mother and see what time they'll be releasing my father. That way I can drive over to the rehab facility and help her get him and the wheelchair into the car."

"I talked to her this morning, Logan. She thinks they might not let him go until after lunch." Mrs. Jenkins walked over and put a platter stacked high with pancakes in the center of the table. "Everyone help yourselves while they're hot. Don't be shy."

She walked back to the stove and started cleaning up. Logan swore, in all his years hanging out in this kitchen, he'd never seen the woman sit down and eat herself.

Tyler glanced around and when no one made a move, he stood and stabbed three pancakes with his fork. "Don't mind if I do. Somebody pass the syrup."

Becca handed him the bottle of maple syrup and then

lifted the platter of pancakes. She took two for herself, and handed it off to Tuck. "If your father gets released this afternoon, that will leave all morning free. Logan, why don't you and Emma go to the store and see how the signs look?"

"You started painting the signs already?" Logan turned to Emma, surprised. "When?"

She glanced up from the plate of pancakes as she passed it to Logan. "Don't forget, I'm used to east coast time. I'm usually awake a good hour before the rest of the household. I sketched the lettering out with a pencil, and then found some old paint in the garage. Here, I have a picture." Emma pulled her cell phone out of her pocket.

Logan glanced over and looked at the screen. "You're amazing. Some old wood and leftover paint and you turned it into that?"

"Don't be too impressed. I only did that one, but I'm almost done with the second. I'll be finished by the time you guys are done with the ramp. You should look at what I've got so far. Make sure you like them."

Logan smiled. "I'm sure I'll love whatever you do."

He glanced up from his breakfast to find he was the subject of scrutiny again and stifled a sigh. Maybe it was obvious to everyone else that he had feelings for Emma. So what? What should be obvious to his supposed friends was that his relationship with Emma, no matter what it might or might not be, was none of their business.

"Here's an idea." Tuck, laden fork poised over his plate, turned to Logan. "You go to the store with Emma and get it all fixed up with the new sign and everything. I'll help your mother with your father, and we can bring him over to the shop on the way home as a surprise."

Again Tuck was pushing Emma and him together. If Mrs. Jenkins' pancakes weren't so damn tasty, this family would have already ruined Logan's appetite. "I don't know, Tuck. That seems like a lot for Dad to handle on the first day."

Tuck shrugged. "How about we play it by ear? See how he's feeling. If he's too tired, I'll call and let you know that your mom and I are bringing him straight home. Then you and Em can meet us at your house."

Logan glanced at Emma, not missing how Tuck had once again included her in his plans without asking either one of them. "What do you think?"

"It won't hurt to go over and make sure the place is all put back together, even if your father can't make it over today. And not to sound selfish, but I'd love to see how my new signs look with the displays."

"You're anything but selfish, Emma." Logan looked at this amazing woman next to him and resisted reaching out to grab her hand. "All right. I guess there's no reason we can't go to the shop. I still have to screw in the grab bars in the bathroom, but I can do that quick. We'll go over right after the ramp is up."

"Sounds good." Emma smiled. The sight warmed his heart, until Logan noticed the satisfied look on Becca's face, the relief on Tuck's, and the interest on Tyler's.

Something was going on here, and he'd be damned if he didn't get to the bottom of it before day's end. Enough was enough.

Logan put his plan to figure out what was up with everyone into action the moment he left the Jenkinses' kitchen. Thinking like the military leader he was, he chose the target he judged would be the easiest to break—Tyler.

He waited until Tuck went to the garage to cut some two-by-fours to length. As the whine of the table saw filled the air, Logan turned to Tyler. "What was going on at the breakfast table this morning?"

Tyler's brows rose. "Uh, we were eating breakfast?"

"I know that." Sometimes Logan had to wonder if this young smart ass who joked about everything was really Tuck's brother. They were such opposites. "What else? Why was everyone acting so strange and staring at me and Emma? And why is it so important to Tuck and Becca that I take Emma to the store with me?"

"Uh, I don't know." The way Tyler avoided eye contact with Logan now was in direct opposition to his casual shrug.

"Tyler. You know something. Spill it." Logan employed the no-nonsense tone he used to reprimand his troops and his cadets.

"Oh, no." Tyler shook his head. "I'm very happily a civilian so you can't pull that army officer shit on me. You can frown at me all you want, Logan, but I can't tell you."

"You can't tell me because you don't know? Or you *won't* tell me, which means you do know something?"

"Stop trying to trick me." Tyler's frown deepened. "That's it. Discussion closed. I mean it, Logan. Drop it or I'm out of here. I love your father like he's my own, but if you don't ease up, you can finish this ramp your own damn self."

Wow. Logan had never seen the smooth talking, easy-going Tyler so agitated. There was something going on, and judging by Tyler's reaction to his questioning, it had to be bigger than just a bunch of interfering friends and relations sticking their noses where they didn't belong.

Tyler whipped out one end of a tape measure. He shot Logan a glance over his shoulder. "Don't you have a grab bar to install or something?"

Maybe Tyler wasn't the easiest target to pick off after all. Logan cocked a brow at Tyler's attitude. "Yeah, I do."

And he would get to it right after he interrogated Tuck. Logan spun toward the garage and stalked his way to his next victim. By the time he reached Tuck, Logan found him frowning down at his cell phone. When Logan walked farther into the garage, Tuck shoved the cell into his pocket and turned back to the board on the workbench.

"What's up?" Tuck asked the question without looking at Logan. Instead, he concentrated solely on the wood.

"You tell me." Logan folded his arms across his chest.

"Just measuring." Tuck shot Logan a glance over his shoulder and then went back to focusing on his work. "You know what they say. Measure twice, cut once."

"Yes, so I've heard." Logan drew in a breath and moved closer. "Now, put that pencil and tape measure down, turn around, and tell me why you and Tyler and Becca are throwing me and Emma together."

One brow cocked high, Tuck asked, "Is that an order, sir?"

"No. You know damn well it's not, so stop with the attitude." Logan blew out a breath filled with frustration. "Tyler wouldn't spill. Now you won't. Do I have to go to Becca next? Is that what you want me to do?"

"Logan, leave Becca out of this."

"Fine. You tell me what's up and I will."

Tuck turned to face Logan. "Here's a suggestion. Go talk to Emma and leave the rest of us out of it."

"Emma. Why? What can she tell me?" All this time Logan had assumed he and Emma were in the same boat. Both in the dark as to why everyone was acting so strangely. But here Tuck was insinuating Emma was the key to getting the answers to Logan's questions.

"That's all I'm going to say." Tuck shook his head, and then leaned again over the board.

"All right. If that's the way you want to play this." Resigned, Logan let out a huff. "I'll talk to Emma right after I finish what I have to do to get the bathroom ready for Dad."

Tuck glanced up from beneath the brim of his hat. "Tyler and I will handle all of that. You go find Emma."

What the hell?

"Fine." Logan turned on his boot heel and headed next door to find Emma and, hopefully, the end of this mystery.

After the short walk, which felt inordinately long today, Logan crossed the back yard and found Emma in the Jenkins kitchen. She'd covered the kitchen table with newspaper, and held a paintbrush poised over the barn wood.

She looked up at the sound of the door opening, and smiled when she saw him. "Hi. I'm just finishing this one. Are you done already at your house?"

"No, they're still working over there. Um, can we talk?"

As Logan asked the question of Emma, Becca walked into the room. She stopped just inside the doorway, wide-eyed. "Uh, I just remembered, I forgot something."

Turning, Becca fled the room as if her life depended on it. There was definitely something going on here.

Emma watched her sister leave. She turned to Logan and put down her paintbrush. "Sure. What's up?"

"Can we sit?" Logan pulled out a chair for Emma. She'd been standing to work on the sign.

"All right." Looking baffled, Emma perched in the chair, watching him.

Logan pulled out a chair for himself, sat and leaned forward. "This may seem crazy, but there's something going on around here. It feels like everyone knows something I don't and—" The expression that crossed Emma's face made Logan cut his sentence short. She was hiding something. He took both of her hands in his. "Emma. What's going on?"

She swallowed hard and drew in a deep breath. "Can I ask you a question?"

"Of course."

"I heard that you were engaged once. I know it's none of my business, but what happened? How come you didn't get married?"

That's what this was about? An engagement that had lasted a week? Just long enough for his mother to announce it to the neighborhood and in church before he had to go through the embarrassment of telling everyone it was off? "Emma, that was years ago. Like twenty years. I was just out of high school. I hadn't even left for boot camp yet."

"Okay." She nodded. "What happened?"

Logan had to wonder why it mattered. To her, it obviously did. Maybe she was so traumatized by Jace acting the ass with his ex-girlfriend that she needed to know Logan wouldn't do the same thing? But the situations were so different, it was almost laughable.

"It's not something I talk about. Tuck and Layne don't even know all of it. I was only eighteen, which made them about eight or nine at the time."

Emma shook her head. "Logan, I don't need to know. I was foolish to even ask. It was so long ago, it doesn't matter—"

"No. You're concerned enough that you asked, so I want to tell you. This girl and I were young and stupid, and careless. And she got pregnant."

All of the color drained from Emma's face. Concerned, Logan squeezed her hand in his. "Emma. You okay?"

She swallowed again, looking a bit ill. "Go on. What happened?"

He shrugged. "I guess she got scared. She and her friend drove to a clinic an hour away, and when she came back she told me there was no more baby. I was angry. Sad." Logan let out a short laugh. "And relieved. We weren't in love. Hell, we weren't even dating, which made it extra stupid we weren't more careful."

It had felt as if his life had been turned on end, not once but twice in a week's time. First, when he'd learned he was going to be a husband and a father when he was about to leave for basic training. Then again when he learned that without his knowledge, she'd made the decision to change all that. She gave him his life back, but at a cost he wouldn't have condoned had he known. And it all happened just weeks before he turned nineteen.

"Is this what's been bothering you? Why everyone's been acting nuts?"

"I think Tyler always acts a little crazy, so . . ." Emma's smile looked forced as she sat up straighter in the chair. She reached over and gave his hand a little squeeze. "Everything is fine, Logan. I apologize for asking about your past."

"It's all right. I want you to be able to ask me anything at any time, especially if it's something that's bothering you."

"I'll remember that." She withdrew her hands from his. "Now go finish your work so I can do the same."

He watched as she picked up the paintbrush again. Their talk had only made the mystery murkier than it had been before. Logan had infiltrated enemy strongholds with less effort than he was expending to get this family to tell him the complete truth. Logan wasn't used to being defeated. He didn't like it. But right now, it seemed as if he'd have to wait them out, and get ready for his father's homecoming.

Something was very wrong when war seemed so much simpler than his home life.

Chapter
Twenty

The back door hadn't been closed two seconds when Becca skidded into the kitchen. "What happened with Logan? Did you tell him?"

"You mean you don't know? You weren't listening from the hall?" Emma realized she was shaking. She put down the paintbrush and buried her face in her hands, ignoring the fact that she had paint on her fingers.

"You two were talking too softly. I couldn't hear."

At least Becca admitted she was eavesdropping. That was something. Emma blew out a breath and lowered her hands. "I didn't tell him."

"Why not?"

"Because he told me he was engaged all those years ago because he got the girl pregnant, and even though he didn't love her, he was going to marry her because of the baby."

"And you're afraid he'll do the same with you." It wasn't a question, but a statement. Becca knew too well how Emma felt.

"Yes." Emma blinked back the tears. "I want the fairy tale, Becs. What you found with Tuck. A man who wants to be with me, not who feels like he has to."

"What are you going to do now? Em, you have to tell him."

Anger replaced Emma's sadness. "I know I have to tell him, Becca. Stop saying that. And stop throwing me at him. All of you. That's why he came to talk. He's noticed something's up."

"I'm sorry."

"I know. " Emma let out a sigh. "And I know you're right. I'll tell him later today. After his father is home and settled. He doesn't need the stress before that."

"I think that's a good idea."

Emma reached for the paintbrush, then let her hand drop to her lap. "I'm shaking so badly I can't finish this damn sign."

Becca stood. "Move over. I'll do it."

"You can paint?"

"Em, you outlined the letters in pencil. All I have to do is paint over them. A child could do it." Becca took the brush in one hand and hovered over the board.

"Keep the edges straight." Emma stood, too, trying to look over Becca's arm. "And try to keep the thickness uniform."

"Emma, stop. Go make yourself a cup of tea and let me finish this so it's ready when Logan comes back to take you to the shop."

The shop, where they'd be alone together. Where she'd have to pretend that nothing was wrong. That she wasn't waiting for the time when she would give him the news that would change both of their lives.

She wouldn't show for a couple of months yet. Maybe she could put this off a little longer.

As Emma waffled on her plan, Becca's motions caught her eye. "Thin, Becca. Thin letters. Here, give it to me."

She would finish this sign and worry about the rest later. She blew out a breath, steadied her hand, and went to work.

Chapter
Twenty-one

The jingling of the bell announced an arrival. The shop door swung open, held by Logan's mother as Tuck pushed Logan's father inside.

Logan put down the hammer he'd been holding in his hand and strode toward the group. "Dad, I thought someone would have called if you were coming."

Tuck shrugged. "We wanted to surprise you."

"Well, you sure did."

"Logan, the store looks wonderful." His mom moved to stand next to the wheelchair.

Watching his father's face, Logan asked, "You really like it?"

"I love it." She looked around her, one hand resting on Logan's father's shoulder. "Honey, do you see what Logan's done?"

Emma had been in the back, sorting through more boxes of dusty old stuff, looking for additional display items. It seemed to be her favorite pastime. She came through the door of the workroom now and stopped, probably waiting as anxiously as Logan for some sort of reaction from his father.

Finally, it came, in the form of a jerky nod. "Good." His father's eyes looked misty as he repeated, "Good."

Logan glanced at Emma. She was biting her lip and

looking a bit teary-eyed herself. He motioned her forward, then turned back to his parents. "I can't take credit for any of it. Emma did everything. The new layout and displays. The signs."

She came to stand next to Logan. "Mr. Hunt, I'm glad to see you looking so well."

"Thank . . . you." His father nodded again, speech and movement still hard for him, but so much better than before.

Logan's mother smiled at Emma. "You did a lovely job."

"Thank you." Emma shot Logan a glance. "I was worried I'd overstepped."

"Don't be silly." Logan laid an arm around her shoulders and watched three sets of eyes follow the motion—his mom's, his dad's and Tuck's. This was ridiculous. "Emma has been spending a lot of time helping out around here."

Why did he feel the need to explain? And why was it so hard to do?

Maybe because they hadn't defined what they were to each other. It felt like they were dating, even if they had yet to go out on an actual date. Sunset sex at the cabin didn't count. Neither did dancing at Tuck and Becca's wedding, since she had been officially Jace's date for that. Logan would have to remedy the situation. Take Emma out on a real date and soon.

"So you're from New York?" Logan's mother asked her.

"Yes, ma'am. Born and raised. But now that my sister is settled in Oklahoma, I've been thinking that I might want to move here myself."

Logan swiveled to stare at Emma. "You have?"

"Yeah." Her eyes searched his. If she were waiting to see what he thought about the idea, she wouldn't need to ask. Logan had a feeling the happiness he felt at the news was written all over his face.

"Um, want a little tour before we head home?" Tuck

leaned down and spoke directly to Logan's father. "Wait until you see what Emma did with that old lumber you had stashed at the cabin."

Logan's mom clapped her hands together. "Oh, I see the signs. They're perfect."

After Tuck had not so subtly moved their audience to the back of the store, Logan turned to take Emma's hand in his. "You'd really consider moving? When did this come about?"

"Recently. The past few days." Emma shrugged. "I guess being around Becca, and everyone else here, made me realize how much I missed having her nearby."

"But your job—"

"I can find work in my field anywhere."

"What about your parents?"

"I can visit them. My dad's retired now. They love to travel, so they can visit me and Becca here." Emma's gaze held his as she watched him.

"So you'd look for work in Stillwater near Becca?" The thought of having Emma around on a permanent basis had Logan's heart pounding.

"Yeah, probably. Stillwater or somewhere close. Or I could work from home for a while. I can probably get plenty of freelance jobs online."

"You'd really be okay with leaving New York?"

"Yes." Emma bit her lower lip. "Would you be okay with having me around?"

Was she really worried about that? The question explained her nervous behavior but not why in the world she would be concerned he wouldn't want her around.

"Are you crazy?" Logan rested his hands on her shoulders, letting his thumbs cup her face. "I'd love it."

"So I guess we should be heading home now." Tuck announced the return of the group a little louder than was necessary, probably to warn Logan that he and Emma were about to be interrupted.

"I'll go home with you." Logan dropped his hold on Emma, just as a customer walked into the store.

"You open? The sign says *Closed,* but I saw customers."

Crap. He needed to keep that door locked. "Actually—"

"Logan, stay and help this gentleman. We're okay on our own. Really." His mom dismissed the offer and turned to the man hovering in the doorway, looking uncertain. "Come on in. Look around. Let us know if we can help you with anything."

Logan waited for the customer to move to the back of the store, then moved closer to his mother and father. "I want to be home to help with the wheelchair—"

Tuck held up a hand to stop Logan. "We're good. I had a lesson with the physical therapist on how to best get both him and the chair in and out of the car. I've got it covered. And the ramp is ready at the house. We're good. He'll be there inside waiting for you when you can get away."

"We're fine, dear. We'll see you at dinner." Logan's mother turned toward Emma. "Both of you. I'd love it if you could join us, Emma."

"I'd like that. Thank you." Emma smiled.

"Good. We'll see you later." Logan's mother pushed open the door and held it wide.

Tuck sent Logan a satisfied nod. "See ya."

A customer, an ongoing mystery, and now, possibly, a girlfriend living right in his town—Logan had trouble keeping up with it all.

Once their sole customer had left, promising to be back again soon, with his wife next time, Logan was left alone again with Emma.

He moved to the door and turned the key in the lock. He turned to see Emma had followed him.

She glanced at the key in his hand. "You're not going to get any more business like that."

"Maybe I don't want any more business today." His head had been spinning with plans since Emma's revelation about moving.

"I understand. You want to get home to your dad."

"I do. Soon. But right now, I want some time alone with you." He tugged on her hand. "Come on in back. I don't want any more customers seeing us through the windows. I'm not going to attack you. I promise."

"I don't like the sound of that." A frown knit her brow. "Why aren't you going to attack me?"

Logan laughed. "Because I want to talk."

He lifted her onto the workbench and Emma's brow rose as she braced her hands on his shoulders. "You sure?"

"Yes. Don't get any ideas. I just want you to sit so we can talk eye to eye." With his hands around her waist, it might have been an effort to stay focused if this conversation wasn't so important to him. "So tell me, seriously, are you really thinking about moving here?"

"Yes."

"Okay." It was hard to control his smile. "Well, if you do, I thought since Becca and Tuck are newlyweds, you could stay with me. You know, while you look for a job or a place . . . Or maybe for longer."

"Longer?" That watchful look was back in Emma's eyes again.

"Mmm, hmm." Yeah, Logan was suggesting she move in with him, and yeah, it was much too soon in the relationship for that. But then again, it was long overdue that he found someone he wanted to get serious with. He'd found Emma late in his life, and he wasn't going to waste any more time.

It was all a little overwhelming. Even Emma looked affected by the enormity of what he'd suggested. They could talk about this more later, after it had sunk in for both of them. Now, while he and Emma had a few stolen moments of privacy before they had to be surrounded by family and friends again, he intended to take advantage of it.

He leaned in, intent on kissing her tempting lips, but Emma held him back with one hand and pressed the other one to her mouth. She swallowed hard as her brow furrowed.

"You all right?" Logan watched as the usual healthy glow of her creamy skin turned pale.

"Do you still have a package of those crackers from my soup the other day?"

"Uh, yeah. I left them over by the coffee machine. Hang on." With one last concerned look at the wobbly woman seated in front of him, Logan turned and grabbed the crackers, quick before she toppled off the workbench where he'd set her.

When she didn't look able to do it herself, he tore into the cellophane wrapping and handed one to her. She took it and nibbled off a corner. Emma raised her gaze to meet his. "I'm sorry."

"Don't you dare apologize. Once again I worked you through lunch." Logan should have known better. It was more than obvious now that Emma didn't do well unless she ate regularly. He wouldn't forget it again. "I'll get you a glass of water."

Her frown deepened as she swallowed another bit of cracker. "No. No water."

"All right. We should head out. Get you something to eat to hold you over until dinner." He eyed the remains of the cracker she was chewing. "Finish that and let's get you in the truck."

"Maybe give me a few minutes. I'm not sure I can take a ride in the truck right now. If that's all right?"

"Of course, it's all right." Logan hated that he'd done this to her. Not once, but twice in one week. "Emma, please. If I ever forget to break for lunch again, you have to remind me you need to eat. You help me so much. You have to let me take care of you. Okay?"

"Okay, I will." She dipped her head, more compliant than he'd ever seen her.

"Good." The thought that he'd be the one taking care of Emma appealed to Logan. More than he'd ever imagined it would.

"So what do you do in New York, Emma?" Mrs. Hunt asked from her seat across the dining room table.

"I'm a graphic designer. It's a lot of computer work." Emma put down her fork and instead reached for a dinner roll. "But I really enjoy the creative parts of my job."

As delicious as Logan's mother's homemade chili looked, Emma's stomach had yet to recover from the roller coaster ride it had taken her on this afternoon. There was no way the spicy, fat-laden beef dish would sit well. Couldn't Emma do anything the normal way? She must be the only pregnant woman in history who got morning sickness in the afternoon.

"Then I'm not surprised you're so artistic. Your signs are beautiful." Mrs. Hunt made small talk while she lifted another spoonful of food to her husband's mouth.

The man looked appalled to be spoon fed, especially in front of a stranger. It made the full impact of the situation Logan had faced for over a month now very clear to Emma.

Emma kept up her half of the conversation, taking a cue from Logan's mother by pretending everything was perfectly normal. As if Mr. Hunt, a once healthy adult man, wasn't being spoon fed like a baby. As if Emma wasn't about to completely change Logan's life with those two simple words that weighed on her like lead—*I'm pregnant.* As if she wasn't holding down the small amount of food in her stomach by sheer force of will.

Emma glanced at Logan and found him watching her. She shook herself out of her morose thoughts and kept her polite face in place. "Thank you, but the signs were nothing. I just went on Becca's laptop and chose a font that I thought would match the style and the feel of the store. Then penciled it onto the wood and slapped on some old paint I found in the Jenkins garage."

"You're being modest, but since you're our guest, I'll let it go." Logan laughed. "Can I get you a drink? There's some beer in the fridge."

"There's even wine. Logan, go get a bottle out of the pantry and open it so we can celebrate your father being home." Mrs. Hunt turned to Emma. "The Jenkinses insisted I take a few bottles of the leftovers from the wedding and of course, we haven't had the time to drink any of it."

"Sounds good to me. I can do wine." Logan stood.

He'd already taken a step toward the door when Emma said, "Just water for me."

"Really? I thought Becca said you love wine."

"Yeah, I do. Just not tonight."

"We have sweet tea, if you'd rather," Mrs. Hunt offered.

"Just water is fine. Thank you."

"All right. Water it is."

Emma allowed herself a breath when Logan left the room and she wasn't under his scrutiny any longer. She glanced at his parents in time to see Mrs. Hunt lift a napkin to wipe a dribble of chili off his father's chin.

She needed to tell Logan, but how in the world could she add one more thing to his already overloaded plate? At least one thing remained a constant in Emma's life—her timing, as usual, sucked.

★ ★ ★

Becca met Emma inside the kitchen the moment she walked through the door from dinner at Logan's. "I haven't seen you all day. What's going on?"

Emma knew what her sister really wanted to know, but hadn't asked, and that was whether Emma had told Logan yet. "What the hell, Becca? Were you sitting here waiting for me like Mom used to when I had a curfew?"

"Don't change the subject. What happened tonight?"

"I texted and told you I was having dinner at Logan's house."

"I know that. I meant what's happening with Logan?"

Luckily, Emma had some news that might satisfy Becca. "I think he asked me to move in with him."

"Really?" Becca's eyes grew wide. "Oh, my God. Emma, that's huge."

It did feel pretty huge, but Emma still wasn't convinced she hadn't read too much into it. "Yeah, it wasn't exactly in those words, but it was close."

"That's wonderful. So you definitely can tell him now."

"Soon. He's got so much happening with his father just getting home." That, on top of the dozen or so other excuses, fears and insecurities Emma's inner voice whispered to her day and night.

"Emma . . ."

"I said soon. Jeez. Just give me a little time." Time for Logan to fall in love with her before the weight of responsibility made him commit to a lifetime with her.

This should be the best part. The feeling of falling in love. The start of a relationship full of firsts, when everything was new and shiny. Emma wanted to hold on to the essence of it before she hit fast forward and they found themselves with a baby.

Tuck walked in from the hall and went to the fridge.

Reaching in, he pulled out a beer, and then glanced at Becca. "She tell him yet?"

"No. Soon." Becca answered, and Tuck had asked, as if Emma wasn't in the room.

Before she could yell at Becca for that, the back door swung open and Tyler stomped his boots on the doormat. "What was for dinner tonight? I hope y'all saved me some. I'm starved."

"Pot roast. Your mother left a plate for you in the microwave." Becca hooked a thumb at the counter.

"Great." Tyler opened the microwave door to peek inside, then turned to Emma. "You tell him yet?"

At least Tyler had asked Emma directly instead of acting like she wasn't there. That was something, she supposed. "No, and I'm tired of everyone asking. I'm going to get changed. While I'm gone, all you people need to get lives of your own."

"I will have a life when I'm an uncle. Wait, will I be an uncle? She's my sister-in-law's sister." Tyler's brow knit in a frown as he tried to reason out the branches of the family tree.

"Stop with that kind of talk before someone hears you. I'm serious," Emma hissed.

Before they did anything else to piss her off, Emma escaped to hide in her room until bedtime. This constant inquisition was getting to be unbearable as was the fear one of them would tell Logan before she got around to it. Her secret was in the hands of people who couldn't seem to keep their mouths shut. It was a dangerous situation. If she didn't want Logan finding out from someone else, Emma would have to tell him herself.

Easier said than done.

Chapter
Twenty-two

Logan had walked Emma to the Jenkins yard, kissed her silly behind the hedge he'd become very fond of, and then made his way back home, a little lighter in his step. He came into the kitchen to find his mother alone, unloading the dishwasher.

"Hey, Mom. Dad all settled in for the night?"

"He is. I got him into his pajamas and into bed without too much trouble."

"Mom, you should have waited for me. I could help you with that."

"It's better if I do it alone. It's hard enough for him not being able to do everything on his own when he wants to."

"I know, Mom, but it's too much for you to do all alone."

"I'll be fine. The nurse taught me how to move him. There are all sorts of tips and tricks health care workers use. You know, how to stand when you lift the patient. Where to position the chair. I practiced with Anna. You remember her, don't you?"

Logan recalled the nurse who was so often in and out of his father's room while he visited. "Sure."

"Such a little thing, and she'd hoist your dad right up out of that chair and get him to the bed all on her own.

Did I tell you? She's expecting her first child. It's such a demanding job, physically, that I wonder how long she'll be able to work before she has to go on maternity leave. I'll have to remember to pick up a little something for the baby and send it over before she leaves." Logan's mother smiled. "So, Emma is lovely. She eats like a bird, though. She barely touched dinner."

Logan had noticed that, too. "I think her stomach was bothering her today."

His mother nodded. "Well, then I understand. Chili isn't the best for an upset stomach. So, are you two serious?"

That not so subtle transition wasn't lost on Logan. His mother asking about his love life used to piss Logan off when he was younger. Strange, tonight he didn't seem to mind the question one bit.

"We're getting there." Logan couldn't help but smile when he talked about Emma. "I didn't think serious was an option until today. But now, she's talking about maybe moving to Oklahoma to be near her sister."

"I'd love to see a wedding in this family. And grandchildren, too, before I get too old to enjoy them."

Logan laughed. "I'll see what I can do. Just don't get too excited. I only met Emma at Tuck's wedding. It's barely been two months—"

Two months. Like the pieces of a puzzle, things began to fall into place.

Emma looking ill at the store and munching on crackers as if they were a lifeline. Her turning green at the sight of his mother's chili, when he'd seen her wolf down an overflowing plate full of drippy, spicy barbecue at the buffet at Tuck's wedding. Her not drinking tonight when he knew from watching her during the wedding weekend that she definitely drank alcohol—wine, champagne, and vodka with cranberry.

The way the color had drained from her face when he told her about his short-lived engagement and the accidental pregnancy that had caused it . . . *Shit.* Logan was up and out of his chair before the pieces had all settled in his brain. There were still questions, but he had an idea who had the answers.

"Mom, I gotta run next door for a minute."

"Sure, sweetie. I may be in bed by the time you get back."

"Okay, see you in the morning." Logan was lucky he was able to hold even that much of a conversation with his mother, as distracted as he was.

He needed to talk to Emma and confirm his suspicion. He pushed through his parents' kitchen door and strode across the back lawn as he had so many times over the years.

The entire walk over, thoughts of Emma played in his head. How he couldn't see her without smiling. How he thought of her day and night, sometimes at the oddest moments, and every time, she made him feel happy and warm. Complete. Content. Jeez, how could he have been so stupid not to notice he'd been falling in love with her? More and more each day. Maybe he didn't want to see it until today, when she said she might not be going back to a home a thousand miles away.

It seemed he hadn't seen a lot of things that had been right in front of him lately. Such as all the clues about what was going on with Emma, and the entire Jenkins family.

Not standing on ceremony, Logan came to the Jenkinses' back door and gave a halfhearted knock while pushing it open.

Tyler glanced up from his plate of food. "Hey, Logan. What's up?"

"Where's Emma? I need to talk to her." Logan didn't mess around with small talk.

"About time." Tyler's brows rose. "She's been sleeping on the pullout sofa in the den. I think she's in there now."

"Thanks." Logan strode to the room he knew well. Years ago it was where he'd watch cartoons and build mock forts made from sofa cushions with the younger kids while he babysat.

A baby of his own . . . What if Emma really was pregnant?

It raised a million questions. He realized among them, one stood out from the others. Why had he waited so long to settle down and start a family? As he knocked on the door to Emma's room and she opened it, looking surprised to see him, Logan knew the answer. He'd waited for the right woman and here she was.

"Logan, hi. I didn't think I'd see you until tomorr—"

He moved into the room. Ignoring the pullout sofa bed sticking into the middle of the room, and the suitcase open on the floor, he pushed the door closed with a click. He palmed the back of Emma's head, wrapped his other hand around her waist and hauled her to him. "Emma Hart, I've fallen totally and completely in love with you."

She bit her lip as her golden brows drew low over those eyes he could stare into for years and never get tired of. "You have?"

"I have." Leaning low, he hovered just shy of her lips. "This is where you're supposed to say something."

He felt it, the love between them. Still, he wanted to hear her say it.

Her eyes shone with unshed tears. "I love you, too."

A smile bowed his lips before he crashed them against Emma's. He kissed her until her tears dampened both of their faces. He pulled back and brushed his thumbs across her wet cheeks. "I hope these are happy tears."

"Mostly."

His brows rose. "Mostly?"

Emma swallowed hard. "Logan, I have something to tell you." She drew in a shaky breath. "I'm scared to death you're not going to like it."

"Nothing you can say will change how I feel." His heart sped as he waited for her to tell him the news he was sure he already knew. He found it so hard to breathe, he couldn't even imagine how she felt.

"The night we were together after the wedding. We didn't use any protection that time in the shower." Emma blurted, "I'm pregnant."

"The shower." Logan felt like slapping himself in the forehead as another piece of the puzzle dropped into place. He'd forgotten. She'd been so tempting that he'd convinced himself pulling out would be safe enough.

"That's when I assume it happened. I can't figure out any other explanation. I haven't been with any other man. I'll take a paternity test—"

"Emma, I believe you. I believe it's mine. You don't need to take any test." It was overwhelming, and exciting all at the same time. He looked down at the woman he held. "A baby. Wow."

"I'm so sorry, Logan."

"Sorry? No. Don't be silly." It wasn't exactly the way he would have planned it, but that didn't mean he wasn't happy.

She didn't look convinced as she sighed. "Anyway, I flew here as soon as I could after I found out, but I didn't want to just dump it on you with your father and all. I can do it alone. I'd rather, if you don't want—"

"Emma. Stop. No, I don't want you to do it alone. I want to be with you. Both of you." Logan shook his head. "I should be upset with myself for being so careless with you and your body. This affects you as much as it does me. More. But I don't have any regrets."

"Really?"

"Really. None." A smile spread across his lips.

Maybe this was the push he'd needed. It was frightening how easy it would have been for Emma to have gone back to New York after the wedding. For Logan to have never seen her again. He could have missed all this. He could have lost her.

Logan was starting to get a little teary-eyed himself. He cleared his throat. "So I guess the only thing left to decide is do you want to come with me to pick out your engagement ring, or do you want me to surprise you? Think hard about that, because you'll have to live with it on your finger for the rest of your life, and I have no experience when it comes to picking out women's jewelry."

"Logan, please be sure you want this. Want me." At the look of uncertainty in her eyes, he squeezed her tighter to him.

"There is no doubt in my mind. I think I started to fall for you the moment I met you." Logan laughed, remembering. "Way back when Jace kept getting in the way."

"Jace. I forgot all about him. We're going to have to tell not only Jace, but your parents, and my parents, and Tuck's parents . . ."

"Please, *please* let me be the one to tell Jace we're getting married and you're having my baby." It was petty. Logan knew that, and he didn't care.

Emma rolled her eyes. "Fine, but you can also be the one to tell Tara. I'm afraid she's going to want to scratch my eyes out when she hears."

"Maybe now she'll get on with her life and find someone who makes her as happy as you make me." Logan watched Emma smile at that and couldn't help but smile himself.

"I hope she does. I truly do want her to be happy." A scowl twisted Emma's beautiful face. "Just someplace nowhere near you."

His little wife-to-be was jealous. Sick man that he was, Logan liked that. Hell of a pair they made. "I can say the same thing about Jace. I truly hope the man finds the woman of his dreams—somewhere far away from you and me and our new life together."

"I like the sound of that. Our life together. But, you should thank Jace, you know. If he wasn't such a jerk, we might not have ended up together."

"I'll try to remember that." Logan remembered something else. "Tuck, Tyler, and Becca—they all know?"

"Yeah." She cringed. "I'm so sorry they knew before you. I didn't tell any of them, I swear. They found out by accident."

"It's okay, baby. It does explain a lot of the strange behavior around here, though." He hugged her to him, resting his head on top of hers.

"So I guess we should go tell your sister you'll be planning another wedding. And soon." Logan stepped back and pressed one palm to Emma's belly, knowing it was much too soon to feel anything. He still couldn't help himself. He had a feeling he'd have his hands on her so much she'd have to tell him to go away.

"Will your brother be able to fly home from Japan for the wedding?"

"I doubt it. Not so soon after he's just been home. That's okay. Layne will meet both of you the next time he's home." Emotions swam through Logan. He wanted to lay Emma down and make love to her, even as he wanted to coddle and protect her and their unborn child. It was a strange mix of feelings. The good news was he had a lifetime to get used to them.

"Can we hide in here for a little while longer?" Emma covered his hand with hers. "I kind of feel like I want to have you all to myself for a bit."

"That sounds very good to me." Logan dipped his head, intent on kissing Emma, when whispers in the hallway had him halting in his path to her lips. "It seems we have an audience."

"I know. I hear it. Ignore them." Emma reached up and reeled him in the rest of the way.

Logan had no problem taking full advantage of their last bit of privacy, real or imagined. Soon they'd have to face the rest of the world. At least they'd face it together. He kissed her, and realized it felt different from before. Better. Deeper. Like it was a promise for the future, not just a pleasure for the present.

Cupping her face with his hand, Logan kissed her thoroughly. His promise to her that he'd love her and cherish her for the rest of their lives. He pressed one palm to her belly again, marveling that there was a life growing inside her. A baby he'd put there. The purely male part of Logan reacted, wanting to take her right then and there. Stake a claim to her body.

He broke the kiss, leaning his forehead against hers. "We can't have sex in Mr. and Mrs. Jenkins' den. I'm sorry, but I can't do it. I practically grew up in this house. They're like my second parents."

"I know. I agree." She leaned back and blew out a breath. "But that means you have to stop kissing me like that or I won't be responsible for my actions."

They'd have to work something out. Somewhere to be alone, because there was no way he'd be able to keep his hands off her until they were married, no matter how soon that might be. Maybe the hunting cabin . . .

As he considered that option, Logan's phone vibrated in

his pocket. He pulled it out and saw *Mark Ross* on the readout. He glanced at Emma, about to shove the phone back in his pocket and call Mark back later. "Sorry. I shouldn't have even looked. I know you hate cell phones."

"No. Go ahead. I think we could both use the distraction." She laughed, sounding a little breathless and as eager as he to find privacy.

"Okay." Smiling, he dropped a quick kiss on his future wife before he hit the button to answer the call. "Hey, Mark."

"Logan. Hi. We've missed you around here. Are you ever coming back to Stillwater?" Behind the joking tone, there was a bit of underlying concern in Mark's question.

"Yes. Don't worry. By the start of the semester I'll be there, but before that—how do you feel about driving back out here for another wedding?"

"Another wedding? Wait. You?"

"Yes, sir." Logan smiled. It felt good to tell his friend the news. Real good. He pulled Emma into a one armed hug. She wrapped her arms around his waist and squeezed.

"Well, I'll be. Let me guess. Becca's sister?"

Surprised, Logan let out a short laugh. "How the hell did you know that?"

"Logan, we play cards together. You've never had a poker face and you never will. I knew the moment you pulled her into the bushes at the wedding that you liked her." So much for Logan thinking he was being so slick and low-key. Mark continued, "My last remaining single friend, finally married. I have to admit, I didn't see that one coming."

"Me, either. What can I say? Love makes a man do things he never thought he would." Logan glanced down at the woman in his arms as she beamed up at him.

Meeting Emma had changed Logan, no doubt about it. As had his father's stroke. Both made him realize he'd been living half a life. He wanted more. Love. A partner. Everything his parents had.

The baby, and Logan's becoming a father himself, was the icing on the cake. It was another piece of his future falling into place.

"I'm happy for you, Logan."

"Thanks, Mark. Me, too." Logan knew for a fact he'd never been happier.

Epilogue

"Logan, it's getting late." Tuck popped his head around the doorframe. "We gotta go."

"I know. I know." Logan blew out a breath and stared at the blank piece of paper on the kitchen table.

"What the hell are you doing?" Tuck took a few steps into the room, the shoes of his military dress uniform clicking against the tile of the floor.

"Trying to write my vows."

"Are you freaking crazy?" Tuck's eyes widened. "I married an English professor, and we didn't even write our own vows. Whose idea was this?"

"Mine." Logan groaned at what he'd thought was a good idea at the time.

"What's wrong with the regular old traditional ones? They've been good enough for people for years."

"I wanted something special for Emma."

"Then you should have written them a week ago." The judgment was clear in Tuck's raised eyebrows. "This thing is supposed to start in like half an hour."

"I know, and you're not helping by reminding me." Logan had hoped something would come to him, but it hadn't. Maybe he should call Mark Ross and ask for help. If an English professor couldn't help him, no one could.

Tuck glanced at the paper in front of Logan. "Come on. Write them in the truck while I drive."

"Logan? We're leaving. Are you driving with us?" Logan's mother called to him from the front of the house.

"No, Mom. I'm not ready yet." Logan blew out a loud breath, frustrated. He wouldn't be able to write if he was in the car with his parents or in the truck with Tuck. A stress-free environment would be too much to ask for today, but Logan needed to at least be alone and somewhere quiet if he had any hope of getting this done. "Tuck, would you mind following my mother and father over? Mom is going to try to get the wheelchair out of the car by herself instead of asking for help. Stubborn as a bull, that woman."

Tuck laughed. "So that's where you get it from."

Logan let out a snort. "Nah, Dad beats Mom in the stubborn department. Hands down. Between the two of them, I never had a chance."

"All right. I'll go and follow your parents over. You finish up. But make it quick." Tuck took one final glance at the blank page.

"I'll try." No pressure there.

Logan heard the front door close behind Tuck, but words didn't magically pop into his head once he was alone. Logan was just considering getting on his parents' computer and searching *original wedding vows* when there was a knock on the back door. Tossing the pen down, Logan strode to open it.

"Tara. What are you doing here?"

"Why? Aren't I invited to the wedding?" Tara's voice rose high, tinged with a bit of hysteria.

Logan frowned. "Of course, you are. But I didn't think you could make it home from school for the weekend."

"I had to come. I had to talk to you before you do this."

She moved forward. "You can't marry her, Logan. Not before I tell you . . . Logan, I love you. I've always loved you."

"Tara—"

"No, listen to me. I know you kept your distance from me all these years out of respect for my family, but I'm an adult now. You don't have to do that anymore. I want to be with you." She pressed her hands to his chest. "We can be together."

Logan grabbed and held her hands. "Tara. Stop. I'm getting married today to Emma."

"Emma." Tara let out a snort. "It's all her fault. Everything would have been fine if she'd never come to town. You and I would have hooked up at the wedding. You would have realized I'm the one you want."

The last thing Logan wanted to do was hurt this girl, but he couldn't let her go on believing that. "No, sweetie. That's not true. You can't blame Emma for us not being together. It never would have happened for you and me."

"How do you know that? You never even gave us a chance." She tried to step closer, tears in her eyes. "Just look at me. I'm all grown up, Logan. Don't you see that? You don't have to be my older brother anymore. I'm a woman now. You can act like a man with me."

She leaned closer, trying to press against him even as he held her away. Horrified, Logan took a step back. When she moved to follow him, he planted a hand on each of her shoulders and locked his elbows to keep her at arm's length. "Tara. I'm getting married today."

"Why are you getting married? You barely know her. What's the rush?"

Tara didn't know Emma was having Logan's baby, but that didn't matter, because the baby wasn't the reason Logan wanted to marry Emma. "I love her, Tara. It took me too long to find her as it is. I'm not wasting any more time apart when we can be together."

"You only think you love her because you didn't know that *I'm* in love with you." The sincerity and pain were clear in Tara's tear filled eyes.

"I know you think you are, but you're not. Not really. You'll find someone worthy of all the love you have to give. One day. I swear to you, you will." Logan continued as tears streamed down her face. "Tara, I'll always love you like a sister, just as I love Tuck and Tyler like brothers, but the man who's meant for you is not me. Never was. Never will be."

She shook her head, and drew in a trembling breath. "No."

He dropped his hold on her. It was getting late. Emma and over two dozen of their friends and relatives were waiting for him. "I have to go. I'm sorry, Tara. I really am. I'd like you to be there for the ceremony, but if you're not, I'll understand."

Logan grabbed the hat for his dress blues from the table, abandoned the blank paper there and turned toward the door. He'd clear his head on the drive over and then he'd wing it on the vows. Speak from the heart. That's where his love for Emma lay. The words would come.

"Hmm. I seem to remember someone, not very long ago, commenting how Tuck's backyard wasn't the Plaza wedding I'd always planned and dreamed of." Becca glanced around them and then at Emma. "But never in my wildest dreams did I picture you getting married at a hunting cabin."

Never in Emma's wildest dreams had she thought she'd be pregnant, marrying an Oklahoma-born army officer, either, but here she was.

They hadn't had a lot of time to pull this thing together, so they'd planned a small wedding lakeside at Logan's family cabin. Just family and very close friends. It was a good place. There was history. It felt right to start their new life together here.

The empire-waist cut of the off-white wedding dress, and the fact they'd planned the wedding in a month, meant she wasn't really showing. Even though her breasts felt huge, Logan didn't seem to mind the changes in her body at all, so Emma wasn't going to worry.

"That's what surprises you most? That I'm getting married outside by a lake? Not that I'm quitting my job in New York and moving to Oklahoma?"

Becca laughed. "Yes. That, too. But no more than Logan's plan to retire next year from both the army and OSU and move here to work at his father's store. With you by his side, to boot. Or that Tyler is going to help run it with some old guys from the veterans' association in the meantime."

Emma smiled. "It has been a kind of surreal summer, hasn't it?"

"You can say that again." Becca glanced past Emma. "Here comes Jace. There's one more surprise, that you invited him."

"He's kind of the reason Logan and I are together." Emma lifted one shoulder in a shrug.

"One day, you're going to tell me that whole story." Becca narrowed her eyes.

Emma laughed. "Don't count on it."

"Hmm. Just wait until you can drink again. A bottle of wine, a girl's night out, you and me alone and we'll see."

"That we will." Emma dismissed Becca's threats and watched as Jace made his way across the grass to meet them where they waited for the ceremony to start.

True to gentlemanly form, Jace tipped his hat. "Becca. Emma. You both look beautiful."

Emma smiled. "Thank you, sir."

"Thanks, Jace. Em, I'm going to go check on some last minute things. You okay here?" Becca asked.

"I'm fine."

When Becca had left them, heading toward where the preacher was talking with their parents, Jace eyed Emma. "So . . . Logan, huh?"

Emma laughed. "Yeah. Logan."

"All that time when I'd hoped and dreamed of me being the one for you, you had your eye on good old Logan." Jace's grin told Emma he was only teasing.

"Well, not the whole time. I met you the year before I met him. Remember? At a certain rodeo?"

Jace hung his head and let out a sigh. "I messed up pretty big that night, didn't I?"

"Yes, you did." Emma could laugh about it now. She was even grateful. Everything that had happened had led her to being with Logan, so how could she be upset with Jace now? Then, though? Then she'd been pissed as hell. "You know, to be perfectly honest, I could have forgiven you that one time if it had been just a friend helping out a friend. But really, Jace, come on. You did it again to me at the wedding."

"I know." He hung his head until the shadow of his cowboy hat hid most of his face.

"I do want you to be happy, Jace. And if it's with Jacqueline, that's great. I guess I'm saying I think you have to commit one way or the other. Either be with her, or make a clean break, because as long as you two are tethered to each other, you'll never be free to find someone else." Emma let out a laugh. "And I'm so *not* the person to be giving anyone advice on their love life, so just ignore me."

He lifted his head and met her gaze. "No, you're right. I guess I have some thinking to do. And she and I have some talking to do, too, I suppose." A frown drew his sandy brows down. "Hey, isn't it getting kind of late? What time was this shindig supposed to start?"

"One. What time is it?"

Jace glanced down at his cell phone. "Quarter to."

"Is Logan not here yet?" Emma's heart gave a little lurch.

"I didn't see him when I pulled up."

Oh God. After her long speech to Jace about relationships, was Logan ditching her at the altar? Had he changed his mind? Emma swallowed hard. No, he wouldn't do that. Yet he'd lived forty years unmarried. Maybe the idea was too much for him.

Were his parents here yet? Was Tuck? Emma needed answers. She needed Becca. She needed her damn cell phone. "Excuse me. I'm, uh, feeling a little bit warm. I'm going to go find some water."

"You okay?"

"I'm fine." Or she would be as soon as she found Logan.

Jace nodded. "A'ight. See you after."

Emma escaped him and strode around the corner of the cabin, feeling ill. This time it wasn't from the pregnancy. Her heart beat so fast and furious, she got lightheaded and was afraid she might pass out.

Logan's truck pulled into the already crowded drive and stopped her in her path. Emma held one shaky hand to her chest. He was here. She should never have doubted him.

She knew the moment Logan saw her. He smiled wide enough for her to see it from a distance, then slammed the truck door and made a beeline toward where she stood. He looked so good in his dress blues it made her heart flutter. She'd had to work hard to convince him to wear the uniform for the ceremony, but it had been well worth the effort.

"Emma. You're perfect. So beautiful." As he reached for her hands, Logan seemed as overcome by the moment as she felt. "How am I so lucky?"

His sweet words had Emma getting choked up. "You're not supposed to see me until the ceremony starts. It's bad luck." Even so, she grasped his fingers in hers with no intention of letting go.

"I'm so late, the ceremony is starting about now, isn't it? I think we found a loophole in that tradition. Besides, I don't need luck." He smiled. "I have you. That's all I'll ever need."

"Please stop saying such sweet things. You're making me cry." Emma looked up at the sky and ran the tips of one finger beneath her lower lashes, wiping at the moisture there.

He laughed and drew her against him. "Don't worry about that happening during the ceremony, because I tried all morning to write vows and I failed miserably."

"It's all right. I failed pretty badly with my vows, too. I even asked Becca with her doctorate in English to help, but nothing felt . . ." She shook her head as the right word eluded her.

"Nothing felt right."

Emma nodded when Logan finished her sentence. "Exactly. Do you want to go with the traditional vows?"

"Yes, please." The gratitude in Logan's voice had Emma smiling as he leaned his forehead against hers. "I love you so much. You're my light. My world."

Those were pretty good words for a man who claimed to have none. She'd be sobbing soon if he didn't stop being so sweet. "Can we go get married now?"

"I want nothing more. Well, maybe *one* thing more, but that's for later." Logan ran his hands down her back and pulled her closer.

She saw the heat darken his eyes and realized just one lifetime might not be enough with this man, but it would be a good start.

Read on for a peek at Cat Johnson's next
Oklahoma Nights cowboy romance,
Three Weeks with a Bull Rider, coming next April.

With a huff, Tara spun on the heel of her cowboy boot, bound for the building. She stepped from behind her car—and directly into the path of a truck going way too fast for a parking lot. It skidded to a stop as she leapt back, and then pulled into the empty spot next to her car.

The driver's side door opened and that's when Tara recognized both the truck and the driver.

Jace Mills. That figured. Chief idiot and number one annoyance from among her brother's roster of friends, and now he'd nearly run her over. "Jeez, Jace. You almost killed me. Slow the fuck down."

"You kiss your mama with that mouth, Tara?" Jace raised one sandy brow high above his blue eyes. "And you stepped right out in front of me. Look where you're going from now on."

Tara clenched her jaw and tried to control the string of obscenities she'd love to let loose on him.

"I was distracted, but you should still be more careful. There are families walking around here with kids and stuff." She frowned at the empty cab of Jace's truck. "Tuck's not with you."

"That is a very good observation."

She rolled her eyes in frustration. "Why isn't he?"

Couldn't this man cut her even one little break? Every tiny piece of information she got out of him was a struggle.

"That is a very good question." Jace grinned.

"Do you have an answer?"

"I do, and it's a doozey. Wanna hear?" He waggled his brows.

"Dammit—yes, Jace. I wanna hear." Tara would need dental work from gritting her teeth if she continued this conversation with this obnoxious, frustrating, annoying man who made her want to scream.

A wide grin stretched across Jace's lips. "Tuck's at a wine tasting with Becca, his BFF Logan, and Logan's wife."

Tara's gut twisted at hearing Logan's name. Having Jace mention Logan in the same breath as his new wife made it even worse. She'd loved Logan for as long as she could remember, and Becca's sister had swooped in and stolen him from her. She swallowed away the bitter taste in the back of her throat, nauseated all over again by the memories of her last conversation with Logan.

It had been on the day of his wedding. He'd told Tara he'd never loved her and never would. That he loved Emma. But she needed to focus on the situation at hand and not her broken heart. Tuck's sudden interest in wine over rodeo left Tara stuck without a ride.

"Crap. I needed Tuck here tonight."

"We're going to have to talk about your potty mouth, young lady." Jace crossed his arms over his chest and leaned back against the truck. "But before we do, why did you need Tuck here? And come to think of it, why are you here?"

"Not that it's any of your business, but I'm working with the sports medicine team to fulfill my internship requirement for graduation."

"Sports medicine? That's what you're going to school

for?" Jace frowned. "Hmm. I thought it was veterinary studies."

"You're so observant." Tara rolled her eyes.

Jace's only response was to lift one shoulder in a shrug. Unfortunately, as much of an idiot as Jace was, it looked like he was also her only hope for a ride to Stillwater, where she could crash for the night at Tuck and Becca's place.

Tara eyed his truck. "Can you tow a car with that thing?"

He hooked a thumb at his truck. "This thing? Tow a car? Uh, yeah. I could tow a tractor trailer if I had to. Why?"

"My car is dead." She tilted her head in the direction of the piece of crap behind her. "One of the stock contractors took a look at it for me and suggested I tow it to the local scrap yard and junk it."

Jace eyed the vehicle and let out a long slow whistle. "That bad, huh?"

"Apparently. And then, I also kind of need a ride to Tuck's place." She'd work on her brother's sympathies when she got to Stillwater. Maybe she could convince Tuck to loan her his truck for the next few weeks.

It's not like he needed it. He and Becca both worked at the same damn place. They should carpool. Save the environment. Reduce their carbon footprint and all that good stuff.

A smug smirk appeared on Jace's face. "So what you're saying is you need my help."

"Forget about it. I'll find another ride." Tara let out a huff. She'd just keep calling Tuck until he answered.

"Stop pouting. Jeez, you're such a child."

Gasping at the worst insult he could have thrown at her, Tara had no words except to deny it. "I am not a child. You're a—"

"Tara, if you'd shut up one damn minute and listen, you'd hear I'm saying okay. I'll help you. I'll take a look at your car and if it doesn't look fixable, I'll tow it to the scrapyard and drive you back to Stillwater."

This man was so infuriating, she'd love to plant the toe of her cowboy boot right where the sun didn't shine, but he was willing to help so she'd have to play nice. "And what would I have to give you in exchange? I'm warning you. I've got no money, not even to chip in for gas. Seriously, like none. I spent it all on that piece of shit car."

Jace scowled. "I don't need your money. I have plenty of my own for gas, thank you."

She didn't trust Jace as far as she could throw him. He wouldn't do her a favor for nothing. He must have some ulterior motive. "Then what do you want?"

"Hmm, let's see. What do I want?" Jace stared up at the sky and tapped one forefinger to his chin. "I know. You have to be nice to me. No name calling. No smart ass comments. None of your usual shit. Think you can do that?"

Not likely. "I don't know. For how long?"

"Until we get to Stillwater. Starting now."

"How about starting the moment we get inside the arena, until we get in your truck to start the drive to Stillwater?"

"You're unbelievable." Laughing, Jace shook his head. "All right. It's a deal."

Jace extended one big, rough hand and, though she'd never willingly touched him before, Tara shook it to seal the deal on this unholy alliance.

One day, far in the future when Tara had a successful career and a happy marriage, she'd look back at this time in her life. At how she'd had her heart broken by the only man she'd ever loved, and she'd survived, become a stronger woman because of it. How, stranded in Shawnee during week one of her internship, she'd hitched a ride with the devil. And how, being the mature person she knew herself to be, she'd even been nice to him for one whole night . . . God help her.